DAUGHTERS OF JUBILATION

BY KARA LEE CORTHRON

SIMON & SCHUSTER BFYR

New York   London   Toronto   Sydney   New Delhi

This book is a work of fiction. Any references to historical events, real people, or real places are used fictitiously. Other names, characters, places, and events are products of the author's imagination, and any resemblance to actual events or places or persons, living or dead, is entirely coincidental.

SIMON & SCHUSTER BFYR

An imprint of Simon & Schuster Children's Publishing Division
1230 Avenue of the Americas, New York, New York 10020
First Simon Pulse hardcover edition October 2020
Text copyright © 2020 by Kara Lee Corthron
Jacket photograph copyright © 2019 by Bernadette Newberry / Arcangel | Back jacket
silhouettes holding hands copyright © 2019 by Klaus Vedfelt / Getty Images | Back jacket
silhouette on left by Yuliia Blazhuk/iStock | Jacket light and trees texture by tomertu/iStock

For information about special discounts for bulk purchases, please contact Simon & Schuster
Special Sales at 1-866-506-1949 or business@simonandschuster.com.
The Simon & Schuster Speakers Bureau can bring authors to your live event. For more
information or to book an event contact the Simon & Schuster Speakers Bureau
at 1-866-248-3049 or visit our website at www.simonspeakers.com.
Book designed by Tiara Iandiorio
The text of this book was set in Electra LT Std.
Manufactured in the United States of America
2 4 6 8 10 9 7 5 3 1
CIP data for this book is available from the Library of Congress.
ISBN 9781481459501 (hc)
ISBN 9781481459525 (ebook)

In memory of my mother

You are horror and beauty in rare combination.

—Octavia E. Butler

1

Savior

HERE'S THE THING ABOUT ME: I AIN'T normal. Never have been, never will be. So? That's my private business and nobody else's. I got no interest in drawin' attention to myself for any reason other than my good looks and memorable personality. They don't understand what I did yesterday, so they're makin' a big fuss. I hate it, but what am I sposeta do? Refuse a newspaper interview, with my mother so proud she's finna combust?

"Can you remember what you were thinking when you first noticed that something was wrong?" a young reporter asks me. If I didn't know better, I'd think he was in high school too.

"Nothin'," I say. "I could just tell it was gonna fall, so I had to get them outta the way." This is silliness. Who *wouldn't* have done what I did?

He asks a few more questions; then he makes me pose for a photo with the family. The Pritchards. They flash toothy smiles at me, their savior. Had I not been there yesterday when a big ol' oak tree was about to fall on them and their new, shiny T-Bird convertible, we would not be sittin' here all sweet and harmonious.

The flashbulb blinds me, and I'm finally free to go. Mr. and Mrs. Pritchard thank me once again. Their toddlers run circles around us, and Mrs. Pritchard's fat with another one on the way. T-Bird ain't exactly a family car, but that's none a my business.

"You should come over to our house for supper one night," she offers. In a fraction of a second, Mr. Pritchard shoots her a look. Ain't no way in hell he's ever gonna let me step foot into his house. Not that I'd wanna go. Plus, white people can't cook.

"Thank you, but I'm just glad y'all are safe," I say in my good-girl voice with my forced good-girl smile. I leave the newspaper office's steps with Mama beamin' beside me.

"Imma stop sayin' it, but I am so proud a you, baby. You're so brave and selfless."

"Honestly, I just didn't have time to think," I say.

"That means savin' folks is just who you are then. Don't lessen it. This is a great thing you done."

We get to the bus stop and wait.

"Whatcha wanna eat tonight? I'll make whatever you want, and you don't even have to help me."

"Maybe chicken and dumplin's," I tell her.

"Shoulda known. I was guessin' you'd say shrimp and grits, but chicken and dumplin's woulda been my second guess," she says.

I mighta said "shrimp and grits," but the last time I asked for it, she complained about the rising price of certain kinds a fish, so I thought it was off limits.

She bumps me with her shoulder, and I can't help but grin. It's a weird affectionate thing she used to do when I was little.

Mama doesn't know the whole story, though. I'm not a hero.

It's the end of a mostly mild spring. There was no storm or high winds. No reason for a giant oak like that to just plummet to the ground. I was foolin' around cuz I got mad. I'd ridden my trusty Schwinn into a neighborhood I didn't recognize. Hadn't meant to, I just wasn't payin' attention. I stopped to figure out where I was and how I ended up there when a man approached me.

"Who do you belong to?" he asked, givin' me the dirtiest look.

"No one. I just got lost," I explained, backing me and my bike away from him.

"I suggest you get *un*lost 'fore you catch some real trouble," he barked, and then he marched across the street to the car where his wife and kids waited for him. The wife was hollerin' at the little ones to get in the car, but they didn't pay her no mind.

When he got to the driver's-side door, before gettin' in, he said something to the woman, and she got closer to him. They talked for a few more seconds—I was too far away to hear what they said—and the wife looked over at me, shakin' her head in disgust. Like the very sight a me was ruinin' their whole day.

That ol' oak tree was big enough and near enough that I thought, *Wouldn't it be somethin' for these folks to have an accident right now?*

It was a quick thought, and I don't think I meant it, but it didn't matter. A sharp headache ripped through me, and the tree started rockin' at the bottom of its trunk. And it kept on rockin,' harder and harder. Couldn't believe my eyes. I tried to make it stop, but then I heard the unmistakable creakin' sound of wood startin' to snap.

I ran over and shoved the family outta the way. All of 'em. And then the tree came down, crushin' that shiny new car.

Once they got over the initial shock, the kids started cryin' and screamin', and their parents tripped over each other thankin' me. I made the mistake of tellin' 'em my name, which is how the newspaper found me.

So yeah. Sure. I guess I saved the Pritchards from certain death. But nobody knows I tried to kill 'em first.

2

Flirting

WELL. SPRING HAS FLOWN AWAY like it was runnin' from the law, and summer has burdened us all again. It is hot as holy hell out here, and ain't nobody bothered to refill the lemonade on account a the flies. But I swear to Christ Jesus they better do somethin', less they want me to melt. My hair! Lord! Just pressed and curled it three hours ago, and it's already startin' to wilt. I don't even wanna think 'bout that daggone kitchen at the back a my head. Nasty li'l tangles for days. Humidity can kiss my sweet brown ass!

Anne Marie means well, but damn. When she first moved to South Cakalacky, she couldn't believe none of us kids had never been to or heard of a Juneteenth party. She's into history, so this holiday is tailor-made for her. She's a sweetheart and my closest girlfriend, so I don't complain about the swelterin' heat. Or the flies. Out loud.

"Did we run outta lemons or water or what?"

"Weren't you the one complainin' about all the flies?" Anne Marie smirks at me.

She's right. I was.

"I'm startin' to think dehydration is the lesser evil," I say.

She makes a goofy face and curtsies low. "What else can I get for Your Highness?"

"*Highness?* Please! I'll make it myself. Just hand over the lemons."

She stands up straight again, giggling. "Kidding. I'm the hostess. You stay put," she tells me as she heads over to the serving table.

I told her I'd get out here early to help her set up, but that didn't happen. I did try, but I was layin' under the fan, lettin' ice cubes melt on my neck and face, and it felt a little too good to just stop so I could come out here to carry chairs and shit. Lookin' at the sad, droopy JUNETEENTH 1962 banner she made with construction paper and glue, I feel guilty. *Some-* body shoulda told her not to put up that raggedy thing, but nobody did, and now it's too late. Oh well. I'll make it up to her at some point.

In my defense, I wasn't the onliest one on CP time. As I was crossing the bridge earlier, I ran into Bernadette, Peggy, Marcus, and a couple others. All of us over an hour late. On the other side there was a thick grove of trees, and we all took a breather to enjoy the glorious shade. We'd been laughin' and cuttin' up and complainin', but then, all at once, we got quiet. We were facing the same direction, and we all saw the same thing: about fifty yards away was a big, gorgeous swimming pool. Kids were over there splashin' around, and it looked like a slice of paradise to me. That big, bright, fake blue. Bet they keep the water nice and cold. We stared like it was a desert mirage from a Bugs Bunny cartoon. Might as well have been. Since none of us will ever be allowed in that pool.

"Um, Evvie?" Anne Marie calls, bringing me back from my pool dreams.

"What?" I'm fannin' myself, tryna sound pleasant.

"I think that's for you," Anne Marie says, lookin' past me. I turn around and—oh come on now! What the hell is *she* doin' here?

"Hi, Evalene! Don't you look pretty," Miss Ethel says, looking me up and down. I know I look pretty. I'm in my new peach-colored swing dress that hugs me in all the right spots and makes my bosoms look like a movie star's. And even though this humidity is doin' a number on my hair, it looks a damn sight better than Miss Ethel's on a good day. I always try to look decent, but I look even better today, and I certainly don't need *her* to tell me.

"Why, thank you, Miss Ethel," I say, because I was raised right. "Thought you wouldn't be gettin' back in town till late."

"We just got in." Miss Ethel smiles a phony smile and

glances around at everybody here like she ain't never seen colored people havin' a cookout in her whole life. Hell, maybe she ain't.

"I just happened to see you out here, and I wanted to make sure you wadn't plannin' on stayin' out to all hours, since I'll need you bright and early. In all her four years, Abigail has yet to sleep in." She tries to joke. Oh, this woman. *Go home!*

"Don't you worry. I'll be there on time like always," I promise, flashing my best, most white-people-pleasing smile. Yes. Always on time to feed and tend to that li'l demon spawn you spat out into the world.

"Well," she adds, "you've been late before. But I know what it's like to be young. You just don't make that a habit, ya hear? Bye-bye." Miss Ethel looks around, a little lost, but when she gets her bearings, she scoots herself back out to the main road. I couldn't imagine why she'd be in this neighborhood at all until I spy the brown paper bag under her arm, tied with blue string. She got herself some grub from Miss Johnnie's. White people will venture into deepest Africa for colored-people food.

"Daggone! Boss lady keepin' a eye on you," Leon teases as he flips some burgers on the grill.

"She needs to keep them eyes to herself," I tell him.

"She pay pretty good, though, right?" Anne Marie asks, bringing out a fresh pitcher of lemonade. Hallelujah!

"You are an angel," I say, grabbing it from her hands and pouring myself a glass. "She pay good enough. She could pay better, and I'm finna tell her so. 'Specially if she wants me to stay on when school starts up."

"You goin' back to school?" R. J. asks, a bit too eagerly.

"Why wouldn't I?"

"Ya know? You workin' now. You sixteen. Seventeen soon, right? You could just quit and work if you want to," he explains.

That comment gets me so mad that for an instant, the ground rumbles beneath us.

"What the hell?" Leon exclaims, holding on to a picnic table for support.

"Language!" Anne Marie scolds, but she also looks frightened.

Leon sucks his teeth at her and I take an easy breath and the earth settles down, like nothin' unusual has happened. Shit. I *must* start watchin' my temper.

"Was that a baby earthquake?" R. J. asks.

"Could be, but I doubt it," I say.

"It *has* been a while since we last had one," Leon says.

"We should watch the news to see if . . ."

And before Anne Marie can finish tellin' us to watch the news for an earthquake report, which won't be there, I shift the focus.

"I am not gonna quit school. Imma get my diploma come hell or high water." I mean it too. Mama didn't make it all the way through school cuz she had to work. My grandmother doesn't trust anything learned from books, so I'm sure she never made it very far. I intend to be the first Deschamps girl to do it. If for no other reason than for my little sisters to know it's possible.

"Diploma's just a piece a paper," R. J. continues. "'Sides,

somebody gonna marry you soon enough, so none a that'll matter," he says with that crooked smile a his. Leon laughs to himself; Anne Marie shakes her head. I ain't in no mood for this today. Does he have no pride? This boy's been following me around since I's seven years old. Wadn't interested then, and I sure ain't now. 'Specially not when there are so many others out there I'd like to be makin' time with. Well . . . one. Just one in particular, who might just be the finest boy I've ever seen in my life. This same one in particular who promised me he'd be at this damn shindig not two days ago, and so far I ain't seen hide nor hair a him.

"It'll matter to me, that's for sure," I say.

"That's good. Give them pretty li'l babies you gonna have a mama they can look up to. Course, you already a famous hero."

I groan. I do not wanna talk about that goddamn article again. It's been over a week since it came out. Enough already.

"Oh, will you give it a rest?" Leon shoves a hot dog in R. J.'s face. "Here. Give your mouth somethin' else to do, please." I can't help but giggle, and I smile at Leon.

Anne Marie fills a bowl with fruit punch in addition to the lemonade. Festive.

"I don't know why you ain't proud," mouthy Bernadette says. "If I'd gotten my name in the paper for savin' some lives, I'd never stop talkin' about it."

That's for damn sure.

"I don't like makin' a fuss, and if people forget about it,

they won't expect me to do it again. Cuz I ain't never doin' that again."

They laugh and let it drop.

Sun's gettin' lower and lower. Dammit. When I see Clayton next, Imma kill 'im!

I shouldn't be surprised. You know how babies can get all excited about a toy when they're playin' with it, but if you hide it from 'em when they ain't lookin', they forget it was ever there? Sometimes I think Clay's like that with me. The first time I can remember feelin' belly butterflies over Clay was when I was eleven. He never paid attention to me back then. But in the last couple years—really since I got to high school—he's been different. He'd nod if he saw me in the halls, and sometimes he'd tease me, but never in a mean way. The first time I wondered if maybe he liked me for real was last summer.

I know it's childish, but somehow I got roped into pla-yin' jailbreak with some neighborhood kids. I was runnin' for home base, and I happened to see Clay talkin' to one of his friends on the street. I didn't slow down, though. I made it to home base: an old Cadillac that probably hasn't been used since Roosevelt was in office.

I'm fast, so I was the first one there, but I ducked down behind the car so Clay wouldn't see me runnin' around like an idiot. I figured I'd just stay hidden, and eventually he'd leave.

When nearly all my team members made it to home base, I will admit I got excited because we won. Jailbreak is dumb, but I always enjoy a victory, and we crushed the other team. They started whinin' about it (sour grapes), but the game was over, so I walked back out to the street . . . and he was still there! On the corner, starin' right at me. I kinda waved then, cuz it was awkward, and he half smiled. I turned to go in the opposite direction, and I tripped over absolutely nothin' and fell on the ground. Right into a mud puddle. A couple of my teammates cracked up. I felt a strong urge to cry, but I couldn't, because before I could do anything, Clay was at my side, helping me up.

"Are you all right?" he asked me.

"Yeah, I'm fine," I mumbled, so embarrassed.

He held on to my hand and looked me over for cuts and bruises. The other kids shut up then, cuz Clay's older than them and far cooler.

"You gotta be careful," he said, and I could see that he, too, wanted to laugh, but he didn't.

"Thanks," I said. I tried to pull away from him, but he didn't let me.

"I'm not hurt. I swear." I tried to pull away again, and he held on again. And he was starin' at me hard, and even though I was sweaty, dressed like a derelict, and partially covered in mud, he seemed to like what he saw.

Then one of his friends from the baseball team came by, and that was it. He let me go, smiled, and went off with his buddy.

But that was last summer. Since then, we'd see each other every now and then and were friendly, but not much more than that. Something happened this spring, and it happened to him.

He has been silly lately. Not me. Ever since school let out, I feel like I run into him just about everywhere I go. Not that I mind, of course. He's cool and casual, like always, but I don't think every time we've bumped into each other has been a complete accident. I mean, I ran into him at the salon. Once in a blue moon, I go to get my nails done without tellin' Mama (she'd be furious if she knew I was spendin' money on somethin' we don't need), and when I went in a week ago, guess who turned up? And I noticed *he* didn't leave with a manicure or a new hairdo. I also believe he asked me three times if I'd be here tonight, knowin' full well I would be, and where is he at?

This cookout started two and a half hours ago. Bein' fashionably late is one thing. Standin' somebody up is another.

"Why ain't nobody dancin'?" Bernadette hollers, and turns up the radio playin' Bunker Hill's "Hide and Go Seek" and proceeds to mash potata like she invented it.

"Too hot," I call back.

"Y'all ain't no fun," she argues, and keeps on dancing, sweat flyin'. A couple other folks join her, and pretty soon this is just a big outdoor dance party. While everybody's occupied, I slide up to the punch bowl and add a few drops a joy from my purse flask. Just enough to stay happy. Smells like the burgers are burnin', and I wanna help out, but it's so hot, and it's surely hotter over by that grill! I keep on fanning myself like I done stepped into Hades. I am South Carolina born and bred. And we are in the *south* of South Carolina (Savannah's just a short ride away). So I can't for the life a me figure why I feel like a withered wild flower soon as the mercury hits ninety.

I do have a theory, though. I think it's got somethin' to do with the haints.

I was seein' haints before I knew I had the strangeness inside me. Probably before I could walk. These are restless spirits that can't seem to get to wherever they sposeta be goin'. A lot of 'em are angry. All of 'em are sad. Not everybody can see 'em. I tried to introduce one of 'em to a neighbor girl when I was about three or four, and she couldn't see a thing. That's when I learned that they weren't people.

I can ignore 'em usually, but I know they're always around. I know this because if I focus, I can know what's goin' on in more than one world at a time. Imagine you could tune your radio so you could hear several different stations at once and understand everything you hear perfectly. That's the best way I can describe it. So I wonder if the heat is such a trial for me cuz I got haints flockin' all around me, crowdin' my atmosphere all the time.

R. J. attempts to dance over to me while looking hip, but he can't pull this off.

"Evalene. You not gonna come out here?"

I pretend I don't hear him and sorta walk-dance with my homemade fan over to the grill to salvage the meat that ain't been burnt to a cinder. I try to overlook the heat as I plate a couple hot dogs, the few burgers that survived, and when I turn around . . .

"Hey, Evvie girl," he says to me, and I try to act cool, like I ain't jumping up and down inside at just the sight of him. He smiles this real shy smile, and I smile back even though I know he's a liar. There ain't nothin' shy about Clayton Alexander Jr. Least I ain't never seen that side of him.

"Hey there," I say back. "Didn't think you was gonna show."

"And miss an opportunity to see you in a dress? Am I a damn fool?"

I roll my eyes but keep on smilin'. Only Clay can get away with flirtin' with me like this.

"I don't know. Are ya?" I flirt back.

He chuckles and looks down at his feet, but he doesn't say anything. I wish to high heaven I had a hand mirror right now and two minutes of privacy so I could pat down my hair in the spots that have poufed up and double up on my cherry bomb lipstick.

From the corner of my eye I catch R. J. watchin' us like a lost puppy. If he didn't look so pitiful, I'd fling a burnt patty at him. I shift my position to cut him outta my view.

Because it's still in my hands, I hold out the plate to Clay. "Weiner?" I offer, regretting the word as soon as it left my lips. I honestly thought that was gonna sound sexy when I said it. Lesson learned.

He just grins. Once again, I think he's tryin' not to laugh at me.

"Well . . ." I try to regain my dignity. "Do you want anything to eat?"

He doesn't answer. He just keeps lookin' at me. The way

he looked at me last summer when he pulled me outta that puddle. I feel dizzy in a good way, but I try not to let it show.

"Okay then." I put the plate down and walk back to my seat and my lemonade. If he has somethin' to say to me, I'm sure he'll say it sooner or later. I ain't gonna beg him to talk to me.

"Evvie?"

I take a big gulp of lemonade before answering, just to show him how much more interested I am in it than him. "Yeah?"

"Will you come dance with me?" he asks. Now, if I didn't know better, I could swear that Clayton was just a teeny bit nervous asking me that question. Did he really think I'd say *no*?

I take one more sip and close my eyes, savoring the sweet, tangy goodness before I look back at him.

"Why not?" I offer him my hand. He smiles and takes it, leading me to the trampled patch of grass that has become the dance floor. Just as we stop, feeling that we've found the optimal dance spot, not too far away from the music and not too close to anybody else, a different song comes on. A slow one. He encircles my waist, and I start to feel another one of them goddamn headaches comin' on.

No. *Not now.* I take a few deep breaths.

"Are you all right?" he asks, his voice full of a particular kind of masculine concern. Not paternal and certainly not brotherly, but somethin' I know I'd never feel from another girl.

No. Honestly, I am not all right. Sometimes—some very unlucky times—I get these special headaches.

Everybody gets a headache once in a while. You just take an aspirin or two and go about your business. Not these kinda headaches. They're rare, but they're bad news. Part of me not bein' normal is my ability to do strange things. Like make the ground shake or knock down an oak tree on unsuspecting bigots. For some cockeyed reason they call it *Jubilation*. It ain't the typical kinda jubilation, though. Not the definition you'd find in *Webster's*. It's a catchall word for the spooky magic shit that runs in my family. The headaches are almost like a warning bell that lets me know I'm about to do something dramatic. Something I probably can't control and probably won't remember.

Took me forever to figure out what brings 'em on. I think I finally know. Fear, anger, and desire. Sounds simple, right? Sounds like if I know that much, I oughta be able to prevent 'em, right? I wish.

Typically, this is how it goes: the pain starts behind my eyes, then gradually moves to the base of my skull, and then . . . then I black out. And time passes like I've been in a coma, but in a coma where my body does things that my mind chooses to hide from me.

The first time it got dangerous, I was just about to turn twelve. I scratched this girl's face so hard she bled. This is what I've been told. I have no memory of ever doing such a thing. I did see dried blood under my nails later on, so it must've happened. I came outta my daze in the church basement alone with my mother, and that's when she informed me that puberty would mean a helluva lot more for me than the birds and the damn bees.

But it's not a hopeless plight. When a bad headache starts, there are two ways I can prevent a blackout. 1) I can nullify it by forcing my mind to focus all of its attention on neutral images. A tomato plant. Hanging laundry. A pair of scissors. Or 2) when it's too far gone for neutralizing, if I make myself vomit, it goes away. I hope number one works, cuz I certainly can't do number two right now.

In the midst of my anxiety, somethin' troubling has just occurred to me. With the Pritchards and that fallin' tree? Not only did the headache come so fast I didn't have time to react to it, I was conscious the entire time. I think my powers are evolving, and I can't imagine that's a good thing.

"Evvie? You need to sit down?" Clay asks.

I catch sight of the grill and think to myself, *Grill. Charcoal. Metal. Spatula. Grill.* Tryin' like hell to go neutral. I start to feel like I'm fading and know my time is running out. I take a step backward, preparing to run, but Clay holds me steady, pulling me even closer, and I'm terrified I'm about to throw up all over him. But I get lost in those eyes of his, and something changes in me. I wrap my arms around his neck, and he squeezes me a little tighter.

And I don't puke. I don't black out. I'm here and present, and I feel good.

At that moment a large ball of flame erupts from the grill up into the air with a loud roar. A few people scream and holler, and then it's gone in a blink. Everybody blames Leon cuz he was the one closest to it when it blew, and he swears he didn't do a thing. Anne Marie throws salt over the hot coals. Bernadette informs her that baking soda is best, and they bicker about it, but there's nothing left for them to fight over. All that remains is a shallow flame. I laugh to myself, nervously. I know I did that, and I know it could've been a lot worse.

"This party's goin' bananas," Clay jokes.

I look up at him, and despite the chaos around us, we share our own secret laugh. My headache's gone. I wonder if Clay has something to do with that.

Fear, anger, desire. Maybe cuz my desire has a real flesh-and-blood destination right now that makes me stronger. Wish I could ask Grammie Atti. She'd know, but she and Mama aren't speakin', and I don't think she's ever liked me much anyway. Don't help that she's terrifying.

"What you thinkin'?" Clay asks.

I smile at him and shake my head. "Nothin' really. Just enjoyin' the song."

We start to sway at the same moment. I ignore the perspiration making our skins stick together and focus on the lyric that tells the truth: I only have eyes for him. I lean into his upper chest. Now he takes a breath, a short breath, like he can't quite keep up with his own breathing. I feel his heart beating like a baby bird's against my cheek. And I ain't worried about accidental magic. I ain't worried about a thing. Everything is fine. Everything is perfect.

3

Juneteenth

ATER IT'S JUST A FEW OF US LEFT. The sun's been down for ages, and we sit around shootin' the shit. Because he's got class, Clay's next to me, but not with his arm around me, tryna show off or nothin'. A few times he brushes my hand by "accident." The third time he does it, we look at each other, and he raises an eyebrow. I just grin and turn my attention back to whoever's talking at the moment. That's about when R. J. finally takes off, which is a relief. Bless his heart, I don't think I could've taken one more second of him staring at me.

Now Anne Marie's complainin' about her uncle. He's always in her business, and now that he's living in her house, he wants to act like he's her second father. I tell her to stand her ground and not to let him intimidate her.

"Easy for you to say," she says.

"Why?"

"Cuz nobody intimidates you," she tells me.

"That ain't true," I say.

"Feels true," she replies. I don't know what she means. I get intimidated by people all the time. Only thing is I do my best not to show it. That's the onliest difference between me and her.

"Well it ain't," I say. "I bet you good money if you let him know what's what, he'll quit botherin' ya. He's just actin' like a big, dumb dog. Show him he's in *your* territory."

She nods but looks down at the ground. I'm probably sayin' too much. Sometimes I do that. Besides, it's always easy to give advice from a distance.

To change the subject, Leon starts tellin' the cheesiest story about seein' Wade Hampton's ghost. We laugh. Nobody here believes him. *I* don't, because I know what it is to see a ghost, and it ain't like what's he sayin'.

"Quit laughin'! Y'all weren't there," he protests.

"What was you doin' in the General's Woods anyway? That ain't nowhere for us to be," Clay says.

"That's beside the point. Listen. I swear on my granddaddy's grave—"

"That ain't Christian," Anne Marie points out.

Leon sighs in frustration. "Whatever! I swear on my *own* life then. Let heaven strike me dead right here if I didn't see Wade Hampton's ghost sittin' on top a his horse in full Klan regalia at the top of a ol' moss tree. You tell me how the hell he got way up there, and, more importantly, how's Wade Hampton gonna be ridin' his horse anywhere when he's been dead a hundred years?"

"Sixty."

"What you sayin' now?"

"Wade Hampton the Third has only been dead for sixty years," Anne Marie says. She's always been a history wiz.

For a heartbeat all the fun and silliness desert us. It's unsettling to think that South Carolina's own Wade Hampton III—Confederate general and one of the KKK's most loyal sugar daddies—died only sixty years ago. When we ain't thinkin' about it, somethin' like that feels like forever ago. When we are thinkin' about it? It was yesterday.

Not that it would matter much if he was still breathing. I'm sure he'd be pleased to know that the Klan is alive and kickin' without his fat checks.

Leon finishes his story and promises to get proof if he sees him again. I can't wait to see what kinda "proof" he'll come up with.

Gets quiet for a couple minutes after that. I know why I get quiet. I can't help but think about the wiry chocolate boy with girl's eyelashes and giant eyes like a li'l baby deer's who's sittin' just to my right and who keeps slidin' closer to me. Maybe everyone has their own version of what I got goin' on in my head in theirs. I look around our little circle and catch Leon starin' at me. He clears his throat and looks away. Then I notice Bernadette looking at Clay like he's a cool glass a water and she's stranded in the Mojave. For the tiniest second, I think about twistin' her head right off her neck, but I glance at Clay, and I don't think he's even noticed. If he did, I don't think he cares. He ain't lookin' at nobody but me.

Anne lights a cigarette and inhales. I try to catch her eye, but she got one a them thousand-yard stares right now. I wonder if she's gettin' sick of us. Ready to put an end to the festivities.

"Y'all wanna hear the thing or not?" she asks.

"Yeah!" I pipe up first, and then the others do too. I don't want her to think we totally forgot what we're here to celebrate.

She takes another drag off her cig, reaches into her pocket, and pulls out a folded piece of paper, from which she reads aloud.

"'The people of Texas are informed that, in accordance with a proclamation from the Executive of the United States, all slaves are free. This involves an absolute equality of personal rights and rights of property between former masters and slaves, and the connection heretofore existing between them becomes that between employer and hired laborer.'"

When she finishes, no one knows what to do at first. Clay looks at me like, *Should we clap?* Real quick I grab a cup of spiked punch, and I hold it up high.

"Here's to absolute equality of rights," I say. And then I add, "When that finally happens!" I was careful to say "when" and not "if." In response, there's a chorus of *amens*, *hear hears*, and *yeses*. Anne Marie smiles at me, and I can tell she's already feelin' better.

Bernadette gets loud again, talkin' about this movie she saw, recountin' every detail. Somethin' about a man so afraid of bein' buried alive that he opens his father's tomb and has a heart attack right there cuz the tomb's empty. I don't care for horror flicks. They don't get anything right.

I yawn, for the first time thinking about my early morning, when Clay gives my pinky a tug. I turn to him, and he tilts his head toward the road.

"This was so much fun," I say to Anne Marie, interrupting Bernadette's endless movie report, "but I gotta get up early."

"Yeah, me too," Clay says, standing up behind me.

"It ain't that late yet," Leon protests.

"Late enough," Clay says with a smile. "I'll walk Evalene home."

"Bye, y'all," I say, but they're already talkin' again. Anne Marie waves. Sad eyes again. I'll call her later to make sure she's all right.

Clay and I walk, his fingers interlaced with mine, and instead of heading to the main road, he gently points us toward the woods. Well, he stops and stares in the direction of the woods, and I lead us that way.

"How many days a week you work?" he asks as it gets harder and harder to see each other, the trees and their shadows surrounding us.

I sigh. Just thinking about work makes me wanna curl up and hide somewhere. "Five usually. Sometimes six."

"Damn. That's a lotta time to be around that brat."

I laugh. "How you know she's a brat?"

"If she was an angel, I'm sure your boss lady would wanna spend more time with her herself," he says. And that is a real good point. I'd never thought of it like that before.

"You're right. She's a terror."

"It's too bad."

"Who you tellin'?"

"No," he says, wrapping his arms around me and pulling me to him, "I mean about your schedule. I was hopin' to see a whole lot more a you this summer."

I stay calm and try not to tremble. But this is it, right? It has to be. All the time I've spent wonderin' if I've been imagining things, wishful thinking and all that, he has never been this overt. I don't think I have to wonder anymore. Clay likes me. He *likes* me. I look down so he can't see the size of my grin. But I can't get too carried away. Nothing's official yet.

"I don't see why you can't," I say.

"*When?*"

"You work too. We'll just have to be . . . creative."

"Oh, is that all?" he asks, eyes sparkling with mischief. "I can be creative."

"Really?"

"Evvie girl, you ain't seen creative yet," he jokes, and I laugh, moving in even closer. He leans down so our foreheads touch. I look into his eyes. I love those big eyes of his. If I had to stare at 'em all day long, it wouldn't be long enough for me.

But now . . . He ain't lookin' in my eyes now. He's lookin' down at my lips.

"You have no idea, do you?"

"Idea of what?" I ask him.

He chuckles and blinks, and his eyelashes brush against my skin. He swallows.

"You're like nobody else," he whispers.

It's slow, but he leans down the rest of the way, following what his eyes desire, and kisses me, and I think my body is finna melt into a pool a heat and feelin' and taste. I kiss back, and we kiss so hard and for so long, my lips start to get tingly, and I don't mind a bit. His mouth finds my earlobes, my neck, my collarbone.

"Oh, Evvie," he breathes.

And the unwelcome thought of Mama pops into my head outta nowhere. She would be *livid* if she knew what her baby girl was doin' right this very minute. I have a feelin' if anyone's gonna put on the brakes, it'll have to be me. I know that we shouldn't be doin' this so soon, but I can't stop us. So Clay does.

"What's wrong?" I ask him.

He still has his arms around me, his hands delicately

caressing my back, but he's pulled back. He's put air between us, and I don't want air between us.

"Evvie," he starts, but he doesn't say anything else.

"What is it? Is it me?" With horror, I wonder if my roll-on has worn off. I *told* Mama not to get the cheap one!

"*No!* God no. I just . . ." He hesitates again. "I just don't want to do . . . anything until you're ready. Ya know?"

I take a breath. "Uh-huh."

Though we can't see each other too clearly in the dark, we keep on starin' in each other's eyes, waitin'. I know what we're waitin' for, and I kinda can't believe we're here already, but here we are. Kissin' just ain't enough. When I woke up this morning, I did not expect to be here. With him holding me tight and close like I'm a diamond. He's probably right. Why rush? It's risky, we could get caught, and I can't even think about how mortifying that would be. Worse yet . . . would he resent me later? If he thinks I'm easy?

"What are you thinkin'?" he asks.

Of all the reasons I should turn around and run home before I miss curfew.

"Clay?"

"Yes, Evvie girl," he whispers.

"I'm ready."

Under the cover of trees and night and cricket songs, Clay's gentle fingers slowly lift the bottom of my dress, as though he's waitin' for me to stop him at any second. I don't stop him. He removes my panties, and I'm glad he can't see 'em. They're covered in childish pink flowers. He parts my thighs. I'm a little scared, I admit, but so excited by his touch, by everything about him, I can't see straight. I can hardly breathe or think. And he's here and he moves into me and it hurts for a second and then it doesn't and I don't know where he ends and I begin and his breathing's coming hard now and we rock against the tree and he groans into my ear, a low deep sound from the far reaches of his throat and I exhale slowly . . . and then I see two eyes watching us.

I scream.

"What? What's wrong?" He can barely get the words out. Though the intense, hot beauty of the moment is now dead and gone for me, somehow it's not for Clay (bless his heart), and he finishes with a tiny cry.

Then there's stillness.

I'm frozen still, lookin' all around us, tryna find those eyes again.

And then I hear a twig break several yards away.

"Come on," I whisper, urgently. I scramble to fix my clothes, and he does the same.

"What's happening?" he asks.

"Somebody's out there," I say, and I scan the trees for any sign of life. I find none. The twig coulda been a critter, but not the eyes. They were at least five feet off the ground, maybe six, but the strangest thing was I could make out the eyes clear as day, but the rest of the face looked . . . blank.

"You sure it wasn't your imagination?"

"No!" I snap. "I know what I saw."

We leave the woods and walk back toward the park. I

start to feel bad for snappin' at him, so I take hold of his hand, and he squeezes back tight.

"Did you see what they looked like?"

I shake my head. "It was weird lookin'."

"It?"

"I don't know if it was a man or a woman or—"

"A bear?"

I swat at him and he laughs, then pulls me close.

"WHATCHU DOIN'?"

I jump a mile high, and Clay clutches me with shaking hands as Marcus and R. J. emerge from the bushes, laughin' their fool heads off!

"You creeps! What is *wrong* with you?" I shout as I give R. J. a good, rough shove, but they both just keep on laughin' at me. I have half a mind to put the hurtin' on them. They don't know who they're messin' with. They don't know the talents I got.

"Y'all a couple a jackasses! You scared poor Evvie half to death," Clay yells, his own voice quivering.

"Ah, can't you take a li'l, bitty joke every now and again?" R. J. asks, batting his eyelashes at me.

"Not funny at all," I say, not daring to let any fear tears fall. "I'm finna stick the church ladies on y'all! What kinda perverts watch folks when they alone together like that?"

R. J. and Marcus stop laughing then.

"Watchin' folks when . . . ? R. J. just saw y'all coming down the path, so we hid and jumped out." Marcus is puzzled. "I don't see how that's perverted at all."

"No before. Back in the woods! I saw you! We heard you runnin' off," I holler. Somewhere in the back of my mind I know what I'm sayin' makes no sense. There's no way R. J. or Marcus coulda been that quiet, and the blankness . . . Still, I'd rather find out it was just them bein' stupid instead of thinkin' about the alternatives.

"We weren't back in the woods," R. J. says evenly. He's telling the truth. So that means somebody else was watchin' us.

"Evalene," R. J. begins, "what was you two doin' alone back there?"

I feel my cheeks get hot. Who the hell is he to be asking me that question?

"R. J.?" Clay cocks his head at him and steps forward. "Think you done enough for one night. Why donchu go on home before I get irritated." Oh shit. I do believe Clay just threatened him. He might be wiry and pretty, but Clay will knock a nigga down if they askin' for it.

R. J. takes a step back, and I can see that he's mad, but also a li'l nervous. He's not a fighter. "I can't ask a simple question?"

"Night, R. J. Night, Marcus," Clay says.

"You can't stop me from talkin' to her. We known each other since we was kids." Damn! He just won't give up.

"R. J.! Go *home*," I finally cry. "Stop pesterin' me and stickin' your nose where it don't belong!" I pull Clay away from the pranksters, not caring about anything they might say in response. Why did they have to spoil everything?

Course . . . somebody disrupted our perfect night before they came along.

Once they're outta earshot, Clay tugs gently at my hand. "He's obsessed with you."

"I don't care if he is. Sick of it." I keep walking fast, and I don't know who or what I need to get away from so badly, but I don't wanna slow down. I don't even wanna think. I just wanna go.

"Evvie girl." He plants himself on the sidewalk, and I'm forced to stop. I look up, and my house is in full view, just a couple steps away. We musta been walkin' a good twenty minutes without sayin' a word. Felt like two.

"You mad at me?"

I shake my head.

He pulls me into his arms again, and I catch a good whiff of aftershave mixed with just a touch of sweat and fatigue, and I swear to Christ Jesus, if I don't faint dead away, I might start chewin' on his face.

"Can I see you tomorrow?" he asks.

I smile and nod. I gotta be careful with him. Can't let him know how much power he's got over me. Guys will walk all over you if they think they can get away with it. I know in my heart Clay's not like that. Maybe it's my mother's voice in my head, urging me to always be cautious.

"Good," he says, and he kisses me again, firm and sincere, just enough to let me know there's more to come. He slides his face near my ear. "I know I didn't do my job tonight. But I will tomorrow."

He kisses my hand and waits until I'm inside. I stumble up the concrete walkway and repeat his words in my head. *I know I didn't do my job tonight. But I will tomorrow.* So mysterious. As I unlock the door and step inside, I look over my shoulder, and he's still there. Right now, he looks like a painting. Beautiful and strong, with just a touch of silliness. He's perfection, and he has no idea. I wave and shut the door behind me.

That's when I get it. His job. Oh. My. Lord.

I collapse against the door and slide down to the floor with this stupid grin on my face. Clayton Alexander Jr. must be from some special sexy planet.

While I'm still in a puddle on the floor, I feel pressure against my back. The door's trying to come open, and I lean back with some force. Sometimes I don't shut it hard enough the first time, and it comes loose. Then there's a knock, and I jump up in case it's Clay.

But when I open the door, nobody's there. Instead, I think I hear footsteps near the side of the house. I don't know what to do, and I ain't especially inclined to go investigate. I strain my ears, listening hard.

Then I get an eerie feelin'. I look across the street, and my insides go cold. Standing there, facing me, is a man. At least I think it's a man. He's thin and pale. Ghostly white. His hair is jet black. He's older than I am, maybe somewhere in his twenties, and he stands so still I begin to wonder if he's a statue. I blink a few times to make sure I'm seeing properly. I am, and still he stands. But the second I venture past the threshold, the figure moves, and it scares the bejesus outta me!

I duck back inside, slam the door shut, lock it, and turn out the hall light. I'm pretty sure I've never seen this man in my life, and I don't know why he scares me, but lookin' at him is like lookin' at the dead that won't stay dead. They always want more than the living can possibly give. They want to devour. He has that look, but to see it in the face of a living person is far more chilling. The dead rarely hurt you. The living do it every day.

After a few breaths, I peek through the window drape.

He's gone. I feel relief for the moment. But somehow I know that feeling won't last.

4

Beautiful

EW. I FEEL DAMP GRASS UNDER MY FEET.
I look down and there it is. How'd I get outside? I
don't remember leavin' the house. And why in the
world am I barefoot?

I figure it out pretty quick. This is a dream, maybe a
dream-vision. Too soon to tell yet.

I look around. Walls. I'm inside a building, but there's no
floor—just grass. It's dingy in here. Ceiling's leaking in one
spot, and the walls are made of ugly wood paneling that's
stained. Scorched, actually.

I hear steps. I turn, and a tall shape whirls past me
and into a wall. *Through* the wall. I hear something like
a giggle or a cry or a hum. Haints. What do they want?
They never show up for no reason.

"I saw you," I call out into the emptiness.

No response. My heart beats faster. I don't know if a haint could seriously hurt me or not, but my fight-or-flight instinct kicks into high gear when they poke at me like this.

Another one's here. I can't see or hear it. Until she laughs low into my ear canal, and my skin's finna crawl off my bones. I cry out, and now I'm flying fast. She must be pushing me—*some*thing is—but my feet hover above the ground. I have no control of my body. We're heading right for the wall.

"No," I whimper. Doesn't she know I can't move through walls?

We are a breath away from smashing into the cheap wood paneling. I cover my face with my arms, and at the moment of impact, I spill out into a carpeted room, walls painted a sickly pink. The first room has vanished. Another faint giggle. If they weren't so scary and . . . dead, the haints might remind me of the munchkins from *The Wizard of Oz* movie.

I don't see 'em anywhere. No odd shapes or blurs creepin' into my view. But I do see somebody, a regular person. She's sittin' in a rickety rockin' chair with her back to me. She's just rockin' back and forth. Then she starts to whistle Perry Como's "Till the End of Time." I hate that song. She stands up, and I stay where I am, afraid to move. She turns to me, and . . . she *is* me. Another me. Comin' toward me, whistlin' a tune I can't stand. She cradles a box in both arms, takin' her time to get to me. Obviously in no hurry.

As she gets close, I realize I do not want whatever's in that box, and I try to run, but I can't move.

She stops just in front of me, her whistlin' now loud,

piercing my precious eardrums. She holds the box out to me. I know I don't have a choice, so I pull open the box's flaps. Inside is a black-and-white rabbit with a pacifier in its mouth. Its throat has been slashed, and blood trickles from the wound. Where its eyes should be are dark mirrors. I scream as hard as I can, and I can feel it. But the only sound I hear is her—me?—whistling.

I sit up so fast in bed, I come to standing. Goddamn haints, givin' me nightmares. I lean against the wall, waitin' for my pulse to get back to normal. Every now and then, I might learn somethin' useful when the haints enter my dreamworld. Sometimes I think they just show up to remind me that they can. They can be sadistic.

Mama fries potatas and onions and a green tomato on the stove and shakes her head, cuz she sure didn't raise me to be a tramp, she says. I don't say too much a nothin', but I listen to her criticize my every choice while I comb and plait the twins' heads.

"What kinda decent girl stays out to all hours with a buncha ragamuffins up to who knows what?"

She knows damn well that that buncha "ragamuffins" includes honor students, churchgoers, and at least one Boy Scout. But what I say is:

"I did get in before eleven."

"I told you be home by ten. Last time I checked, eleven

and ten was two completely different times. Have they changed that? Is that the new math I keep hearin' about?" She angrily places the food all on one plate and practically throws it on the table.

"This is how girls be actin' right before they turn up pregnant," she informs me.

"Ow," Coralene whines when I yank her hair harder than I mean to. Doralene snickers.

"Almost done," I mumble.

"So? Donchu got nothin' to say for yourself?" Mama challenges.

"I'm sorry. I don't know what else I can say."

She stares at me with her arms crossed. "How many a y'all stayed so late?"

"Just a couple."

Mama watches me suspiciously, eating a forkful of potatas. Even though she's chewing, I can see her face relax. She's already less mad. This feels like the perfect time to remind her of how brave and selfless she thought I was not so long ago, but that's the kinda smart-mouthin' that might get me smacked. I decide it's better to keep my mouth shut.

"You have the curse," she says quietly. "You know that?"

I dip some fingers into the hair grease and rub it into Doralene's scalp. Despite her resistance, we have talked about the strange talents we Deschamps women share, but I never heard her call it a curse before. I don't think that's right. Nobody should feel bad about shit they can't help.

"It's a curse now?" I ask her.

"Always has been." She sighs. I'm shocked when she takes my face in her hands and looks deeply into my eyes. I'm so unprepared for whatever this is that I get the comb caught in Doralene's hair, and she cries out.

"Evalene," Mama says. "You're beautiful."

"Uh." I don't know what to say to this. "Thank you, Mama."

"Don't thank me." She is not playin' around. Deadly serious. "It is a curse. A beautiful face and a beautiful body can bring no good fortune to a colored woman. Men always see the beautiful things. And they think they got a right to have 'em and do what they want with 'em regardless of how the beautiful thing feels. There's a lotta ugly men out there, and sometimes their ugliness is hidden by a handsome face, but they ugly deep inside and they see that beauty and they want to steal it for themselves." Mama leans on the counter for support, and her eyes travel far away for an instant. I wonder if she's thinkin' about men from her own life. I'd ask, but I don't want to upset her. She doesn't like talkin' about the past.

"I want you to be careful. I mean it."

"I will be, Mama."

I know why she's scared, and I know what she thinks. If I wasn't worried it'd break her heart, I'd tell her that being with Clay isn't like that at all. He makes me feel loved and whole and not like he wants to own me or hide me away from the world for himself. But I can't tell her I did in fact do that thing that could make me pregnant. I also can't tell her that I know I'm not pregnant, so that's somethin' else she needn't worry about. I'm not. There's a trick to it.

"You already been . . ." She stops.

"I been what?"

"Mama, she hurtin' me," Coralene whimpers.

"Me too," Doralene says. I'm 'bout to smack both of 'em with this brush if they don't shut up.

Mama releases my face, and I finish up their plaits right before they both jump up at the same time and run out the door to play. No doubt their hair will look like a couple a birds' nests by noon, but that ain't my problem.

I clean up the hair stuff and realize I have to get moving before Miss Ethel claims I'm late again. I bend down to slip on my flats, and I feel a kick in my rear, and I fall forward. On my hands and knees, I turn myself around and see that Mama's still standin' over by the screen door munchin' on a green tomato, a good ten feet away from me. Oh. I see how it is.

"Mama, *what*? I been listenin' to you all morning. And I will be careful. I promise."

"Who was it?" she asks, narrowing her eyes at me.

I dust myself off and stand, finally getting my shoes all the way on.

"Imma be late if I don't leave right now."

Her eyes flash, and without moving a muscle, she pushes me backward into a chair and scoots it up to the table, just shy a knockin' the wind outta me.

She's playin' with me. I don't have time to play, and she's gettin' on my damn nerves. I take in a short breath, and I lift Mama off the floor about a foot or so, for about ten seconds. Then I let her drop easily like she's landin' on a pillow. Just so she knows that I can play too. Her eyes widen. She's surprised, but not completely shocked.

"You jube on the regular now?"

Do I jube on the regular? Sounds like she's askin' about my monthlies.

"Kinda," I tell her.

She nods, and I can see her rearrangin' everything in her mind to line up with this new information.

"Anybody else know?"

"Who would I tell?" I ask her. I can't imagine braggin' about it around town. "I mean, nobody would understand anyway if they ain't our blood."

Mama swallows. She's holdin' somethin' back.

"What?" I say. "It's true, ain't it? Nobody knows about Jubilation except the Deschamps women, right?"

She shakes her head slowly. "No. It ain't just us. I've heard about it showin' up in others," she explains.

This is news to me. I always understood it as our weird family affliction that we just have to endure. At least that's how Mama explained it to me back in that church basement when I scratched that girl's face. I thought it was only ours.

"And . . . these others? They're not related to us?"

"Not that I know of. Though we are all God's children, so I suppose we're all related."

"Shouldn't we know who they are?"

"No," she snaps. "That is why I want you to keep it to yourself. You gonna be volatile enough on your own. You don't need no partners."

Damn. She makes it sound like I'm finna hold up a liquor store!

"Do you think we should tell Grammie Atti?" I ask.

"No indeed. Evvie, your grandmother is—she'd make all this harder than it needs to be. You know how she is," she tells me, though I rarely see her, so do I really? I can't help but wonder if Mama's mostly worried about what her church lady friends would say if they knew her daughter was spendin' time with crazy ol' Athena Deschamps. That's how a lotta folks see her anyway.

"You don't think she could help?" I ask.

"We can handle it without her. Just keep it quiet. Never use it unless you have to."

I sigh. Mama don't like usin' magic for nothin'. She's one a those good Christian ladies. Tell ya the truth, I'm surprised we been talkin' about it this long, since she's always avoidin' the subject.

"What about accidents? The times when I don't mean for it to come out, but it does?"

She eyes me, almost suspiciously. Like I'm lookin' for an excuse to jube. Does she think this is fun for me?

"If you keep your feelings under control, you shouldn't be havin' no accidents," she warns.

This makes no sense to me, cuz last time I checked, feelings aren't something we can just control like a light switch. But I choose the path of least resistance.

"Sure, Mama."

"You're gonna have to be real aware a yourself, Evalene.

You're too old for accidents. This ain't a blackout here and there no more. This is the real thing."

I fight hard to not roll my eyes. "I know, Mama."

"Oh, do you?"

I wait a few seconds, and then I slowly rise, grab my purse, and head out to work.

"Evvie," she calls.

She is drivin' me *crazy*! I turn around to face her a little too fast, and somehow, the force of my feeling shoves my mother several feet backward. She has to grab the table to keep from fallin' over. I can't breathe. The last person I want to hurt is my mother.

"I'm sorry, Mama. That was—"

"An accident?" she whispers.

I can feel a few tears burning in my eyes. I'm terrible with magic, and I don't know how to get better. I dab at the corners of my eyes with a handkerchief from my purse, and I put it back in with shaking hands. Mama keeps starin' at me, not speaking. She's scared. So am I.

"Mama, I have to go. I'm sorry. I—I'm really sorry. I didn't mean to do that." I honestly didn't. As I grab the doorknob, she regains her voice.

"Evalene Claudette Deschamps?"

I draw in a breath. "Yes, Mama?"

"Don't hurt nobody."

5

Stranger

I MAKE IT TO THE HEYWOODS' AT JUST SIX minutes past eight. I expect Miss Ethel to get on my case about it, but she don't even seem to notice. She barely leaves me any instructions before she flies out the door, and what Clay said last night about her returns to my mind. What does she need to do so early? Her husband's a dentist, and far as I know, she does not have a job to go to. Maybe she's foolin' around.

"Evalene, I want some milk."

"Okay. What d'ya have to say first?"

Abigail makes a face with her tongue hanging out. "Please," she says, as though the word is choking her. I reach for her Donald Duck cup that nobody else in the house is allowed to use, and I fill it with milk. I set it in front of her, and she stares at it.

"Now what d'ya say when somebody gives you what you ask for?"

"Evalene, let's have some ice cream," Abigail says.

"Nope. You just had breakfast, and the ice cream's for after your supper."

She clenches her jaw and scrunches her eyes at me like a wildcat.

"Mommy said I could have it. She said it before you came here."

"I don't think so. She has never once said you could have ice cream durin' the day, so why would she change her mind now?"

Abigail blows air out through her cheeks, like I'm the most frustrating person on the whole earth. She takes a meager sip of milk, barely a drop, and then she dumps the rest out all over the floor, smiling at me.

I close my eyes and take a deep breath. Looks like it's gonna be one a *those* days.

I wash up the breakfast dishes and keep a clear view of Abigail out in the backyard on the swing set. The neighbor girl, Patty, has come over with her naked baby dolls, and they talk their little-girl nonsense. This oughta gimme a few minutes peace until they start to fight and I have to go out and separate 'em.

With them still in my view, I reach over for the telephone and dial Anne Marie's number.

"Hi, Miss Alice, how you doin'? It's Evalene," I say into the receiver. She sounds happy to hear from me and asks how my summer's goin' and all that. She mentions she saw me in the paper and she's so proud. I wonder just how long my dumb thirty seconds of fame is gonna last.

"Thank you, ma'am," I tell her. After that, she puts Anne Marie on the line.

"Hello?"

"Hey, Anne. How are you?"

"All right."

"Your uncle still botherin' ya?"

"Huh? Oh that. Nah. I just been ignorin' him."

"Good. Good for you," I say. I'm not exactly sure what to say next, but somethin' told me I should check up on her today.

"Evvie? You there?"

"Yeah. Yeah, I'm here."

"What's wrong?"

"Well, last night when we left the park, you seemed . . . a li'l bit down or distracted or somethin'. I sure hope we didn't spoil Juneteenth for ya." I glance out the window. A game of Mother May I. Patty is twirling in circles at Abigail's behest. Naturally, Abigail is Mother.

Anne Marie takes a second. She sighs. "I'm fine, Evvie."

"You sound kinda not fine."

I hear what I think is a laugh, but I'm not sure.

"Anne? Are you upset? About me and Clay?"

"*WHAT?*"

"I mean—" Oh shit! Maybe I am way, *way* off base!

"Why would you say that?" she asks, her voice guarded.

I feel my pulse racing, and my hands shake. I did not expect such an intense reaction. The kitchen table starts vibrating, and the floral centerpiece on top bounces up and down.

"If I'm completely wrong, I'm sorry, and I hope you're not mad. I just wondered if maybe . . . you liked him. And you never told me. I just never, ever want a guy to come between us, ya know?" It honestly never crossed my mind that she might like Clay until I noticed her lookin' sad last night when I left the party.

The vibrating escalates. I reach for the vase, but the phone cord ain't long enough, and I watch it tip over, spilling water, peonies, and daffodils all over the place.

But then . . . she starts cracking up. No mistaking this for something else: she is definitely laughin'. Instantly the table stops moving.

"No! I am not interested in Clay. You don't need to worry about that."

"Then what is it?"

She clears her throat, which makes me think she's about to lie.

"Can we talk about it some other time?"

Now she's scarin' me. She tells me everything. Why not this? I grab a dish towel to mop up the water on the floor. "Is it somethin' serious?"

"No . . . ," she says, but trails off like there's more to the answer than a simple no. She sighs. "I don't like Clay like that, Evvie. But I guess I do wonder sometimes what it's like to be you."

"Why?"

"Cuz everybody wants you!"

Where did *that* come from? She's never said anything like this to me before. "That is not true," I tell her.

"It is, actually."

"How do you know that?"

"Because I have eyes and I can see with 'em. It's hard sometimes, cuz it ain't fair. But it's not your fault."

I stop fussin' with the flower mess and sit on the floor. I feel light-headed. Is this new, or has she always felt like this? I dab my forehead with the wet dish towel. I tend to feel a bit ill when I think I mighta hurt someone's feelings without meaning to.

"Evvie? You there?"

"Anne? Can you come over here? I'm at the Heywoods'."

"Why?"

Why? Because you basically just said you're jealous of me, and I'm afraid you're 'bout to drop me as a friend!

"I don't know. Talkin' on the phone is limited. I wanna see your face." It's all I can think to say.

"Maybe. Where is it again?"

I have to pause and swallow. Feels like tears aren't too far away, and I don't understand why I keep gettin' all emotional today.

"Thirty-Five Sutton," I tell her.

Outside, a gentle breeze blows through the elm leaves. I spy some dandelion dust floatin' on the air and settling in the pile of dirt where Abigail and Patty were just playing.

Were. Just. Playing. They're gone.

I drop the phone and race to the back door, throwing it open.

"Abigail? Where y'all at?"

Nothing. A dog barks from somebody's yard.

"Abigail! Patty! Answer me!"

Nothing.

I run up and down the yard, snaking through the swing set, the sandbox, the seesaw, and around the front with the tacky wooden sheep lawn ornament announcing THE HEYWOODS. They're nowhere. *Nowhere.* I run as fast as I can go down Sutton Lane, looking in every yard I see. Down one side and up the other.

"What's the matter with you, gal?" some old white man watering his grass calls out as I fly by him. They were just there! Where could they've gotten to so goddamn fast?

I run right through Patty's yard, her mama hollerin' out the back door, leap over the low hedges back into the Heywoods' backyard, and I look inside. I see a tall, pale figure walking toward the front of the house. There's a strange man in the house! I wanna turn and run in the opposite direction, but I have to take care of Abigail. I rush in, ignorin' all the alarm bells screamin' inside me. But once I get all the way through the kitchen, dinin' room, and sittin' room, he's gone.

"Evalene!"

I jump outta my skin.

"Oh, Christ Jesus!" Abigail and Patty sit on the front hall stairs staring at me all innocent. So cool and calm, as if butter wouldn't melt in either of their mouths.

"I was scared to *DEATH* lookin' for you," I shriek, shakin' like a tree caught in a hurricane. "How many times I gotta tell ya not to leave the yard without me?"

"But we didn't leave the yard," Abigail argues, eyes wide and questioning. Both girls got their filthy hands wrapped around ice cream cones, vanilla for Abigail and zebra swirl for Patty.

"Where did you get those?" I ask, tryna catch my breath.

"The man," Patty says, as if this is a dumb question.

"What man?"

Abigail scampers down the stairs and opens the door. Sure enough, out on the sidewalk, in the bright light of day, is the man I saw last night. He's closer now. He is not a statue. His eyes are concealed by dark shades. His lips bend unnaturally into a ghoulish smile. He cocks his head to the left, and I don't know why, but this gesture doesn't look human to me, and I drag Abigail back inside as fast as I can before slamming the door and locking it.

That pale face. It looks just as blank up close.

"Why did you do that?" Abigail asks.

I'm not sure how to answer that question. What did he do just now that was so wrong? I can't explain it, but it felt like . . . it made me think of old stories I'd hear as a kid, about the boogeyman. They said he ate children who misbehaved so he could steal their souls. When I saw that man out there, I felt like I was lookin' at a person who would surely eat me to steal my soul.

"Ha-ha! You told me I couldn't have it, but I got ice cream anyway, Evalene!" Abigail gloats.

I lean against the banister, using it for support. I try to sound calm.

"Do you know who he was?" I ask.

"Huh-uh, but he was nice," Patty says. "He got us ice cream from the ice cream man when you was on the phone forever, and then he made us hide with him. He said it was a game."

"He said you'd think it was funny. Isn't he your friend?" Abigail asks me.

I shake my head. "No. He's not my friend. I don't know who that man was."

"He knows you," they both say in unison. A shiver passes through me. My throat is raw and dry. I hold my hands together to stop the shakin'. I'm scared, but above all, I'm tired. Tired and relieved that the kids are safe. I don't even wanna think about this weirdo right now. Or ever. I slump down to the bottom stair, the girls above me. The man. The stranger bearing gifts. Who *is* he? And why does he frighten me more than any haint ever has?

"Do not talk to grown-ups you don't know. Don't follow 'em, don't hide with 'em, and don't take ice cream or anything else from 'em. Understand me?"

"I will if I want!" Abigail shouts back.

I swear to baby Jesus in the manger . . .

"Not if you're smart you won't. Smart folks know better than that. I thought you's intelligent, Abigail. Guess I was wrong."

Abigail sticks her tongue out at me, but when she goes back to licking her ice cream, I can see she's actually considering what I said.

There's a knock at the door. My heart stops, and so does my breathing. I jump to my feet and shuffle the girls into the kitchen.

"Why's there water and flowers on the floor?" Abigail whines.

"Be quiet." I hide them in the broom closet.

I throw open every kitchen drawer searching for the biggest knife I can find, but before I can grab one, something zips past my face, and then I hear a loud thump. I run into the living room, and, between the door and the window, I see a seven- or eight-inch serrated knife sticking outta the wall.

A memory overtakes me. I'm eleven, and I'm out in the woods with my grandmother. She hands me an arrow, and I shoot it straight into a tree trunk. Without a bow. Or my hands.

"Do you know how that happened?" she asks me. I'm looking up at her, and she's leaning down toward me. I feel nervous, like I done somethin' wrong.

Before I can answer, somebody grabs me from behind.

Mama. She yells at Grammie Atti and tells her not to show me how to do anything else. She wants me to grow up right. Not like a heathen. Even now, I can hear my grandmother laughing at us in the background as Mama dragged me away.

My current sixteen-year-old self yanks the knife from the wall and studies it. I did that. I made it happen without meaning to, or even knowing I was doing it. This is me. Has this always been me?

If one of the girls had been in the path a that knife . . .

Another knock at the door, louder this time. I peek through the curtain. Oh, good lord, it's just Anne Marie.

I open the door. "Hi," I say, and pull her inside before slamming the door and locking it again.

"What in the Sam Hill's goin' on in here?" she asks while I run to lock the back door. She follows me into the kitchen and stares at me standing there with that big ol' knife.

I glance down at it, stagger over to the counter, and throw it in a drawer.

I open the broom closet. "It's okay," I assure the girls. I tell 'em to go wash their hands and play in the nursery for a while. For the first time I can remember, Abigail does what I say without argument, and Patty does the same.

"We had an unexpected guest," I explain to Anne Marie.

"Was it the wolf man?"

I hold my palm up to Anne so she'll give me a minute. I know I shouldn't, I *really* shouldn't—I'm too young, and it don't belong to me—but I open the liquor cabinet and pour myself a whiskey neat. I offer her the bottle, but she shakes her head in thinly veiled revulsion. I sip it as we sit in silence for a few moments. Eventually, Anne Marie busts out laughing.

"What? It ain't funny!"

"I'm sure it ain't. And I wanna hear the details and I promise I'll stop laughin', but I have to tell you—" She comes over to me and gives me a big, goofy kiss on the forehead. "It is so nice to see you lookin' like an unholy mess for once in your life!"

6

Stars

I LEAN BACK IN THE TUB AND CLOSE MY eyes, so glad this day is done and not ready to think about tomorrow yet. Me and Anne Marie had a long talk after I told her about losin' the girls and the strange man in the house givin' out ice cream. I don't know if she got everything off her chest that she wanted to, but she said a lot. She was beatin' herself up a bit for feelin' jealous of me sometimes. Both because she loves me and because it's one of the seven deadly sins. I told her *envy* was a deadly sin, not jealousy, and they're two different things. I learned that from somewhere. She wanted to know the difference, and I couldn't quite remember, but it's somethin' like wantin' something somebody has versus already havin' something and bein' scared to lose it. She looked more confused after I explained it, so I told her to forget about it. I just asked her to quit bein' hard on herself. We can't help how we feel.

She also said some stuff I didn't really feel like hearin'.

It's no big secret that Clay's been with girls. A lotta girls. Unfortunately, Anne seemed to know many more details than I did, and she decided to share them.

"Ya know that girl Prissy? Gap toothed, long wavy hair?"

"Her too?"

Anne Marie nodded solemnly.

"And, I wasn't gonna tell you this, but I think you deserve to know," she dramatically began. "Remember Deacon Samuel? His wife Ida and their four kids?"

"What about 'em?"

Anne Marie gave me a knowing look.

"Wait a minute. *Ida?* Mrs. Samuel?"

Anne Marie raised her hands in that *don't kill the messenger* way.

"I don't know if I believe that one. I mean, ain't she like *thirty-five?* That don't make sense to me."

"Evvie? Why do you think they moved?"

I stayed quiet. I didn't know why they moved, and I'd never given it any thought before.

Anne Marie didn't have much else to say after that. She didn't have to; she'd made her point. I guess she's just worried about me. I heard some things, sure, but . . . *Ida Samuel?* I would never say this out loud, but let's just say

Ida ain't exactly . . . easy on the eyes. She's not hideous or anything, bless her heart, but . . . I don't get it.

Regardless, it doesn't do to put too much weight on the idle words of idle tongues.

About that time the girls started screamin' at each other and throwin' breakable shit, so I sent Patty home, and Anne headed home too.

The bathwater is murky from my filth of the day and the Soir de Paris I sprayed in it while the water was runnin'. Clay and me didn't make solid plans for tonight, but he asked if he could see me. And that would be the onliest reason for the Soir de Paris. But I doubt Mama will be inclined to let me go out again after gettin' in late last night. That is *if* he comes by at all. Who knows? Maybe some nice deacon's wife is keepin' him company tonight.

Coralene walks in the bathroom without knockin', and I shoot her a glare.

"How many times I gotta tell you to knock when you know somebody's in here?"

Keeping her feet planted, she leans sideways back to the door and knocks on it from the inside. Smart-ass.

"Mama says you takin' too long, cuz other people gotta use the bafroom," she informs me.

"I'm almost done."

"No! You gotta come outta there *now*."

"Li'l girl, you bes' watch your tone with me."

"I'm just tellin' you what Mama said."

I feel a strong urge to teach her a real lesson. Like maybe

reach out and tug on one a them pigtails without usin' my hands, but then she'll be havin' nightmares and wakin' me up at all hours. The twins are still too young to know what powers they'll soon have. They got a good six or seven year before the jube comes for them. About the time they'll be gettin' their periods. Jubilation and menstruation are inextricably linked in our family.

"I'm comin'. Get out."

"No, I'm sposeta bring you back wif me."

"*Out*, or Imma dunk your head in here and wash that mop a yours!" This is enough to send her squealin' from the room. I empty the tub and dry off. I get into my nightgown and make a firm decision. If I don't hear from Clay tonight, I *refuse* to cry. Not gonna happen. I will not be the girl who can't have an enjoyable evening without the attentions of a boy. Man. Either one.

In my bedroom (which ain't too much bigger than a closet, but it's mine and I love it), I look over my little bookshelf. I don't have a whole lotta books, and most a the ones I have, I already read at least twice. There's just one I've barely touched. That damn *Ulysses*. One a the old white ladies Mama used to work for gave us this box of donations once, and that book was in there. Books are rare cuz books ain't cheap, so we cherish them. But this one I have yet to make heads or tails of. I pick it up again, just outta curiosity. I read the first seven lines. Nope. I slam that thing shut and shove it back on the shelf. I don't think me and James Joyce'll ever be on friendly terms.

I smile at my worn-out copy of *The Golden Book of*

Astronomy, a childhood gift from an old auntie who has since passed on. I know it's really for kids, but it's still my favorite book. It's always here for a reread when I need comfort. Just not in the mood for it right now.

I plop on my bed and sigh. I know *Wagon Train*'s on, so I could go out and watch that with Mama. Then again, I hate *Wagon Train.* Whatever it takes, I will find something to do tonight!

My door flies open. "Mama says gimme a bath," Doralene announces.

Great.

"Didn't you have one last night?"

"No, that was Coralene."

"Give yourself a bath. You're big enough."

"Mama says you have to make sure I wash my butt and my bird."

"Jesus," I say under my breath.

"I'm tellin' Mama you said Jesus."

"What can I say? The holy spirit just hits me sometimes," I mutter. She still wants to tattle, but now she's confused. I go into the bathroom to run her bathwater.

"Mama says I can see my daddy on Sunday," Doralene says, stepping into the water. "Too hot!" I know damn well that water's barely tepid, but I humor her and sprinkle in a few drops of cold. Then she sits down in it.

"How comes you don't never come wif us?"

"Because he's not *my* daddy," I say. "I tell you that every time you ask me."

"Nuh-uh. You told Coralene."

"I told the both a ya."

"You don't like him?"

"It's not about that. If he lived with us, that'd be one thing, but he doesn't. So he's your family. Not mine."

"Why ain't he your daddy too?"

"Because I already had one before you were even a thought. Wash."

Mama opens the door and walks in, because nobody in this family knows how to knock.

"You got a visitor," she says.

"Tell 'em I'm busy," Doralene instructs.

"Not *you!*" Mama frowns at me. "What you want me to tell him?"

So he did show up.

"I don't know. Am I allowed out tonight?"

"Oh, that's right! I almost forgot! You can wait 'til the weekend to go out."

Goddamnit! She'd already forgotten about last night! I'm an idiot.

"Then I guess you can tell him I'm sorry, and I'll call him later," I say, tryna sound like it's no big deal and I'm not devastated.

"You'll call him?" she asks.

I nod and point out some dirt that Doralene's missed on her leg.

Mama's lips curl into a sly grin. "You didn't even ask me who was at the door."

My cheeks flush.

"Why don't you go down and tell him yourself," she says, taking my place by the tub. "Tell Coralene she can come in here with us. And cover up first," she warns, glancing at my chest. My nightgown ain't see-through, but it is rather flimsy.

I throw on a robe before I shove a complaining Coralene into the bathroom and shut the door. I run down the stairs, terrified he might be gone by now and momentarily terrified that it could be R. J.

I get to the door, and there he stands. Not R. J. Thank the sweet lord.

"Hey, Evvie girl," he breathes with that smile a his. "Thought we had a date."

"Yeah." I step out onto the porch and pull the door closed behind me. I must look quite interesting in my flip-flops and robe. It's a black satin kimono robe with dragons of different colors on it. It once belonged to Mama, but she gave it to me. Said it made her feel old to wear it. It's pretty, but looks like somethin' a madam in a whorehouse might wear.

"Sorry 'bout that," I say. "I guess cuz we didn't make no definite plans, I wasn't real sure—"

And Clay interrupts me with a kiss. A soft, quiet kiss, but intense nonetheless. He pulls his lips back, but his face remains so close to mine I could probably count his pores if I wanted to. It's right, him bein' this close to me. So right, it feels like we've always been like this.

"You sure now?" he whispers.

I nuzzle his nose, not wanting to lose this physical contact.

"I'm not sure I can get away tonight," I finally say.

"Why?"

Such a simple question. Why indeed.

"I'm kinda in trouble," I say, and then laugh at how baby-ish that sounds. He smiles at me.

"What did ya do, wild child?"

"Came home an hour past curfew last night. Cuz I was with *you*."

"Just an hour. That ain't nothin'."

"Maybe you should explain that to my mother."

"Maybe I should," he says, and he kisses me again. I feel like I got the sun inside me.

"Know what?" he asks.

"What?"

"Pop lent me the Plymouth tonight. You know how often that happens?"

I pretend to think about my answer. "Not that often?"

"That is correct." We both laugh. Kiss. Laugh. Kiss again.

"Tell her you'll never miss curfew again. Come on! Let me take you somewhere. Anywhere you wanna go," he says. "Where you wanna be right now?"

"Hawaii," I tell him, and we both crack up. I know what I'll be doing this evening, and I'm already planning out what I'll say to Mama in a matter of seconds, because there's no way anyone or anything can keep us apart tonight. Let 'em try.

***

I hop into the passenger's seat. I told him I'd be ten minutes, but it was closer to twenty-five, and even so, I'm still just wearin' some pedal pushers and a matchin' top, nothin' too special. But my cherry bomb lipstick is freshly coated, and my hair looks pretty sharp.

Mama wasn't too tough to handle. She has trouble sayin' no when she can tell how important something is to us. But if I don't make curfew this time, she threatened to punish me in a way I haven't even imagined, and I don't think she was kidding.

I turn and flash him a grin. He grins right back.

"I'm not gonna tell you you're stunning," he says.

I'm cool on the outside. Inside, I'm swoonin' like I'm in some old movie.

"Why not?" I ask.

"Cuz I don't want you to get a big head." He winks at me then and pulls away from the curb.

"Where we goin'?"

"You'll see. Ain't far."

It gets quiet for a few seconds, and I panic. I don't want him to get bored. I quickly try to come up with a conversation topic.

"You like workin' at the garage with your dad?" I ask him, and I almost want to take it back. I wish I'd thought harder. This is just generic small talk.

"I wouldn't say 'like,' but I could do worse. I can't do it much longer, though. Too risky."

I nod, confused at first, but then I know exactly what he's talking about.

"Have you ever hurt your hands before?"

"Not so bad it affected my playin'. But it's only a matter of time. That's why I gotta retire," he says.

"You should play for me sometime," I tell him. "Just me."

"I will," he says with a smile.

Clay's a real talented musician. He can play a few instruments, but his trumpet is like a part of him. I glance at the back seat, and there it sits in its sharp-lookin' case, like a third passenger.

"So you gonna go professional?" I ask.

"That's the plan. Not around here, though. Wouldn't be able to feed a squirrel on what I'd make here. Gotta get up north. Wailin' in a Chicago nightspot like the Regal Theater or at the Strand Hotel? That's my dream."

"That's a hip dream," I say. I bet it's wonderful to have a dream that could come true for real.

"It's a hard life, though," he muses, "bein' a musician. But I'd love to give it a real shot. At least then I'll always know I tried, ya know?"

"Yeah," I say, tryna imagine him moving from town to town just carrying his trumpet case. For some reason, the image makes me sad.

"What about you?" he asks. "You thought about what you gonna do when you graduate?"

I'm surprised by this question, and for a moment, I don't know what to say. This is the first time anybody's asked me.

"No. Not really," I say. I don't reveal my secret wish to go to college. Any college. My grades are mostly good, and I love to learn new things. Mrs. Abernathy, the tenth-grade science teacher, thinks I might be able to do all right in college.

My bigger secret is that I'd love to study the stars and the planets. I love my astronomy book, but it only goes so far. I've read a few others from the library, but they're all outta date. I'm sure in college they have modern books written by real astronomers workin' today. I'd love to get ahold a those. But there's no way in hell we'd ever be able to afford it.

"Not at all?" he pushes.

I shake my head. A few seconds later, we pull off onto a side road. He turns off the engine and doesn't make a move to get out yet.

"I always thought you'd make a swell teacher," he says. I'm shocked. Not only has nobody ever said this to me before, I never woulda guessed in a million years that Clayton Alexander Jr. sits around dreamin' up career paths for me.

"Really?"

"Sure! You're patient. Probably the smartest person I know. You'd be great," he says. I take a deep breath. He must be joking. This is some kinda flattery trick.

"Clayton? How you figure I'm the smartest person you know? We don't know each other *that* well."

"Quiz me," he says.

"Do what?"

"Ask me a question about you and see if I know the answer. Then decide how well I know you."

This is just silly. I think for a minute. I really wanna stump him.

"All right. Which one a my sisters is older?"

Clayton looks at me like I'm bonkers. "Twins! They the same age!"

"Ha! Nope. One of 'em's just a li'l bit—"

"Coralene is two minutes older than Doralene," he replies smoothly, and I'm stunned speechless. How could he possibly know that?

"Ha yourself! I know you," he says proudly. "And just to clarify? I said you were *probably* the smartest person I know. Jury's still out. Could go either way."

I laugh and just shake my head, not knowing what to do with him.

"Well? Did you know I hate kids?"

"Doesn't everybody till they have 'em?" he asks, and then opens the door and gets out. I start to open mine, but then I see him pick up speed and race around to open it for me. Only thing is, I still got hold of the handle and he's got momentum, so he nearly tears me outta the car just by force.

"Shit," I laugh, stumbling to catch my balance.

"Sorry," he says, and then smiles self-consciously. "I wanted to be a gentlemen. You gotta gimme a chance." He reaches out for my hand and I give it to him, and he walks us up to a squat building I've never noticed before.

"What is this place?"

He puts a finger over his lips but beams. He leads me down a few steps to a side door below street level. He turns the knob, and the door opens with a mild screech. Apparently, nobody locks this place up. We go inside, and it is pitch black.

"Don't move," he says, and I hear his footsteps walking away. I put my hands out in front of me and immediately bump something hard. Not as hard as a wall, but it doesn't budge. I don't like being trapped in small places. I can't hear his steps anymore, and I can't see. It feels like I'm trapped in a shrinkin' box. Clay's absence is makin' me nervous, and a thought takes me by surprise: this is the same kind of fear I felt earlier today when the Stranger appeared. The memory of him fills me with dread, and now I'm hyperventilating. I know I am gonna die if I don't get outta this place. Whatever has caged me in starts to quake, and I feel a headache moving in.

"Clay?" I call.

Then: light! Faint at first, but it slowly gets brighter. Candles. I can now see that I'm stuck between the wall and huge stacks of heavy boxes. They stop quaking and sit perfectly still as the headache passes. I take a moment to collect myself and allow my breath to settle.

Clay comes and helps pull me free. I feel so much better to be in a larger space again, I almost jump for joy.

"You all right?" he asks.

"Yeah. Yeah, I am now," I tell him breathlessly.

That's when I take in our surroundings. Clay has lit over a dozen old candles, and they're spread all around . . . books. Books everywhere. The ghostly light illuminates big cardboard displays with painted animals and pictures of children. A border at the top of one wall displays the cursive alphabet.

"Clay? What *is* this?"

"You never been here?" he asks.

I shake my head. He claps his hands one time and does a little dance, seamlessly transforming into a far younger version of himself.

"I was hopin' you hadn't. Come here," he says, pulling me over to one section. "This used to be the colored children's library."

"What? Why didn't nobody tell me 'bout this?" Good lord! If I'd known about this place, I'da spent just about every day a my childhood hiding out here readin' everything in sight. Why was this a big secret? A second later I gasp at the sight of a mouse emerging from a wall. Clay stamps his foot at it, and it disappears.

"Yeah, a lotta people don't know. Closed down before we were born. Look at this." He points to a decrepit shelf. My eye goes right to *The House at Pooh Corner*, and I pull it out. It's dusty, and some of the pages are frayed, but I can tell it was nice once. The cover feels like leather, and the drawing on the front looks similar to other Pooh pictures I've seen, but it's fancier, more like an engraving.

"I useta love this book."

"Look up there." He points to a faded, yellowing sign at the top of this section. I have to squint to make it out, but then I see it. NEW BOOKS FOR 1928. Wow. Hard to imagine that these old books were new once.

"Crazy, right?" he asks. "Most of 'em are older than these. At some point, they closed it, but nobody ever did anything with it. Never redistributed the books. Never fixed up this old space. It's almost like . . . like they'd rather lose money on a property, let all this perfectly good furniture and these perfectly good books rot, than give colored kids a chance to read. A place to go." He picks up a copy of *Rebecca of Sunnybrook Farm* and, my god, I do believe that Clayton just wiped a tear from his eye.

"How'd you find this place?" I ask him.

He grins. "Playin' jailbreak this one time."

I glance away from him, embarrassed. Hearing the word "jailbreak" come from his lips instantly transports me back to last summer and me fallin' in that damn mud puddle.

If he's also rememberin' that moment, he doesn't act like it. "I got the door open easy so I thought it'd be the perfect hidin' place. Then I figured out what it really was. I gave myself up so I wouldn't have to share my discovery with anyone. My team was pissed," he finishes.

"I don't blame 'em," I laugh.

"You like it?"

"Uh-huh." I kiss his lips like I'm tryna inhale 'em. He backs me up against one of the bookcases, and a humungous cloud a dust kicks up, and we cough like crazy. Then we laugh so hard it hurts, which defuses the moment, but we don't mind.

"Clayton?"

"Yeah?"

"Thank you for sharin' this with me." He traces the length of my face with his index finger, and I wanna bite it off.

And then the strangest thing happens.

"Do you feel that?" Clay asks.

"Feel what?" I barely get the words out before I feel it too. Moisture. Like a rainy mist, but inside the building. Clay looks up at the ceiling for a leak, which wouldn't make a bit of sense, cuz you don't get mist from a leak, and it ain't even rainin'. That's when my eyes put the pieces together.

"Clay. Look."

He looks where I'm lookin', and he sees it too. The colors. We're not in a mist. We're in a *rainbow*. Clay's mouth falls open. This defies the laws of nature. There's no rain or sun. And yet here we are. Surrounded, embraced by water, color, and light. Instead of going out, the candle flames shine brighter. I feel tears of joy slide down my cheeks. We are not only seeing a rainbow up close in real life, we're feeling it. We are *in* a goddamn rainbow!

The thought crosses my mind, but it couldn't be, could it? Then again, what else could it be?

I grab Clay's hand. I don't want to close my eyes to this sight, but I have to know if this is me. I close my eyes, take a deep breath, and I look again.

And it's gone.

"What— How— What was that?" Clay asks me.

"I don't know," I say, almost to myself. I can't believe my own senses. If Clay hadn't just witnessed this, I'd seriously think I had bats in my belfry. But I'm not crazy. I am powerful in ways I never imagined I'd be. Ways I never imagined I *could* be. It's as thrilling as it is frightening.

"A natural wonder is my guess," I say, trying to explain

it away. "These things can happen. I've read about bizarre weather events happenin' in different parts of the world, but I never thought I'd see it myself."

Clay smiles a new smile: a shy, youthful smile.

"Feels like the world is much more magical when you're around," he says.

I try to smile back, but it's hard. I'm not ready for him to know the truth about me. I don't wanna scare him. I want him to think I'm normal for as long as possible. But how long can I keep it hidden? I made up all that poppycock about weather. I'm jubin' on a whole new level, and it's too much for me.

7

Chivalry

CLAYTON AND I TAKE TURNS READing to each other from *Rikki-Tikki-Tavi* in the dim light. We're sittin' all cozy on a miniature version of the tea party table from *Alice's Adventures in Wonderland*, and we're both wearing what we can only guess were birthday party hats kids wore back in the teens or twenties or thereabouts.

"Where we goin' next?" he says.

"Mmm. I gotta be gettin' home soon," I say, wishin' it weren't true.

Clay nuzzles my neck with his nose and then playfully nibbles on it. "Okay," he says, though he's clearly not happy about it, "but we must do one more thing. Then I'll take you

71

home." I plant a silly *mwah* kiss on his forehead. He raises an eyebrow at me.

"This has been perfect. You don't need to take me nowhere else," I tell him.

"Yeah, I do," he says, and he hops off the table. We put the books and the party hats away, and I help Clay douse most of the candles. Once we're outside, he blows the last one out and leaves it inside near the door.

"I didn't mean we had to rush," I say.

"I don't wanna get you in trouble. Don't worry. We'll come back here sometime. Come on." He takes my hand, walks me to the car, and opens my door. I get inside and wonder where we could possibly be going now. Wherever it is, it may be nice, but there's no way it's gonna be as special as the colored children's library. Maybe if it's safe enough, I can take the twins there for their birthday. *If* they behave.

He gets in and turns the key in the ignition.

"How long you been drivin'?" I ask.

"Psh," he scoffs, looking over his shoulder before pulling out. "I could drive since I's twelve. Legally? Only for two years."

We ride along and talk about school and stuff. Clay just graduated, and he's pretty happy about it. I'm not ready to think about what that means for the future—*our* future—so I tell him the guys on the baseball team will sure miss him. He agrees, but it don't seem like he'll miss them. He only played cuz his dad pressured him to take up a sport. Somehow he was good at it, even though he was always bein' careful with his hands. His fingers are meant for trumpet valves, not catchin' ground balls.

Eventually, he turns off on a windy road going upward. My ears start poppin' cuz a the elevation shift. Now I know exactly where he's takin' me. It's the lookout. Some folks call it "lovers' lane." It's my favorite place in town because it's the perfect spot to watch star formations, and I've come up here a few times to do just that. But I've never been here with a date before. I love this place, and I feel warm and giddy at the thought that I'm gonna be here with Clay.

I hope he ain't turnin' me into a fool.

At the top of the summit, Clay parks the car and gets out. Now that part I wasn't expecting; people on dates don't usually exit their cars at the lookout. But I sit tight this time, giving him the chance to come over and open the door for me.

"M'lady," he says as he opens it. I smile and step out, and he guides me to a specific spot, close to the cliff's edge. We're up so high, that I can't see the ground below. It's just darkness when I look straight down. There's no one else around, and to be honest, I'm not sure how safe this is, but I trust Clay, so I relax.

"Look down there," he says, pointing. From here, we can see all the lights of our town. I've never seen it look so beautiful. In fact, I ain't never seen it look beautiful at all. Truthfully, I only ever look *up* when I come here on my own, so this is all new to me.

"Wow. It's so pretty from up here. I can't believe it," I say.

"Yeah, it's pretty, but notice anything else?" he asks eagerly. I look again and look hard this time.

"Oh, I see it! That new Dairy Queen place!"

"Not *that!*"

I roll my eyes but look once again and see nothing except all the lights.

"I give up. What am I sposeta be seein'?"

Clay sucks his teeth. "It looks like a big map a the United States."

"What?" I look again. I squint. Okay. When I squint, I can maybe, kinda see it, but . . . no, not really.

"Well, yeah if Florida was shaped like a toothbrush."

"It ain't exact, Evvie!"

"Sure ain't. Cuz Maine looks like a drumstick and California seems to be broken into two islands and a daggone peninsula. But other than all that, the likeness is uncanny," I tease. He responds by tickling me, and I nearly fall out on the ground laughing, but then I shove him away cuz I've had enough, and he stops.

I glance back at the lights, really tryna see what he sees. But I can only see this map's flaws now.

I sit on the hood and sigh. Clay sits next to me.

"Well," he says.

"Well indeed," I say back.

"So? Now you seen my two favorite places. When I'm gonna see yours?" he asks.

I hate that I can feel myself startin' to blush. "This is my favorite place, Clay."

His eyes widen, stunned.

"You serious?"

I nod my head, staring deep into his eyes.

"Why?" he wants to know.

"*Why?* Why do you ask?"

Clay sorta coughs and tries to chuckle. "Just wonderin'." His eyes wander back out toward the view as he casually asks, "So? You been up here a lot? With—uh—friends?"

I frown, puzzlin' over what he's tryna say. When I get it, I'm flattered, not slighted, the way other girls might take it. He wants to know if I've been up here foolin' around with guys.

"No. I usually come by myself. Probably sounds silly, but I like lookin' at star formations, constellations, meteor activity. Comets. That type a thing."

"Really?"

"Yeah. Despite the lights from the town down there, this is the best place I've found to make out the stars clearly."

Clay stares at me a long time, not sayin' a word.

I feel a little exposed. I just never talk about this stuff with anyone.

"So. Yeah. That's why this is my favorite place."

He's still just starin'! Does he think it's *that* weird?

"How come you ain't sayin' nothin'?" I finally ask him.

He leans in and kisses me softly, then he pulls back, barely enough to free his lips from mine.

"There's just nobody else like you."

My whole damn body must've turnt burgundy by now with how much he's makin' this brown girl blush.

"I think—I think you've said that before."

"Don't be surprised if I say it again," he whispers.

I can't believe the intense way he's lookin' at me now. Like he's finna swallow me up. And then I can't help but wonder how many other girls he's looked at, just like this.

He attempts another kiss, but I pull away.

"What's wrong?" He looks like I just smacked him.

I tuck a loose strand of hair behind my ear. I start to speak but can't. How do I say what I wanna say? I can't just come out and ask him if he's been with dozens of girls. Even though, in a way, he just asked me the same thing. I fiddle with the belt loops on my pedal pushers. He takes hold of both my hands to keep me from fidgeting.

"What's goin' on, Evvie?"

I think about it a different way, puttin' the focus on me instead a him.

"We've known each other since before I can remember, but you never—uh—paid me a whole lotta attention. No more than anybody else, I mean. What's different about me now?"

He seems completely shocked. I guess I am a little bit too. I didn't realize that the suddenness of him, while like the dreamiest of dreams, had been eating at me. Making me think it could all end just as suddenly.

"Nothin'," he says.

"Then it's you that's different?"

"No, there's no—nobody and nothin' is any different. Really."

"Then damn, Clay! What the hell took you so long?"

He makes a strange face, somewhere between wantin' to laugh and wantin' to throw up. Maybe I shouldn't be pushin' him. I do want to know, but is it worth upsetting him? Of course, if he gets all worked up over a few simple questions, what's he gonna do when we have a real fight?

"Evalene? I wanted to be somebody you'd be proud to have on your arm, ya know? That kinda thing takes time. I didn't wanna mess up. With you," he says.

"That wouldna happened."

"You don't know that," he whispers. Then he clears his throat. "Anyway, I'm here now, and I ain't plannin' on goin' nowhere." He leans in so fast to kiss me this time I don't have a chance to pull away at first, but eventually I do.

"Thing is? I've heard things, Clay," I tell him. "And it ain't all so good."

"Like what?" he asks sharply. I'm caught off guard by his sharpness.

"I've heard that you have quite a few . . . lady friends."

Clay stares straight ahead. A cloud of sadness passes over him. "That what you heard?"

"Yeah," I say, now wishing I hadn't brought it up, cuz he looks so hurt, it's killin' me.

"It's none a my business," I tell him. "You're free to be with as many girls as you want. But," I begin carefully, "I don't wanna be one among many. I feel like I gotta be honest about that."

Clay nods, and he looks down at the ground for a few seconds.

"This somethin' you already made up your mind about?"

No! I haven't hardly thought about it at all. Forgive me for sayin' anything! I can't lose us.

"Yes." I swallow hard. Did I just lose him? Could it happen that fast? He looks down at the lights of the city and smiles a sad smile.

"Okay," he says.

"Okay. What?"

He turns to me, all seriousness. "You will not be one among many. You are the only. Okay?"

I take a deep breath and feel like I'm on the verge of tears. I wasn't entirely confident that he'd choose me over the masses. Maybe I had a feeling, but I wasn't sure. "Okay," I say.

"Wanna hear a secret?" he asks.

"Yeah."

"You shouldn't believe everything you hear," he says. Then he gets back into the car. He just gets into the driver's seat this time, so I guess he's run out of chivalry for the night. I open my own door like a regular person.

I sit down.

"You sayin' it ain't true?"

He turns to me, and I can't read his expression. All I know is it ain't makin' me blush no more.

"In every rumor that's ever been, there is a ounce of truth. Not a *pound*, but a ounce. Do you know what I mean?"

"I think so."

"I've seen some girls, Evvie. Probably not as many as you've heard, but some." He gazes out the windshield and sits very still. "I wish I was a clean slate, but I'm not."

I don't say anything, cuz I don't know what to say.

"Is that a problem for you?" He asks it so softly, I almost wonder if he didn't want me to hear him.

"No," I tell him. "It's not. I'm sorry, Clay. Who you been with in the past is none a my business. I didn't mean to insult you or nothin'. Did I insult you?"

"Well? You basically just called me a tramp."

I cover my mouth to hide my unintentional laugh, but then he smiles. We look at each other, and I simply can't hold back anymore. I practically tackle the poor boy, and he giggles.

"Damn, girl!" But he reciprocates everything I throw his way and more. He comes up from burying his head in my neck and says "back seat" into my ear, and we clumsily crawl into the back. Clay slides the trumpet case to the floor to give us more room, and then he's kissing me again. And he's everywhere, moving down my arms, my belly, tasting my navel, and then he's—

"Clay?" I resist the strong urge to jerk away from him. I'm not sure what this is, what he's doin' right now. This is unfamiliar territory for me.

"Yeah, baby?" he pants, and I think I'm just gonna dissolve into a puddle right here.

"What're you doin' . . . down there?

He kisses my upper, inner thigh and glances back up at me.

"I told you: didn't do my job last night. I'm doin' it now."

And then he starts to . . . I feel like a naive child right now, cuz I have never even heard a the thing he's doin' to me. It's sorta like making love, but . . . with his mouth? I have to keep holdin' back laughter, cuz it feels so ticklish and foreign at first. And nice. And then more than nice. Better. More than better. And—

"Oh dear god," I holler out before I can stop myself, and then I fall back against the seat. Clearly, I was floating above it. Clay gently kisses my belly again, my kneecap, my elbow, the palm of my hand. I caress his cheek ever so delicately and sweetly hold on to his head to prevent any more kisses, because I can't take any more. I need a second to collect myself and find my way back down to planet Earth.

After what might be an hour, or two minutes, or twelve seconds, he speaks.

"How you feelin' now?"

I blow air through my cheeks, then snicker. "You actin' like I'm your patient."

"That's no answer."

How can I possibly answer that question? Didn't my every move and breath answer it for him? Maybe he wants a special medal or somethin'. To be fair: he's earned it.

"Better."

He lets out a huge laugh. "Better? That's it?"

"Better than I ever felt before. Happy now?"

He nods and kisses my palm again.

"Where in the world did ya learn how to do that?" I ask. I really wanna know. This cannot just be innate knowledge.

"I follow my gut," he says.

"Wait. What about you?" I ask. I must be back on this planet if I'm thinking this logically.

"It's all right. We got time."

I close my eyes. I cannot believe these last twenty-four hours. I just can't. How can life change so fast? Don't seem possible. Thinking on time and what it means, I briefly think about checkin' my watch. I am still wearin' it. Not wearin' much else, but my watch is still on my wrist. I could so easily raise my arm and take a tiny glance. I don't wanna worry Mama, and I do have work in the morning . . . but I can't look at it right now. Too scared to break the spell.

And then something thumps, on the roof of the car.

"What the *hell*?" Clay shouts. We scramble to get our clothes on and check the windows, but nobody's there. I struggle with the buttons on my top cuz my hands are shakin' so bad, and I think for a split second that if this is R. J. and them, I will cut their throats!

Clay opens the door and gets out, and I hurry after him.

"Who's out here?" he calls with authority. It's his man's voice, and it gives me chills. He's angry. "Show yourself!"

No one seems to be around anywhere. We only hear the wind. Neither of us says anything; we're both on high alert. Could it have just been a branch blown by the wind? Sounded harder than that. I'm looking along the ground to find the object we heard when something else hits the car, just missing my head.

Clay grabs me, pulling me toward him as another rock

comes our way but misses the car this time. Then we hear laughing above us. A couple rednecks—I can see them necks glowin' red from here—are perched up in the maple beside the car.

Oh Jesus.

"Why are you causin' trouble?" Clay asks them, his voice so sharp it could draw blood.

The two of 'em swing down from the tree like monkeys.

"Just playin' around," the blond one says, gettin' way too close to Clay for my liking.

Clay don't back down, don't back away. But he don't step forward, neither. He's smart, but he's got pride. I'm worried about his pride.

"Do not come near my vehicle again," he says slowly and clearly. He talks differently to them than to me. He's like a whole other person right now.

Blondie laughs. A redhead steps up from behind him.

"Clay, let's just go," I say as quietly and firmly as I can.

Redhead spits a brownish liquid onto the ground, *very* close to Clay's oxfords.

"C'mon, Clay. Donchu got no sense a humor? Donchu know when somebody's just havin' some fun with you?" Then Redhead glances at me. "She looks like *she* knows how to have fun. Am I right?"

A deep infinite darkness crosses Clay's eyes. I attempt to pull him away, but it's like pullin' on a cement wall. He ain't movin'.

"Uh-oh. Looks like somebody's mad," Redhead says to

Blondie, eyes sparkling. This is honest-to-God fun for them.

"Sure looks that way. We better watch out. This boy's liable to run us both over with this nice car a his," Blondie says back.

"He just might," Clay says, menacing. Now I'm pullin' with all my strength, and he's finally startin' to budge. *Clay, don't be stupid!*

The Redhead stops smilin'. "You think you could repeat that, nigger? I'm a li'l hard-a-hearin'."

"You gonna run us over? With *this* here car?" Blondie asks, and then he keys the whole right side, leaving a nasty scar in the baby-blue paint.

I whip Clay's face around to look at me.

"Clay. Clay? Let's please leave right now. *Please*," I beg. He looks from me to the rednecks, the rednecks to me. His anger's so thick, I can feel it pulsin' through his skin. But, gradually, he starts to do as I say.

"Go on and follow your whore," Blondie calls after us, still laughing. Clay pauses, and I hold on to him like his life depends on it. Because it does.

"If you so mad, wonchu come back an fight." Redhead spits more brown juice.

"That's enough," a new voice says. It comes from several feet behind the other two. There's another one standin' there. I see him, and terror I can't describe shoots through me.

As though they're trained dogs and him their master, Redhead and Blondie forget about me and Clay and walk right over to the black-haired stranger, flanking him. The

Stranger that keeps turnin' up like a creature in a nightmare. For the first time, I realize that the creepy vibes I've been gettin' from this man up to now are a trifle. His ocean-blue eyes are dull, vast holes, and when I look at them directly, I know he has never felt compassion in his life. He is malevolence in the shape of a human being.

I push Clay into the car through the passenger's side and slide in when the Stranger grabs the door handle, preventing me from closing it.

"Stop it," I whimper, struggling to rip the door from his grasp. His henchmen appear and hold it open with their weight.

I have no choice. I focus my energy. I'm scared for Clay to know about the things I can do, but this is an emergency. I breathe deep and envision a wall protecting me and Clay and repelling these beasts like an electric fence.

But nothing happens. It's not working.

Nightmare Man stares down at me for a few seconds, cocking his neck to get a better look. He smiles, and a winter chill rolls down my spine. No trace of a headache. No sense of my talents at all. All I have is my fear, like any other person.

"Who are you?" I ask him.

He smiles, brighter. "Evalene Deschamps." He knows my name. My god, how does he know my name? I'm screaming inside. Wailing for my mama. Paralyzed and helpless.

He leans down close to my face, and I feel myself shrinking into nothing.

His eyes. Those vast, blue holes. Dead eyes. Looking into his face is like staring into a corpse. There ain't nothin' there.

"Notre destinée se rencontre fréquemment dans les che-mins mêmes que nous prenons pour l'éviter," he says.

I can't move; I can't think. I can't do anything. Where is my Jubilation? *Why can't I summon my power the one time I need it?*

Nightmare Man winks at me and closes the door. Clay turns the car around so we can get back down the hill, and as he pulls away, the Stranger waves to me with no expression on his face.

Clay slams his foot on the gas, and we tear the hell outta there and back toward the main road so fast, I think we're gonna hit a tree. We don't, though.

Finally, he slows down. My thoughts are coming back. My fear is still alive, but frozen for the moment. Over-shadowed by relief: We're alive. They didn't kill us.

Clay pulls over. Turns off the engine. Takes a deep breath. And punches the shit outta the steering wheel while loudly cursing. When he's through, he collapses into it weeping. I pull his head into my lap and stroke him while he cries.

There ain't nothin' I can say. Nothin' I can do. I'm six-teen. I'm a colored girl. I don't have the words to help him when a couple of scary crackers can do what they want to him and to me, and there's not a goddamn thing he can do to stop it.

8

Visiting Day

MAMA PULLS RANDOM ITEMS OUT of her pocketbook. Two wrapped peppermints, a skate key, some loose change, and a button that looks like it's from my old coat. She places them on the table, arranges them, and then methodically puts them back. She pauses before repeating the whole exercise.

"Don't worry, Mama. He sounded good last time I talked to him," I try to reassure her. She nods but keeps fooling with the contents of her purse. She's always doin' this when we wait for Daddy to come out to the visitors room. She gets nervous, and her fidgeting just makes me more nervous. I get nervous just bein' here at all. The difference is I feel better as soon as I see him. She doesn't.

A guard looms over us, occasionally looking at Mama's items to make sure she didn't somehow smuggle in any contraband after bein' thoroughly searched. I wanna tell him to back off, but I know better than to start trouble here. They send me away for smart-mouthin', they liable to never let me come back.

"My beautiful girls," Daddy says, comin' though the door. I notice his blue-gray uniform startin' to fray at the cuffs, and I hope he can fix 'em. Otherwise the sleeves'll start unraveling.

"Daddy!" I smile big. I want to grab him and hug him so badly, but it's against the rules. I hate the rules.

"Y'all ain't been waitin' long, have ya?" he asks, a little apprehensively.

"No, just a few minutes," I tell him. More like fifteen, but I don't want him to feel bad. Especially cuz it's probably not his fault he's late. Sometimes guards will mess with inmates. Set 'em up to miss precious time with their families. They can all rot.

He glances at Mama. She stares down at the table.

"So tell me the latest."

I try to fill him in on everything I think he'd find interesting that's happened since the last time we talked. It's funny. I always want to impress him with my maturity, but as soon as I see him, I turn into a little girl. If I let myself think about it, it's kinda embarrassing.

"And then she had the nerve to tell her mother *I* was

the one that broke that ugly doll! Right. Cuz when I go over there to watch that kid, I'm really just there to play with the toys. Ridiculous!"

Daddy laughs so hard, I can see the holes in his mouth where a few rotted teeth had to be pulled. I try to make my stories funny to keep him laughin'. I don't know how much laughin' he does when I'm not here. I do whatever I can to keep the smile on his face for as long as possible. Because when it's time for us to leave, he always looks a little broken. A few times, he's cried. Not even botherin' to wipe the tears away.

It might sound like a small thing, but I haven't hugged my father in four years. I wish I knew how to put into words what that feels like, but I don't think those words exist. As much as it kills me, I suspect it's worse for him.

"What about you?" Mama asks, surprisin' us both. "How you doin', Jesse?"

And there goes that smile I worked so hard to maintain.

"I'm survivin'. Mostly." He tries to chuckle. "Been readin' some. Just finished one called *As I Lay Dying.*"

"Oh, I know that book! We're sposeta read that in English this year," I tell him.

"You won't be sorry, pudd'n'. I'm not gonna lie to you: it's mighty sad, but one a the best books I read in a long time!"

"What about classes?" Mama interrupts.

He snorts. "Yeah. Takin' history right now. Ancient history. We been studyin' the Macedonian Renaissance."

"I meant job trainin'."

"I know what you meant," he snaps. They look at each other for a long moment, and I wish Mama could come here just once with nice things to say to him.

"Daddy? Did I tell you that Anne Marie's cookout was on Juneteenth? Do you know what that is?"

He breaks the shared glare with Mama.

"I certainly do. I like her. She seems like a smart one."

"I've noticed there's somethin' you ain't told your daddy," Mama says to me. I frown at her. She's actin' like I did somethin' and I'm tryna hide it, when I haven't done a thing.

"What?"

She gives me a look and then turns to him.

"She got a boyfriend now."

Oh. That. I feel my cheeks burning.

"He doesn't wanna hear about that," I mumble.

"Oh, yes he does," Daddy says. He's smiling again, his eyes bright and alert. "Who's the lucky fella?"

"Clayton Alexander," I say. I do *not* want to discuss this with my father. This is just makin' me feel even more like a little girl.

"*What?* He's older'n I am!"

"Clayton *Junior*! Not the one you useta know," Mama corrects. I hate how she says "useta know." Like anybody he knew before prison is lost to him now.

"Well shit, I thought he was only 'bout eleven or twelve."

"They grow up, Jesse." She says this with a grin. Not unfriendly, though.

"Wow! So he's— Oh. Okay. He better be treatin' you right."

"He is, Daddy."

"I'm serious, cuz . . ." He pauses and glances up at the guard. He seems to rethink whatever he was planning to say. "Let's say, for his own good, he better not hurt my baby."

I smile and look away, more than ready to talk about anything else.

"My baby," he says, and shakes his head, and I see the sadness creepin' back in again. "You know? I still remember the day you were born?"

"I know, Daddy."

"You came with the hurricane. Made one grand entrance." He laughs then coughs hard.

He's said those two sentences to me I don't know how many times. I never know how to respond.

"I'm comin' back, though. Just gotta keep my eyes open and my head up high. It won't be much longer now."

Outta the corner of my eye, I see Mama sink a little in her chair. I know she loves him, but things were never simple between her and Daddy.

"I can't wait," I tell him. It's true.

"You think *you* can't wait? Lord, child you have no idea how—"

"That's it. Let's go." The guard appears without warning. Daddy lingers in the chair, lookin' at me with so much love in his eyes, I think I might cry.

"Move it!" The guard kicks my father's shin, and his jaw tightens; the kick hurt him. I notice for the first time the chain connecting his ankles. They don't usually bind his ankles. This motherfucker kicked my father, *AND* he knew he was chained and defenseless? Uh-uh. No.

I think I hear them giggling. The haints. It could be in my mind. But if they are present, are they daring me? Encouraging me?

Time is crucial. All you need is a second, a half second, to get your mind right when it's all wrong. But sometimes you don't even have that.

Between the kick, Daddy's wince, and me seein' them chains, no time passes at all. And in that no-time-passin' place, the guard grabs his own throat, cuz he can't breathe, and his eyes bug out and he starts flailin' around like a fish on land, tryna get somebody's attention. Somebody who gives a damn. Mama and Daddy glance at each other, and they both look at me. I hear that giggle again. I'm certain it's them. They are here, and they're on my side. I have to hold back a smile. I know this is wrong, but the feelin' I feel, watchin' that piece a garbage fight for his life, is so complete, so vibrant, so new. It's like I've touched another orbit of existence, and I feel happy-happy.

"Evvie!" My mother hisses my name, and her face is all horror. The guard crashes to the floor, chokin' and sputterin', and his pink skin turns a sickly purple. I guess somebody went to get help, cuz a nurse, two new guards, three medics, and a guy in a suit bound through the door and drag the sputterin' man through it.

Now that they're gone, a silence has fallen over the visiting room. I expect to feel drained or scared, but I don't. The happy-happy feeling has passed, but I feel . . . fine. I feel like he got what he deserved.

A couple seconds later, excited chatter starts up around us. Families shocked by the drama they just witnessed. My daddy stares at me, but the love on his face is replaced with fear.

"My baby," he says, like this time he's tryna figure out if that's still who I am.

Soon another guard appears to take my father away. This is usually the saddest, most painful moment for him and me, but now he just seems bewildered. And I still feel a hint of happy-happy.

"I love you," I say.

"I love you, too, Evalene," he replies. Just before the guard gives him a shove, he turns to my mother and says, "Indigo? You gotta fix her. Before she gets locked up too."

9

Training

NEITHER OF US HAS TAKEN THIS PATH in a long time. At least a year for me. For Mama, it's been years—emphasis on the s. She is none too happy right now.

We open the rusty gate and enter the yard. Instantly I feel unwelcome. Is this a mistake? I pause before going any farther.

"Mama?"

"Uh-huh?"

"Maybe we should forget about it and go back home."

She peers up into the tree with shiny blue and green glass bottles covering every branch.

"We can't. I wish we could. It's just too big for us."

She walks up the crooked cement path, and I follow, watching the ground to make sure we ain't about to step on anything that could hurt us. No sharpened animal bones or coyote teeth shrines today. A couple chickens peck at corn kernels, and then they look up and all around. Not a thought between 'em. No clue why they're here or whose supper table they might wind up on. Poor dumb animals.

When we get to the back door, Mama looks at me.

"It's gotta be you," she says.

I swallow and steady my breath. I knock on the door. Three times, take a second, and then two times. We wait. No sounds or footsteps or voices or anything. It's creepy. Then again, you'd have a hard time findin' anything on this property that *ain't* creepy.

We wait some more. It's strange. She's never out. Even when she is, she somehow manages to be home at the same time. Mama swears that she's seen her out at the market only to hear from a cousin who was with her at the time that Grammie Atti hadn't left the house in days. This has happened more than once. She's just like that. Mama nods at me, and I try again: three knocks, a second, two knocks. Then from inside the house, we finally hear somethin'.

"Quit all 'at knockin'! I know it's you. Just come in already."

I open the door, and there she sits at her converted card table in this old-timey kitchen. Wrought-iron pans hangin' from nails so big they look like railroad spikes. A *wood* stove. All kinda roots and herbs danglin' from the rafters. It's so old-timey, there's a claw-foot tub in here. Who takes a bath in the kitchen?

"Hi, Grammie Atti," I say, soundin' guilty, like I came here to get absolved of all my sins when that's absolutely not why we're here. I hope against hope that my grandmother can help me understand Jubilation. I hope she can answer my questions. But for all I know, she could throw us outta here without givin' it a second thought.

"Uh-huh," she replies skeptically. Pointin' to the jar in Mama's hands, she asks, "What's 'at?"

Mama sets it down on the counter.

"Thought I'd make ya one a your favorites. Mother."

Of course, Grammie Atti knew exactly what it was before she asked. She knew before we came inside. Now she watches Mama with a little smirk on her face. Yes. Mama made one of her favorites: pigs' feet. Disgusting. Stank up our whole house. That's how you know we really need help.

"How thoughtful," Grammie Atti says. Sarcasm in every syllable.

"It's good to see you, Mama."

"Is it now?"

Mama purses her lips and closes her eyes for a second. She's tryin' her best to be patient and civil with my grandmother, which ain't easy.

"All right. I know it's been a while—"

"Three years, it's been. Almost four! My grandbabies must be runnin' around and talkin' in full sentences by now." For a moment her fury is interrupted by confusion as she glances behind us. "Where they at? You bet' not tell me you left them babies home alone."

Mama tries to smile. It doesn't take.

"No. They're spendin' the day with their father."

Grammie Atti explodes in loud, spiteful laughter.

"You might as well've left 'em alone if *he's* what you call a babysitter!"

"He's not babysitting. He's *fathering*," Mama says sternly. This shuts down my grandmother's laughter.

"If you say so."

"I said it, didn't I?"

"You ain't even been here two minutes, and you already sassin' me!"

Mama nods to herself. She seems to be thinkin' something that she won't say aloud.

"You're right. I'm sorry."

"He's a drunk, Indigo."

"No, he's not, but that ain't why we're here," Mama says as evenly as she can. For the first time, I feel real sympathy for her. I can't imagine what it must've been like to be raised by Grammie Atti. When you think about it, it's amazing that Mama's as kind to me and the twins as she is. Considering the model she had.

"We don't mean to bother you, but we're here cuz—"

"I know why you're here," she cuts Mama off. She likes to do that. "I knew you'd be over here before you did."

Finally, she offers us some seats. A wooden stool and metal folding chair. Clients she takes through the beaded curtain into the nicer room. The one with the cushioned wicker furniture. We don't rate that high.

"So? You jubin' like a wild woman, aintcha?" she asks me.

"I don't mean to," I mutter. "It useta not be a big deal, but lately, it's gotten worse."

"It's serious," Mama adds.

"Of course it's worse. Of course it's serious. You growin' into a woman and—" She stops for a second, leans forward in her chair, and glances at me below the navel area.

"And as I thought, you been fuckin'."

"*Mama!*" My mother is scandalized, and I want to slither under this cheap card table and die.

"Evvie is a good girl. A decent girl. Don't put that on her," my mother argues on my behalf. If an asteroid hit this shack at this second, that would be fine with me.

"Oh please! Be offended all you want, you *know* it's true. And you know you were doin' the same thing at sixteen and so was I. She ain't special," Grammie Atti retorts.

My mother looks like she's finna pass out.

"That's us. Don't have to be Evvie," she says, barely audible, and it feels like years have just fallen offa her and she's about my age!

"Oh, yeah, you right. Evvie's different from us," my grandmother concedes right before winking at my mother with her whole face. Mama leans her elbows on the table and rubs her forehead.

"So what d'ya want from me?" Grammie Atti asks.

"Mother," Mama starts. She takes a pause to reset.

"Mama? You and me don't get along and we probably never will, but—"

"Wouldn't be that way at all if you didn't insist on believin' in White Jesus."

Here we go.

"That's not what he's called, and you know that."

"That's what he is. That's what your church is about. Pleasin' the white man. You pray to White Jesus."

"And who do you pray to? Nobody."

"Don't need to."

"No, you got it all figured out, right? Fifty-two-years-old livin' alone in a shack tellin' fortunes like the warm-up act at a freak show. What a sweet life you lead!" Mama shakes her head and sighs. She doesn't usually go off like that.

Grammie Atti says nothing. She fills her pipe with tobacco. I wait for her to retaliate somehow, but she stays quiet for longer than I expect. It don't make her less scary, though.

"How's 'at sayin' go? Somethin' about people in glass houses," she says softly.

"You're right, Mama," my mother says. "I shouldn't have said that, and I'm sorry."

Grammie Atti nods, the closest she can come to reconciling. She lights her pipe and inhales. The orange glow briefly illuminates the tiny tobacco leaves. Mama starts to say something else, but Grammie Atti raises a finger to stop her. She exhales blue-gray smoke and regards me.

I try to concentrate for a second. Try to read her thoughts. It ain't that hard to crawl into somebody's head and read their thoughts if you really want to. I've done it, but not much, cuz if I wanna know what somebody's thinkin', I usually just ask. I can almost see into her mind when a spark pops from her pipe, flies through the air and lands on my cheek.

I squeal and swat it off me. Mama jumps up to wet a dishcloth and tells me to hold it on the spot so it don't turn into a burn. She glares at Grammie Atti, who just smiles.

"That's whatcha git. Don't be sneakin' into my thoughts less'n you's invited. And you will never be invited. Ya hear me?"

I nod, holding the rag. I feel a li'l bad for trespassin', but also annoyed. She is always at least five steps ahead of everyone else in the world.

To avoid any further calamities, Mama quickly tells Grammie Atti about what happened when we visited Daddy. At first, the idea of attempting to strangle a white man—a white man in law enforcement at that—even gives my grandmother a momentary scare. It's subtle and it's fast, but I see it. But then she laughs so hard, tears roll.

"It ain't funny," Mama warns her.

"The hell it ain't," she argues, instantly snapping back to a scowl. "We was trained to be all polite and deferential with it, but that's a load a shit! Jube ain't polite. Jube ain't deferential. Jube ain't a goddamn ice cream social! It's our survival!" she bellows. The walls tremble. I bet they're afraid of her too. But Mama doesn't back down.

"We don't need to rely on our magic to survive no more," she argues. "Progress is slow, but times have changed."

"Oh, have they? Wonchu go tell that to Mamie Till[1]? Bet she coulda used some magic." Grammie Atti stares my mother down, and Mama shrinks in her seat. I'm floored by this. I never imagined that that was what Grammie Atti meant by "survival."

"Regardless," she begins again, softening her tone ever so slightly, "the girl needs to learn control. Discipline. The rest is up to her."

"I agree," Mama sighs.

"Why not teach her yourself? Afraid White Jesus won't be your friend no more?" Grammie Atti asks her.

"I'm too long outta practice," Mama mutters.

"Right," Grammie Atti says with more than a little acrimony.

"How comes I can't jube when I'm scared?" I ask. They both look at me as though they forgot I could speak.

"You can. You just don't know how to yet," Grammie Atti says.

"Can you show me that first?"

"Hush," they both say.

"Your impatience will be your ruin, you ain't careful. One thing at a time," Grammie Atti lectures.

Inside I'm mad and cussin', but on the outside, I simply nod and stare straight ahead. My eyes land on a gris-gris bag adorned with a tiny silver skull. I wonder what it's like to have a regular grandmother, who bakes cookies and sews quilts and indulges her grandkids with presents. I will never know.

---

[1] Mother of Emmett Till, who was murdered by a lynch mob at age 14 in 1955. Photos of his horrifically disfigured body were famously published in Ebony and Jet magazines.

"Okay. I got it," I say. I'm in a chair, blindfolded, and my grandmother is makin' me find things and touch them with my mind.

"No, you don't. Do it again," she commands.

She wants me to "see" her ugly cuckoo clock on the wall behind me, and I do. They built it wrong: the bird's facin' backward, and his feet are goin' forward. It looks ridiculous. It's one of them things that you see once and you can't ever *un*see.

"I see it."

"No. You don't. You see your memory of it. Quit bein' lazy! See it. Right now."

Of all the ways I could be spendin' a Saturday afternoon, this has to be the worst. I'd rather be in school. I'd rather be at the damn doctor! She sent Mama home a while ago. Said she could get more done if she was alone with me. I feel like Helen Keller.

"Now?"

"Don't sound too sure a yourself," she taunts.

"Now. I see it now."

"I don't believe you."

This crazy old woman! One of these days, I swear to Christ Jesus, Imma—

I jump when I hear a metallic sound like a spring bein' stretched past its limit and then a dull thud. And then nothin'.

"Grammie? Grammie Atti?"

"Take it off," she says quietly.

I remove the blindfold.

"Turn around and look at my clock."

When I see it, I think I'm halluncinatin'. The cuckoo is gone. Like he done flew away. And the spring he was attached to is stretched and stickin' straight out in the air, ready to impale somebody. I open my mouth to speak but can't think of any words.

"Now turn back around," she tells me. So I do that, too. I look up, and there he is. The backward cuckoo bird's smashed into the wall with both his face and his ass stickin' out. Guess there was too much friction for him to keep flyin'.

"Um . . ."

"Yes. That is your doing."

"Sorry."

"You know what your problem is."

"What?"

"No, I'm tellin' ya. You know what your problem is. So you know you got work to do."

I scratch my head and gaze up at the bird's ass. I have no idea what my problem is, but I ain't foolish enough to tell Grammie Atti that.

"Fix it."

"Huh?"

"Fix my clock. You broke it. You fix it."

Great. Like I know how to fix a daggone cuckoo clock! I try to stand, but she stops me. Literally. I can't move.

"Stay there," she says. "Fix my clock." This time it sounds like a threat.

I don't know what to do, and she won't help me. My eyes move all over the room while I ponder what I should do. I find myself looking again at one of her shelves of whosie-whatsits— more gris-gris bags, candles, poppets, spooky dolls—wishing I knew how to make some a this junk work for me.

"You might as well settle in, cuz you ain't goin' nowhere till you do it," she informs me. This makes me mad as hell. This makes me wanna break things. But I know that when I get angry, bad shit happens.

So what's that mean? I can never be angry? That's impossible.

"Don't be a dummy," she grunts. She's starin' out the window. Maybe she's wonderin' if she got enough garbage decoratin' her yard yet.

"Ain't about stoppin' up your emotions. It's about how you use 'em."

I wish she'd stop readin' my thoughts.

"Wish in one hand, piss in the other. See which one gets filled up the fastest," she says, not missing a beat.

Damn. How I use 'em. Shit. All right then. I give more thought to the clock and the wall and how it got to be that way. I resign myself to the obvious fact that this ain't gonna be easy, and that actually allows me to relax. I'm still angry. I can feel it. I can feel it in different parts of my body, but mostly my stomach. My abdomen, I think.

As an experiment, I mentally collect all the pieces of my anger from all of its hiding places inside me and move them all to my abdomen. Treatin' it like a home base. Now I look at it all down there, the pieces scatter, and I concentrate on them. Focus as hard as I can. They scramble for another minute or two until they form a solid band.

Whoa. It's a pulsing red-orange glowing thing that enwraps me, but it doesn't hurt. It feels weird, but not painful. It wants to move so badly, I'm vibrating. I nearly fly off the chair, but I clamp myself down.

I can do this.

I aim the vibrations up to the wall behind me. Up to the clock. As if on a rope and pulley, the clock smoothly disengages from the wall, slides downward, and lands itself in front of me on the table. Instinctually I start to grab it with my hands.

"No," she says suddenly. "Put your hands down. Now."

I do as I'm told. I'm gettin' tired, but I go back into the anger band I've just made and let it do what it needs to. I watch the clock wind itself up again, and it starts ticking. It works fine. It's the bird who's suffered the most. I point my band toward him, pull him from the wall, and slip him back onto his spring. The spring recoils itself and screws the cuckoo back into his place. This takes a few tries, but I manage to get it in there. The last piece is his left eyeball. The tiny thing snapped off and now sits on the table, mocking me. I honestly don't know how to fix this part without an adhesive. I can only do so much.

I hear Grammie Atti get up and start putterin' around behind me. She opens a drawer and sets something down on a surface. Harder than necessary.

"There's a tube a glue over here. Use it."

I'm too tired to waste any energy bein' annoyed so I reach around the kitchen behind me. First touchin' a bottle a castor oil, then a tube of . . . paint? What *is* this?

"Keep movin'," she orders.

Finally I come to it and bring it to the table in front of me. Opening it and applying it to the ceramic is tedious, but not too hard. I hold the eye to the bird's head for a good thirty seconds or so, and when my thoughts release it, it stays in place.

I'm so relieved, I almost cry. Sometimes I try to fix somethin' broke with my own two hands and it don't seem to work this well. To finish, I glide it gently back up the wall behind me where it's lived for as long as I can remember. Once it snaps back into place, the deformed cuckoo instantly pops out to announce that it's now five o'clock.

"What about my wall?" She walks by me and indicates the small hole in the wall the bird created.

Dammit! Will this never end? I search the floor below the hole and gather up all the pieces of wall I can find. They're too tiny and crumbly to glue.

This is an impossible task! But Grammie Atti won't let me go unless I do *something*. I place all the pieces from the floor (including some dirt and shit that wasn't part of the wall) and cram them into the hole so that it's sealed, with me holding it all in place. It's ugly, it's temporary, but at least the wall is repaired. At this second.

"Good try, but you right. Fixin' that hole is an impossible task. Let it go," she says.

I exhale, and all the pieces fall outta the hole back down to the floor. The little hole is the perfect size for an enterprising mouse if she's willing to climb up the six feet and change to get there.

I take another breath and discover that my red-orange band has faded and that I don't feel angry anymore. I feel pretty good. Better than I did this morning. Though I'm tired as hell and not proud of how much I'm sweatin'. You'd think I just ran a marathon.

I turn to face Grammie Atti. I'm kinda proud a myself. If you don't count the hole, the operation was a success.

"So? I did it."

"Yeah. Good work. Now you just need to learn how to do all that in the blink of an eye instead of a goddamn hour."

10

Girlfriend

MY MONTHLY VISITOR CAME THIS morning. I woke up to dried blood on my inner thighs and stains on the sheets. My monthly visitor loves to surprise me. I call her Ambushina.

I run down the hall to the bathroom, and then I get an idea. I reach down low inside me, and for a few glorious seconds . . . I stop the flow. I block its path as though I've done it tons of times before. For a second I'm drunk off the power, but it's exhausting and I have to let it go.

However . . . I get another idea. What if I could expel five days worth of bleedin' right now? I try it, and I start to fill the toilet, but as soon as I do, I feel really, *really* sick. I slow down the flow to its normal speed, but I collapse on the floor, too weak to pick myself up.

Why did I do that? I close my eyes and count to calm down, ease my breathin', and keep myself from vomiting. I hear the door open and close, and I sit up so fast, I hit my head on the bottom of the sink.

"Ow!"

Mama starts laughin' at me! Here I am, practically unconscious from blood loss, and now I might have a concussion, and she thinks this is hilarious!

"Why you laughin'?" I whine, rubbing the sore spot on my head.

She notices the streaks of red on the floor, glances at the toilet, and winces.

"Did you try to jube your monthly outta ya?"

"Uh-huh," I admit.

She shakes her head. "Don't get cocky," she says. Then she hands me a giant maxi pad and a belt.

"This is not the way to use your abilities," she says, all somber now.

She helps me stand and leaves me to tend to myself. So much for sendin' Ambushina on her way with a single flush.

That afternoon, Anne Marie flips through the newest arrivals at Lowcountry Records, looking to buy a new one. She's meticulous, inspecting every detail.

Every. Detail.

"Did ya see this one?" I say, handing her a record.

She studies the cover and the song list for several seconds. "I like Neil Sedaka, I think. But his songs all sound the same to me," Anne Marie reasons before handing it back to me. I'm gettin' tired a bein' in this store. She needs to make a decision or give up.

"How 'bout this one?" I ask, handing her another one I just grabbed at random.

She glances at it and then stares at me in disbelief.

"Stonewall Jackson? You're suggestin' I buy an album recorded by a man who calls himself *Stonewall Jackson*?"

"Oh, I—I thought it was somethin' else," I lie, and toss it back in the general direction of where I found it.

"What you gonna recommend next? Greatest hits a the Confederacy?"

"Well shoot, I might as well. So far nothin' has impressed you. Are you sure you actually like music?" I ask.

Anne Marie makes a face at me and continues to scrutinize every record in sight.

"Evvie, what do you think a Dee Dee Sharp? Too teeny bopper?" she asks me.

"I think she's fine."

"Seriously!"

"I seriously think she is *seriously* fine," I tell her. I'm sorry, but it should not take forty minutes to pick out and buy one record. One! But this is what shopping with Anne Marie is like. I wouldna come at all, but she guilted me into it. Sayin' she's hardly seen me since her cookout, and she values my opinion. I don't want to hurt her feelings, so I don't tell her that I feel like we see each other all the time. And the party was only. . . well. Huh. Now that I think about it, that was like three weeks ago. Or four? Damn. Feels like it was a couple days ago.

That might be cuz I been spendin' every single free minute I have (with the exception of the last forty) with Clay, and he makes the time go fast. So fast that I want it to slow down. I want the minutes with him to last as long as possible, but I guess that ain't scientifically possible. Unless—

"EVVIE!"

"Oh. What?"

"What's wrong with you? I been callin' your name."

"Sorry. Jeez!"

She's standing several feet away and gestures urgently for me to come over to her. It takes all my strength not to roll my eyes as I join her by a stack of 45s.

"What's the matter?" I ask.

Her eyes dart around behind me like she's lookin' for somethin' she don't wanna find. I start to turn around, but she grabs my arms, preventing me.

"What the *hell*?"

"I was tryna get your attention, cuz somebody was standin' behind you."

I feel a slight chill despite the July heat. I have a feeling I know what she's about to say.

"He was just starin' at you, and then he came up close

behind you, and I yelled out for ya and he just turned around and left. It was the spookiest thing!"

I swallow. "What did he look like?"

"Weird. He was white. Real pale. And he had black hair and—"

A small involuntary cry leaps from my throat. "Oh my god." I pull her to the back corner of the store and hide us behind a tallish shelf. I peer out to see if I can catch a glimpse of him, but I don't see him anywhere.

"He's gone, Evvie. What's goin' on?"

"Remember the day you came to the Heywoods' and I had the knife?"

"Wait! That was *him*?"

"Shhh!" I don't know why, but I'm scared for anyone to overhear us. Though there's hardly anybody in here, and Billy's over behind the register bobbin' to whatever's playin' in them giant headphones he's got on. Lookin' like a spaceman.

"Yes," I whisper. "He—he just—he keeps on—" I can't seem to spit it out, and I'm all shaky. I can't explain what he's doin', cuz I don't even understand it.

"Okay," she whispers, as though I'd said something coherent. "Do you feel safe walkin' down to the drugstore?"

I nod automatically, but I do not feel safe right now.

"Why don't we go get a soda, and you can tell me about this freak if you want to. Only if you want to, okay?"

"Okay." I usually do feel better when I talk things out with Anne. She can get on my nerves sometimes, but she's a good listener and she really cares. Not like a lot of people, just waitin' for their turn to talk.

She links arms with me, and we start to walk out of the store. Until she stops short.

"What is it?"

She picks up a record album and stares at it like she's hypnotized. It's Eartha Kitt's *Bad But Beautiful*. Looks like a collection of her hits. Not somethin' I would choose, but you never know what Anne Marie's gonna like.

"You should get it," I tell her.

Anne Marie traces the photo of Eartha with her index finger and just keeps starin' like she's in a trance. I nudge her and she jumps, lookin' at me like she forgot I was standin' there.

"Yeah. Lemme get this real quick," she says, making a beeline for the register. I follow her. Billy finally removes his headphones to take her money. Then he looks over at me.

"What's wrong? Didn't you find nothin' you liked?"

I shake my head. "Nah, I'm broke. Just here for support."

"You sure? Cuz maybe we could work out a deal or somethin'?" he says.

I sigh and cross my arms over my chest to keep his roaming eyes from gettin' a good look.

"No. Thanks."

I try to rush Anne outta the store once she's paid up. It's hard. She keeps on lookin' in the bag to check on Eartha. Like she's scared her new friend might hop out and run away. Never knew she was such a fan.

* * *

I sip my cherry soda. We can't sit at the drugstore counter on account of our abundant melanin, so we sit in a booth in the back and take our sweet time. Anne nurses her lime rickey and watches me, concerned. I told her all about the incident at the lookout. All about how this weirdo has been appearing in places where I am. How he knows who I am.

"And you have no memory of ever meeting him before this summer?"

"None. Clay don't know who he is either."

"Wow. That's so scary."

"I know." I sip the last of my soda, wishing I had more. Not because I *want* more, but just to have something else to focus on.

She picks up her cigarette from the ashtray, inhales, and when she exhales, she tries to blow the smoke away from me. I still get some and try to cough as lightly as I can. She looks at me sheepishly.

"Sorry, Evvie. You're smart for never pickin' up the habit," she says. She sticks her arm out and flicks the cigarette, away from me. "And now they say it can cause *cancer*? It's terrible. I wanna quit. I wish I had your willpower," she says, inhaling again.

I don't tell her that it has nothin' to do with my willpower and everything to do with my vanity. I've seen the yellow stains between Mama's fingers and the permanent tint of gray on her teeth. Also, after a while, smokers start to stink. Not for me, thanks.

"Well, for starters, I wouldn't go up to the lookout anymore, if I were you. Especially after dark," she says. I don't say anything, and I know she just wants to help, but this bit of advice is ludicrous. Why in the world would anybody go up to the lookout during daylight hours?

"And maybe you and Clay should stick to more populated areas. Or go out on some group dates? There's safety in numbers."

I crack up for a second, but she just stares at me, confused.

"Why's that funny?"

I wipe the smirk off my face cuz she looks so sincere.

"That could get awkward," I say.

"Why?"

I take a deep breath. "Anne? You honestly don't know why Clay and me like to be alone?" I keep lookin' at her, until it finally sinks in.

"Oh," she says. It's one little sound—"oh"—but it's filled with such melancholy. Her body drops back against the seat, and she just stares at me. Is she disappointed in me? Judgin' me? Probably. I just don't need to hear some sanctimonious no-sex-before-marriage lecture right now. We'll just have to agree to disagree.

I shake my head and fiddle with my straw.

"There's nothin' to be done about it," I say, ignoring the look she's still giving me. "The only thing I thought maybe I *could* do was . . ."

"What, Evvie?"

I wanna tell her. I wanna tell her about the strange magic that I *know* can protect me as soon as I figure out how to control it.

"Nothin'," I mutter.

"No, tell me. What were you about to say?"

I shift in my seat and think of what she might like to hear. "I was about to say, I thought I could . . . pray. Ask God for protection or whatever. But I don't think that's gonna be enough."

Anne reaches across the table and squeezes my hand.

"I'll pray too."

I've never had any intentions of sharing my secret gifts with most of my friends. They'd just think I was crazy or puttin' 'em on. But I have thought about telling Anne Marie. And I would, if it weren't for one problem: Anne Marie is a real churchgoer. An old church lady in trainin'. Now, I go to church myself, but only because I have to. She goes because she *wants* to. I've often wanted to tell her about me, but I always chicken out. What if she decides I'm possessed by the devil or somethin'? I'd hate for her to start seein' me differently or, worse yet, to be scared a me. So I keep it to myself. As for her, I don't mind her being devout, but if she starts fallin' down, speakin' in tongues and shit, I don't know. That might be a bridge too far.

"You should tell your mother, Evvie."

"So she can lock me in the basement for the rest of my life?"

"You need to get an adult involved. I can tell my parents. Maybe my dad'll have some ideas. He was in the army."

"Please don't. All you gotta do is tell one person, and before ya know it, half the town's in my business!"

"Then what are you gonna do?"

I don't feel like discussin' this anymore. I have to handle it my way. Mama has enough to worry about, and I truly hate the idea of becoming fodder for gossip. I don't know what to do yet, but I'm not gonna figure it out right now, so it's best to let it go and move on. She listened, which is what I needed. She can't do anything beyond that.

"Maybe I'll talk to Mama about it," I lie, to end the conversation.

She sighs, instant relief. I think she still believes parents can take care of everything. Bless her heart.

We head for the door, and Anne stops to flip through a *Life* magazine. The woman behind the counter glares at her, cuz I'm sure she wants Anne to cough up the twenty cents instead of readin' the whole thing in the store. Psh! I hope she stands there and reads every word. While she's distracted, I visit another aisle and pick up a box of tampons. I haven't been usin' 'em for long; I don't think Mama knows yet, but I had to make the switch. I'm just tired a wearin' pads that feel like big ol' diapers. Like the one I got on right now.

I place it on the counter and take out my wallet. In a heartbeat, Anne Marie's by my side, eyeballin' my purchase. She turns to me, and I do believe her eyes are about to pop right outta her head.

"What?"

The register girl gives me the same look she gave Anne a few minutes ago. Maybe that's just her face. She stuffs the box in a brown paper bag, then wraps it in another one. Just to be safe, she drops it into an even larger paper bag. She slides it across to counter to me like it's radioactive waste.

I sigh and take it. We leave.

"You goin' home or what?" I ask her.

She shrugs with this weird, haughty expression.

I stop in the middle of the sidewalk. She's surprised but stops too.

"Why'd you stop?" she asks me with that same haughty air.

"I'm not takin' another step until you tell me what's wrong with you."

"Me? Nothing at all."

"Oh for the love of—will you just say it already?"

"Fine! I've never met somebody who uses tampons before! It's a little odd."

"Not really! I just got sick a the damn belt! That's all."

"I just thought this would be somethin' that you mighta discussed with me before just doin' it."

It takes all my strength not to start laughin', but I manage. She's truly upset about this.

"Maybe if we were twelve. I can make my own decisions now, and I know you can too."

Her mouth draws into a line, and she starts walkin' real fast.

"Why are you mad at me?"

She increases her speed, so I have to do the same. It is another hot day, and I am in no mood for this foolishness!

"Anne Marie, stop it right now."

She halts, arms crossed. She turns toward me but won't meet my eyes. All I have to do is put some heat in my voice, and she'll listen. She's like that. Programmed to comply instantly with anything resembling authority. I'm glad, cuz I was a second away from stopping her in an entirely different way.

"Tell me why this is a problem for you," I demand.

She taps her foot on the ground. She's shaking.

"I feel like—I feel like you're changin' so fast, I can't keep up." Her voice quivers now.

"I'm not changin'. Really I'm not. Just cuz we prefer different feminine hygiene products, doesn't mean we can't still be friends."

In spite of herself, this makes her laugh. Then we both break into laughs.

"No." She regains her grave face. "Don't make fun a me."

"I'm not makin' fun a you," I assure her. "I just wanted you to laugh. I'm tryna understand where you're comin' from, and I'm havin' a hard time."

Anne looks at me now, but instead of lookin' angry, her face is apologetic.

"You've never had a boyfriend before," she mumbles.

Her thoughts are all over creation today!

"No. I guess not. I did go out with that kid from St. Mary's last year. Eugene? Was that his name?"

"Yeah, once or twice. That doesn't count. You can't even remember his name, which was—"

"Wait wait wait! Lemme try again." I concentrate, tryna remember this poor boy's name. Even his face I'm strugglin' to picture.

"Emery!" I say.

"Close. Chester."

"Oh yeah," I giggle, a little embarrassed. "Well, I knew there was a *e* in there somewhere."

"Yep. You got the vowels down. Now ya just gotta work on rememberin' the consonants."

We're both laughin' again.

"Regardless, boyfriend or not, you're my girl. That ain't gonna change."

She smiles at me.

"Before you know it, somebody's hairy knuckles'll be knockin' down your door—"

"No, they won't, and please don't do that," she says. "I can handle a lot, but please don't condescend to me."

I nod. Feelin' chastised and rightfully so. I didn't mean to do that, but it's no excuse.

"Well. I hope Mr. Clayton Alexander Jr. appreciates all the time he gets to spend with you," she says.

"Come on." I throw my arm around her shoulder and lead her down the street.

I think we've talked enough about boyfriends and tampons and creepy guys for one afternoon, so I try to think of a new subject. Up ahead, I spot the old post office, and I wonder if my history buff friend knows its story.

"Anne? Do you know how long the old post office has been there?"

She squints for a second, thinking.

"I don't know too much about the foundation, but the building's been standing since 1796." She tells me about its many incarnations, and I enjoy learning about each one.

11

Haints

DREAMS UNNERVE ME. 'SPECIALLY these days. Most nights, I just wanna sleep. I don't want dreams gettin' in the way a that. Cuz I honestly can't always tell the difference between my dreams and my realities. So how the hell am I ever sposeta get any rest?

Early this morning, for example. I was out in a big field. You'd assume that this was just a typical dream. Except every one of my senses experienced that field in a real, concrete way. The wet dew on my bare feet (I wish my subconscious understood the value of shoes). The smell of hay and saturated earth, like from a pond or river, though I saw none of the above. Sounds of birds from overhead. Pigeons, sandpipers, and whip-poor-wills. The sight of nothing but unkempt grass for miles in every direction. I didn't put anything in my mouth, so I didn't taste nothin' special, but all my other senses were wide awake and occupied in this three-dimensional landscape. Another dream-vision that felt all too real.

I walked for a long while. I can't say why, but I knew I had to walk. The farther I went, the more it seemed I was goin' nowhere. Nothin' but grass and an unfriendly gray sky. At least I didn't spot any mutilated animals anywhere. Soon I heard more sounds. Like cars speedin' by, but I couldn't see 'em or any roads that they could be on. The bird songs faded away as the cars overpowered them. And then I heard stranger sounds. A booming loud noise, like somebody had a record player and turned up the volume way louder than it should go and made the bass dominate all the other parts of the music. I'd never heard anything like it before.

The flatness of the land edged into an incline, so I found myself walkin' uphill. More sounds. Cars honking, people shouting or laughing, more bass booming. A cacophony I couldn't decipher.

When I reached the top of the hill, I stood there. Not stunned so much as puzzled. I looked down on a bustling city. Buses, cars, big stores with neon signs, power lines, and people walkin' on sidewalks, talkin' to themselves. Too many sights and sounds in this place. Giant commercial advertisements filled whole sides of tall buildings. One of which I still can't hardly believe. If I was stunned at any point during this trip, it was when I saw that advertisement.

The words said "Lancôme Paris," and the girl on the poster? She was as dark as licorice! Her hair was cut short and nappy. She was gorgeous. I'd never thought of skin that dark or hair short and tight as gorgeous before. Her head was about the size of a Cadillac on the side a that tall, tall building, and people just passed her by. Like it was no big thing. Like they see gorgeous Negro girls the color of midnight on signs everyday!

This strange, familiar place. A nondescript block of a building displayed a gaudy yellow sign that said POPEYES, but it looked like a place for food, not a movie house where you might watch the cartoon. Then I understood, though I couldn't understand. Not really. This Popeyes was where Lowcountry Records stood just yesterday.

This was my town, and I didn't recognize it.

"Are you okay?"

I just about fell down that hill, I was so startled by another voice! There was a girl sittin' on the grass below me, and I'm certain she just scared ten years offa my life. Had she been there the whole time? No idea.

"Yeah," I told her. "I'm okay."

She gazed up at me for a bit. Long enough for me to realize that somethin' was off about her. For one thing, she was wearin' denim jeans like a farmer, and sneakers, but she didn't look like she'd been runnin' anywhere or doin' any sports. Her shirt was purple with what looked like the words to a poem written on it in silver. DREAM IF YOU CAN A COURT-YARD, AN OCEAN OF VIOLETS IN BLOOM. Somethin' like that.

Pretty. At the bottom it said REST IN POWER. She had these little white things in her ears with wires connected to a tiny box. At first I thought she looked like a martian, but then I wondered if the white things were some kinda fancy hearin' aids and I felt bad.

"Is your name Evalene?" she asked me.

"Yes."

"I know you."

That's when I finally figured out the oddest thing about her: she looked like me. A *lot* like me. Well, me if I dressed like a hobo. I thought she might be a cousin I'd never met. A close cousin.

She stood up then, right next to me. Almost the same height, but she was a shade taller.

"Do you think we have the power to alter the direction of our lives?" she asked me.

"I don't know. Maybe."

"Good. That might make things easier for me."

"What?"

"I apologize, but I have to do what they tell me," she said.

"Do *what*? Who?"

She grabbed my shoulders and flipped me around so I was facing back the way I came. Only it was not the way I came. My heart leapt into my mouth, and loud cackling laughter danced on the air. Flames. Trees burning. Meat . . . flesh burning. And all these shapes. Foggy shapes. Women. Haints, of course. They all laughed like witches from a child's worst nightmare.

"Evalene!" one of them screeched.

I shut my eyes in a vain attempt to make them go away. I opened my eyes, and not only had they *not* gone away, one of them had taken the place of my weird friend-cousin. She dug her talons into my shoulder, and the sensation was pain and arctic cold.

I tried to turn to see her face, but when I did, I swear to God, her head started spinnin' like a top! Then her body did the same thing. She was impossible for my eyes to perceive.

"Notre destinée se rencontre fréquemment dans les chemins mêmes que nous prenons pour l'éviter," she hissed.

I'd heard that sentence before but couldn't place where.

"What does it mean?" I dared to ask.

"Don't you know? 'We meet our destiny in the very paths we take to avoid it,' ignorant girl." She laughed. And the others laughed behind her and none of them had faces and the fire roared in my ears.

"Take what's yours, Evalene. You know you want it," said another one.

"Want what?" I asked. I don't know how I said anything, my teeth were chatterin' so hard from her icy grip.

"Jubilation. There's only *one* way."

"What is it?"

"You got a taste of it at the prison, remember? *Happy-happy* you were, when you thought that man would die in your presence. *Happy-happy* you'll be again, and it's going to huuuuuurrrrt. . . ."

I didn't want to hear any more. Somehow I broke free from her subzero grasp, and I ran. From the sky, a thousand voices shouted down to me: "THERE'S ONLY ONE WAY."

I kept running. I ran like I've never run in my life, and I had no idea where I was runnin' to, but I had to get as far away from them as I could. I saw a gorge comin' up ahead and there was no way around it, so I held my breath, and, at the last second, I jumped as high as I could. I landed on my butt on the edge of my bed, just about to squeeze these tired legs into my good Sunday shoes.

I look down at myself and I'm ready for church and I hear the girls singing some Bible song out in the hall, and I don't know how I arrived here. I also don't know how to speak French, but those words come back to me about destiny, and I remember where I heard them.

The Stranger.

I rub my eyes, stretch, yawn, wiggle around. Anything to shake off my early-morning ordeal. I stare at my reflection in my li'l vanity mirror. I don't know if that was all a dream. That would make the most sense, but why didn't I wake up in my nightgown, sleep crustin' the corners of my eyes, if it was only a dream?

I slide the neckline of my dress down slightly, exposing my upper arm.

And why do I have a sore, purple bruise where the haint dug her fingers into my shoulder?

* * *

This morning's sermon has something to do with reachin' for higher ground when the devil wants to pull you down to his level. I've heard this sermon before. More than once. No need to listen to it again. Anne Marie and her parents are in the front row, and she seems riveted. Bless her heart.

On the way here, I was relieved that everything on the streets looked the way it always had and not like what I saw in my dream-vision. The horrors I experienced this morning feel far away. Mostly. That I heard the Stranger's words in the mouth of a haint fills me with dread. But I try to put it outta my mind for now. There are more important things to focus on.

Like Clay. He came to church with us today and sits next to me. Just bein' near him makes me feel safer. He ain't payin' attention to this sermon any more than I am, but he's leafing through the hymnal, so he at least appears to be engaged. I stretch and stare at the parishioners in the pews all around us and try to spot the ones noddin' off. Clay starts scribblin' something, and I can't imagine he's takin' notes, and I sure hope he ain't defacin' the hymns!

On my left, Coralene's head falls into my side, passed out like she's drunk. I adjust her head so her barrettes aren't diggin' in my ribs. I wish I knew what time it was, cuz it feels like we've been here for four hours already. Reverend Henry hits a high note, and folks chime in with "amen" and "yes, Lord," and Clay taps my arm to show me what he's been working on. He's made a stick-figure drawing of Jesus with a conk and shades, playin' the sax. A bubble coming from his face says, *I'm king of the Jews and king of the JAZZ!*

I snort-laugh a little too loud. Mama leans over from my far left and gives me the evil eye. While she's there, she pokes Coralene awake. I cover my mouth and sit back against the pew to avoid her face. Out of the corner of my eye, I can see that Clay's tryna show me somethin' else, but I just stop him with my hand and shake my head without lookin' at him, tryna get rid a the damn giggles. I don't want my mother to decide he's a bad influence.

Unfortunately, once I get the giggles, gettin' rid of 'em is a real challenge. I stare at the floor and try to focus on the sermon for a few minutes.

"I bet some a y'all were tempted by the devil just last night," Reverend Henry says. "The devil loves Saturday nights! The devil wants you to get in all *kiiiiiiinda* trouble with him, don't he? He wants you to go out drinkin' and chasin' loose women with him when he knows you got a wife and four kids to raise. Ladies, the devil wants you to wear your tightest dress and strut all around town with him while your husband works the night shift."

I'm still lookin' down at the scuffed-up hardwood floor when Clay slides another drawing into my view. This one is the devil with a sad face, a teardrop in his eye, and a bubble that says, *Please come and make trouble with me. I'm very lonely.* This time I lose it. A legit loud laugh erupts outta me. I cover my face completely so I don't see the scowls, but mostly so I don't see Mama, who is surely ready to strangle me right now. I start coughin' up a storm as a distraction, and that gets the twins laughin'.

"Stop it," my mother scolds. And then every child in the church starts laughin' all at once. At first I think it's funny, but then I realize it's *all* of 'em. It's like a mass hysteria of giggles for every person under the age of—I glance around to see.

Looks like everybody sixteen and under. Reverend Henry's given up on sermonizing and just stares out at us in confusion. Parents reprimand kids and drag 'em outta there, but nothing seems to make the laughter stop.

"Holy shit," Clay whispers. He's not laughin'. He's seventeen and too old to catch the virus.

My mother jabs me in the shoulder. "Evvie??"

I turn to her, alert, and just as suddenly as it began, the laughing stops. People chatter, tryna figure out what just happened. Reverend Henry God-blesses the children and says that they're here to teach us about joy.

Mama looks at me mournfully. Without speaking, she tells me, *You cannot do things like that.*

I know she's right, but I honestly didn't mean to, and I tell her so with the jube voice only we can hear.

It was an accident.

12

Bold

"I'M JUST TELLIN' IT LIKE IT IS. I HAVE YET to see any real differences," Uncle George says, and he shoves some more corn bread in his mouth, makin' a damn mess.

"Things don't happen right away. You know that. Supreme Court said segregatin' any kinda transportation is unconstitutional, and that's all there is to it."

"Yeah. In *February*. Here it is July, and if you get on a crowded bus, you know who will always get the seats while the rest of us stand."

Mama shakes her head, swallowing her bite of collard greens. "Things are changin', George. Accept it. Told ya things would improve once Kennedy got in office."

"Kennedy didn't have nothin' to do with that! Need I remind you how long it took him to send troops to Birmingham last summer? Them kids coulda all got blown up. He didn't care till papers in other countries started callin' us 'the land of the free' in quotations."

"That's just cuz he thought the governor—"

"Yeah and if he believed that bootlicker was gonna step in against some rabid crackers, I'm Queen Elizabeth the First. Kennedy. *Please!* He don't even know how to keep *white* folks safe; how he sposeta be worryin' 'bout coloreds? Soviets is in cahoots with Cuba. If he tries somethin' else dumb as the Bay a Pigs, y'all kids gonna wind up speakin' Russian and salutin' Khrushchev. Course we might all just get blown off the face a the earth." Uncle George laughs bitterly.

Mama sighs. Though her words have been focused on Uncle George and the progress of civilization (and its possible decimation), her eyes keep shifting over to me. And Clay. And me and Clay. Like she tryna catch us misbehavin' at the daggone dinner table. I try to keep my cool, but she can be so nosy!

"Mama? Doralene's chewin' wif her mouf open again," Coralene tattles.

"No I ain't," Doralene protests, spitting half-chewed pieces of ham all over the table.

"Y'all better act right while we got comp'ny here," Mama says, using her stern voice. Coralene whimpers a little, since she didn't get the response she was after, and Doralene grins at her, grease all over her mouth. These kids are just too disgusting for me. I know I never acted like that when I was their age. I *hated* kids that acted like that when I was their age.

"Don't make no never mind what Kennedy *say* he gonna do for colored people if he don't do it. How many of us we know still can't vote? We are among the fortunate, Indigo, and don't forget how they treat us when we show up at the polls," Uncle George says, ending his tirade. This causes the table to go quiet for a second. Mama stares out the window, saddened. The threat of nuclear war is too big for us to comprehend, but being forever locked outta democracy? Shoot, we feel that every day.

Mama gets up to make some more iced tea. We don't need no more iced tea, but she has to keep her hands busy when she gets upset. I wish Uncle George hadn't come over today.

Then Clay does something that shocks me. I'm just sittin' here, mindin' my business, when I feel his warm hand on my thigh. With Mama and them not two feet away! He got more nerve than a nun in a cathouse!

"What about . . . the Voter Education Project?" he asks. This is the first thing Clay has said since we sat down to Sunday dinner other than "thank you, Ma'am" and "please pass the sweet potatas." Uncle George smirks.

It could be considered a minor miracle that Clayton's over here at all. Mama's not too keen on guests, Uncle George bein' the exception cuz sometimes he helps us with bills. She also wasn't too thrilled about me seein' the same boy so much. She likes the Alexanders, though. Alexanders have done well for themselves in this community the past few generations, she's said.

Tryna get in good with her was all Clay's idea. That's why he came with us to church today like a good li'l lamb of God, and why he's joinin' us for Sunday dinner, and that's a treat; it's the one meal of the week that really matters to Mama. Most days we just have "catch what ya can" suppers, and in lean times PB&J, but Sunday is the day she goes all out. And here I am sittin' with the most beautiful, sexy boy I've ever seen in my life with his hand on my thigh, and he's pissin' off mean ol' Uncle George. Today is a good day.

"Yeah. I'd like to see you go down to the courthouse and remind *them* 'bout the VEP. Boy, they'd bash your head in," Uncle George scoffs.

"Be worth it," he says. Then he looks at the twins. One of Doralene's plaits has come undone, and Coralene's fixing it for her. It's a sweet image if you can ignore all the food and shit she's gettin' in her hair. "If it means *they* might be able to vote when they old enough without bein' disrespected or punished for it," Clay finishes.

Mama brings the iced tea back to the table.

"Enough a this kinda talk. It's a Sunday. God don't like ugly, and neither do I," she says. But when she thinks I don't notice, I see the tiniest smile pass her lips, and it's meant for Clay, even if she ain't lookin' at him.

Clay helps me clear the table as Mama and Uncle George get into it again. This time it's about baseball.

"Clay? Wanna see the pitchers I colored?" Coralene asks.

"Yeah, sure. Let me just help Evvie first."

"Clay Clay Clay! Can I show you the pitchers I drawed?"

"I just said I would after I'm done helpin'—"

"You said that to Coralene," Doralene growls. I grab a plate from him, and he looks at both of them again like maybe they're tryna trick him.

"You can go with them. I got it," I tell him.

"Nope," he says as he fills the sink. I watch in wonderment as he begins to wash dishes like he's done this every day of his life.

"You wanna dry?" he asks me, and I nod in a daze.

Mama comes back into the kitchen, slippin' into her apron, but she freezes. Her and me both just starin' at Clay. That's when it hits me: neither one of us has ever seen a man washin' dishes before. The first time you see such a thing is a marvel to behold.

And it don't end with dishes, neither. Uncle George complains about our '56 RCA set, cuz the Yankees are playin' and he wants to watch Mantle, and he can't hardly get no reception. Nobody asked him to do a thing, but Clay just walks on over to the TV, looks at the knobs, then pushes it out from the wall and slides around in back of it. "Boy, if you don't know whatchu doin' back there," Uncle George starts to say, but before he can finish the thought, Clay's got the picture coming in like it was a new set straight outta the Sears Wish Book. Mama looks at him like he just landed a spaceship.

"How you know how to do that?" Mama asks.

Clay shrugs. "You just gotta play around with electronics a li'l bit."

"Well. Thank you, Clayton. I gotta tell ya: picture looks better right now than when we first brought it home."

Clay smiles shyly. Uncle George kinda shakes his head like he can't believe what he just witnessed, and Mama don't say a thing when Clay thanks her for the meal and I walk right out the door with him.

"You just charmed the shit outta her!"

He laughs. I got my arm through his, and we just walk. I don't know where we're goin', and I don't care.

"Never thought I'd see the day when my mother would be so charmed by a young man, but I knew if anybody on the green earth could do it, it'd be you," I tell him. He gives my arm a squeeze.

"Girl, you better quit flatterin' me. You know I already got a pretty high opinion a myself."

"Guess you just gonna have to live with your big fat ego," I say, and kiss his cheek. He offers the other one to me, and when I lean in to kiss it, he quickly turns his head and catches me with his mouth. Ain't that somethin'? Crazy as I am about him, the fool still thinks he needs to trick me into kissin' him proper. I could eat him alive.

"Wanna go drivin'?" I ask him, knowing what I'm really asking. *Can I be alone with you and eat you alive?*

He makes a face like he just got bit by a mosquito.

"Wish I could, but I got work in the mornin'. Told Pop I'd open the shop. Five a.m."

"*Five a.m.?* What kinda lunatics need their cars worked on that damn early?"

He chuckles and kisses my nose. "The dumbasses of the world."

We walk downtown just talkin', and it's nice. Even doin' nothin' at all is nice with him.

We're passin' Brickney's Music World when Clay stops us. He stares in the window with somethin' like longing.

"What's wrong?"

He inches to the side.

"Come here," he says. He points to somethin' through the window, inside the store. It looks like a small trumpet, but it's silver and shiny.

"That is an E-flat soprano cornet. It's meant to play delicate, mellow music, but it's a work of art just sittin' there without makin' a sound."

He's right. I don't know a thing about instruments, but it is a beautiful sight. We both look at it until a man on the other side of the glass steps into view and glares at us. We back away.

"Evvie. The music I could make on that thing would knock you out!"

"Looks pricey," I say.

"Yeah it's about an arm and a leg. And a neck and a foot." He slowly nears the window again. "But that I could deal with. It would take a mighty long time, but I could save up. I've done it before."

He keeps starin'. He wants it bad, but this is not a store for us.

"Have you asked Mr. Rance at the pawn shop?" I ask, even though I'm pretty sure I know the answer.

He laughs to himself. "Couple times. Last time, he told me to stop askin'. I've checked around. Seems like this is the only soprano cornet in the county. Hell. Might be the only one in South Carolina." He sighs, and I'm struck, not for the first time, by the blind stupidity of Arthur Brickney and all the others like him. It ain't illegal for me and Clay to go into his shop, but we wouldn't dare.

Over the years, Brickney's made it quite clear that he's only interested in white customers. The few times Negroes tried to patronize the place, he wouldn't let 'em touch any merchandise and tripled—sometimes quadrupled—his prices on the spot if they showed any serious interest in makin' a purchase. Anything to get rid of 'em. I'm sorry, but my nigger money works exactly the same as their white-people money, because guess what: it's the SAME money. Now, if you run a business, the object is to make money, ain't it? Jesus. I think years a hatin' colored people so hard must cause some kinda brain damage.

I take Clay's hand and lead him away from this idiotic establishment and walk us toward the park.

"Someday you'll be up north, where I bet they got tons a them cornet things! Just hundreds of 'em all over the place."

Clay snickers. "Yeah, I heard they grow up there like weeds."

"That's right! You can have one for every day a the year!"

Just inside the park is a playground for li'l kids. Since

there ain't no kids here right now, Clay and I sit in the swings.

"Tell me about your thing, Evvie."

"My what?"

"You know! Your *thing*. The thing that gets you excited when nothin' else does. The thing that can take the blues away. Stars and such for you. Right?"

I almost forgot I'd told him about that.

"I don't know how much of a thing it is. I just find it interesting. Ain't like playin' a instrument. Not like I can carry the stars with me wherever I go."

"You don't have to. They already there," he says simply.

"Still. It's just somethin' I like. A hobby."

We dangle in the swings, kickin' up small puffs of dust from the ground.

"But? Couldn't you be like . . . an astronomer?"

I grin and restrain myself from laughin,' because he's bein' sweet right now, but as soon as he said that, I got this goofy picture in my mind of me in an old-timey observatory takin' notes from Galileo, who's wearin' an old-timey wig and green stockings. I'm sure that's not really what being an astronomer looks like.

"I can't do that," I say.

"Why not?"

"Cuz! You gotta go to school and study for a long time before you can be somethin' like that!"

"Here's an idea. . . ." He playfully kicks my foot. "Go to school and study for a long time."

I can't even let myself imagine it. How many years would

I have to watch Abigail before I could pay for such a thing? By the time I'd have enough saved, *she'd* be ready for college.

"Clayton, I can't afford a damn telescope! How you figure I'm gonna pay for *college*?"

"They got these new things called scholarships. I hear they give 'em out to smart, passionate people, so . . ." He looks at me expectantly and then adds, "So it's too bad we don't know anybody like that."

I shake my head at his silliness. "You gotta be brilliant for all that," I tell him.

"I feel like if the want is bad enough, it's gonna happen."

Impossible as it is, just the thought makes me smile, and that makes him smile even bigger.

"Excuse me?"

A white girl about our age stands in front of us next to a small boy.

We both hop off the swings so she can push her little brother or whoever she's got with her.

I ask Clay, "You think we should turn around or keep—"

"I've seen you before," the white girl says to us.

We look at each other, unsure who she's talkin' to.

"You." She points to Clay. "You work at Alexander Auto, doncha?"

"Higher, Betsy! Higher," the child demands.

This Betsy pushes harder, but her eyes remain on Clay.

"Yeah. It's my pop's place."

"Wow. Good for y'all," she says. I can't put my finger on why, but I'm gettin' a bad feelin', and I wanna go.

"Clay," I whisper, "we should go."

He nods, and we start to head in the other direction. I hear the squeaking of the rusty swing behind us, then the boy whining, then fast footsteps.

"Hold on a second." Betsy is back.

"You two know where I could find any parties around here? You know, like"—she lowers her voice—"Negro parties?"

I turn my attention to the ground to prevent myself from doin' somethin' I'll regret. She got a lotta nerve.

"We don't go to parties," Clay explains. "It's against our religion."

I clear my throat and pretend to look for somethin' in my purse to keep from laughin'.

"Betsy, I'm tellin' on you! You can't leave me," the boy hollers.

"I have to go," she grumbles. "I'm Betsy, by the way," she says.

"We know," I say. Not that she's noticed my existence. I feel the tiniest hint of a headache, and I try to focus on somethin' neutral. Swing set: seat, chains, poles.

She looks at Clay. "And your name is . . . ?"

He sighs. "Clayton."

That red-orange band in my gut starts pulsing. My mind, determined *not* to jube in this moment, fights for neutrality. Ladder, slide, teeter-totter.

"Nice to make your acquaintance, Clayton." She puts her hand out for a shake, and my blood boils. I can tell he doesn't want to do it, but Clay lightly shakes her hand.

Like a reflex I didn't know I had, I dip down into that angry band and touch it. Just a light touch. Betsy suddenly gasps, clutching her stomach. She quickly recovers, but seems different now. Less sure of herself.

"I should go," she says vaguely.

I didn't hurt her. It was just a light touch. And nothing terrible happened. Everything is fine. The looming headache dissolves, and I don't feel sick or anything. Maybe it's better to embrace it instead of fighting.

"See ya around," she says, and heads back in the other direction, no longer experiencing any discomfort. "Don't be a crybaby," I hear her yell.

When I'm sure she's out of earshot, I exhale. "I didn't think she was ever gonna leave," I say.

"Yeah," he says, but he's distracted, searching all around us.

"What you lookin' for?"

"Come on." He grabs my hand, and we walk, fast. Before I can question our pace, Clay tosses somethin' in a garbage can.

"What was that?"

He shakes his head. "Betsy's phone number."

So that's what the handshake was about. Christ Jesus, white girls are bold. Cuz they never have no consequences. It's infuriating.

"I had to make sure nobody saw that," Clay says. "I ain't in the mood for no trouble."

I exhale again. I was close to doing somethin' regrettable to that girl. Somethin' to make up for all the years she's lived without any repercussions for her actions. And I didn't.

I gave her a warning, and it was enough. But I wanted to do more and . . . I got all this excess energy now. I have to use it. How? On *what*?

"Evvie? What's up?"

"Nothin'." Can I make it go away? Can I ignore it?

"I'm sure nobody saw nothin', if that's it," he says.

"Mmm." *What the hell do I do?*

"You actin' real funny."

I have to do somethin' before it takes over. I don't think I'm angry anymore, but I remember how I settled into my anger at Grammie Atti's, and I try that again. Instead of a mere touch, I allow my inner self to sit in it. To really *feel* it. The wind starts to blow, howl, and the howlin' sounds like strange music notes. Off key. Hundreds of green, yellow, and brown leaves spin toward us forming a funnel, and then they blast into our faces. Clay and I cover our eyes, and in a heart-beat, the wind quiets and the leaves all softly land at our feet.

"Damn! You think a hurricane's comin'?" Clay asks, worried and pullin' leaf bits from his hair and off his clothes.

I stare at the ground just ahead of us. I can't move. Clay follows my gaze, and I know I'm not seein' things, cuz he goes silent. The leaves have fallen in such a way that they perfectly form the words "HAPPY HAPPY."

13

Cyclone

LATE. LATE LATE LATE. THEY SAID ON the radio there's sposeta be big deal meteor showers tonight and we might be able to see 'em around two forty-five this morning. I know I shouldn't be going out this late, but I figure this might be one of those once-in-a-lifetime things, so I decide to take my chances. Mama sleeps like the dead once she's out. The twins are more of a concern, but if I make it all the way out the house without wakin' 'em, they should stay asleep till I get back.

I slip on some old pants and my flats and pull a jacket over my nightshirt. I creep down the stairs as slow and quiet as I can be. Lifting my house key from the key hook is the scariest moment. I hold my breath and one, two, three . . .

got 'em. Not a sound. I sneak out the door and close it gently behind me.

Next hurdle. I bear down, and using all my strength, I hoist my bicycle from the back porch and carry it, clamping down on the chain and all, out into the street. I set it down to take a brief rest. Then I pick it up again and carry it to the end of the block. I make sure I'm well on my way before I finally put it down and ride.

Free. I know it ain't the safest time to travel, what with rednecks out at all hours, but there is something fun about wheelin' around town in the middle of the night. The streets are empty. Nobody's around, thank Christ Jesus. It's like the meteor showers are happening just for me. Wish I could share this with Clay, though. Hell, he'll be gettin' up to go to work in a few hours, since his dad keeps makin' him open up the shop.

Takes me about forty minutes to get out to the edge of town and just under ten more to get myself up to the lookout. That last mile is all uphill. I'm huffin' and puffin' when I'm done. I know I couldn't have used it tonight noways, but someday, I do hope we get a car. Mama says who needs it when I got the bike and we both got the city bus? But I bet it feels different to have your very own car. That might be why Clay feels like a man compared to the other boys his age. Technically it's his dad's car, but still. Close enough. Probably closer than I'll ever get.

I watch the sky. I use the binoculars that Uncle George gave me last Christmas—a thoughtful gift until he made sure to let me know how much they cost him. They're not the best quality, but it's what I have, so they'll have to do.

I focus them. A few clouds drift by, but for the most part the night is clear. When I was younger, I dragged Mama and the twins outta bed to look for Comet Arend-Roland from our back yard. They were still babies and screamed the whole time and Mama complained, and we could hardly see it at all. I made up my mind then not to share this stuff with the family anymore. So even if I'm a little lonely, at least it's peaceful.

I see something. I adjust both lenses to get a better look, and I see movement growing in intensity. So bright, I don't even need the binoculars. Then they all start to fall through the sky. Dazzling streams of light. I can't believe how many there are. How beautiful this sight is. When I don't think I can handle any more beauty, they start to swirl in a circular motion. A cyclone of light. This is a rare atmospheric phenomenon that has to be seen to be believed. Because I know what magic looks like, I know this is pretty damn close, but it's not magic. It's the elegance of the universe.

Without moving my eyes, I reach down to make sure the bike is securely leaning against the tree before I edge closer. I know moving a few feet closer can't possibly make much of a difference, but it feels like I'm nearer to touching the sky when I do. I take a few more steps, and when I'm convinced my view can't possibly get any better, I plant myself and stand, still in awe.

I stare as long as I can. I try not to blink. I want to sear this image in my mind so I can always remember it. If I was artistic, I would try to draw what I see, but I'm not so good at art. I wish I had a camera, but there's no way a photograph could capture the motion. I just wanna be able to always recall this picture. I'll do my best to describe it to Clay and Anne Marie. And Daddy. Maybe one day, well into the future, I'll describe it to Mama. Maybe my own kids, if I ever have any.

After a while, my head starts to hurt a bit. Not like the dangerous headaches, but from eyestrain. Truth be told, since I discovered that connecting with my red-orange band makes 'em go away, I haven't had any bad headaches at all. I think that can only be a good thing.

I know it's about time to go, so I soak it in for one more minute, feeling lucky and smart and part of a cosmos too vast for any of us to ever fully understand.

The showers begin to dim. Finally I drop my arms, shake 'em out for a second, and then I turn around to head home. I check my watch and see that it's nearly three thirty. Later than I thought, but not so bad. I'll be home long before anyone's awake.

I stretch and let out a huge yawn as I walk back toward the path, and then I stop and almost laugh in my sleepiness. Until I get back to the tree where I left my bicycle.

It's gone.

Sure it's dark and all I have is a flashlight to guide me as I go from tree to tree searching, but I know *exactly* which tree I propped it up against. Now I'm runnin', but where the hell can I run to? The bike didn't just take itself for a joyride! And I know ain't nobody been up here or I'da heard 'em. The sweat from biking uphill earlier has now dried and makes me shiver in my thin jacket.

How could this have happened? Of all the things I was worried about, losing my bike wasn't one of 'em! I just stand there like a moron, not knowing what to do. I can't go home without that bike. To make matters worse, I'm suddenly so tired I can't keep my thoughts straight. I return to the tree where I know—I KNOW!—I parked my bike. I slide down to the ground, lying back against the trunk. I rub my hands together for warmth and close my eyes. If I could just rest for a few minutes, maybe I'll have a better idea of what to do.

In my eyes-closed world. Stars and meteor showers and distant galaxies right up in my face. I'm floating up to greet 'em. I'm up high in the atmosphere, and when I look down below, there's Clay. I wave at him, but he don't wave back. He looks like he's shoutin' something at me, but all I can see are his lips movin'. Can't hear a word. I notice I'm gettin' closer to the nexus of the swirling circle of blue, and I can feel its heat. It's the opposite of what you'd think: blue stars are the hottest and red are the coolest. I look down again, and where Clay was, Daddy now stands. He smiles and waves up to me with a cigarette danglin' out the side of his mouth.

"Daddy? Look at me! Look up here!"

"I see you, pudd'n'," he calls. "I see you."

I look up again and now see that I'm headed straight for a giant ball of blue flames and I'm picking up speed and I don't know how to stop myself. I scream for Daddy, but now his body is wrapped in chains from his neck down to his feet. His eyes full of tears. He can't protect me.

I awaken to a weird feeling, like breath. I start to fully wake up, glad that what I just experienced was a regular dream and nothing more. I focus my eyes and jump, but steady myself just as quick. Something sits on my chest, breathing warm tiny breaths into my face. A little cottontail. I've never been this close to one before, but here she is, sittin' on me like we're old friends.

"Hey there," I say as softly as possible. Her breath comes quick, and I can feel her tiny heartbeat going a mile a minute.

"You scared?" I whisper to her. She stares into my eyes. Then she takes her little back foot and she tap, tap, taps it on my abdomen.

"What are you doin'?" I ask her.

She stares at me and doesn't answer, since she's just a rabbit. Then she does it again, the tap tap tapping. I'm about to try to go into her head (never done that with an animal before, but how hard can it be?) when she hops off me and scampers away at the hint of a sound and then a blur sails past my line of vision.

"Hello?" I call out, not sure what I just saw, but it's a lot clearer than it would've been before I closed my eyes, because the sky is starting to lighten. I check my watch. Five after five. This is not good.

From the other direction, it comes again, but slower this time. Slow enough for me to see that the blur is riding my bike.

"Hey!" I yell. "*HEY!*"

The bicycle thief pedals backward this time until his eyes meet mine.

Oh. Shit.

"You call? I come," says the black-haired stranger with his slimy smile. I cross my arms around my chest as tight as I can to keep my hands from trembling. I try to casually look around to see if the rest of his cronies are here, but he seems to be alone.

"That is my bicycle. Give it back."

"Oh, this? This is yours?"

I nod like a fool. Of course he knows it's mine.

He squints his eyes at me like he's tryna put me into focus.

"You don't remember me, do you?"

"Yes, I do!" As if I could forget! "You and your friends were messin' with me and my boyfriend. We never did nothin' to you." I hate how desperate I sound, but I'm scared as hell and of *what*? This pale, skinny bully can't be worth this much fear.

He lets go of the bike, and it falls to the ground with a clatter. I shut my eyes and wish him gone. I open my eyes. I don't get my wish.

"No. Before that. We knew each other a long time ago."

I haven't the foggiest idea of what he's talking about, and for all I know he's lying, so I'm just thinkin' on how I can snatch the bike back and hop on it before he can stop me. I ain't figured this out yet.

"We used to play. Games. Hide-and-seek. Red Rover. Freeze tag. You gotta remember some of it?"

I don't remember. Can't remember. Why can't I? Who is he? Why can't I—

He moves closer to me. "Doctor. I know you remember that."

A surge of something painful and hot and sharp rips through my whole being, and the world around me goes dark. I'm in darkness, and I see my red-orange band deep inside, but it's as far away from me as a star.

Then I see, hear, smell flames. I smell flesh. I hear the cackling laughter, and I scream.

Just like that I'm back in the regular world again. I raise myself up (since I somehow wound up on the ground), coughing and gasping for air, and I feel like I'll never get enough back in my lungs. The first thing I see is not what I expected to see. The man is several feet away from me, up against a tree. His arms are wrapped around the trunk in a queer way. He looks like somebody stuck him there with cement. Clearly, that somebody was me.

He still watches me. I can't tell if he's scared or annoyed.

"Think you could at least loosen your grip?" he asks.

How does he know I'm doin' it?

I don't move. Am I able to jube in his presence now? Why doesn't it feel right?

"You're even more fascinating than I remember."

"Stay away from me." I hurry onto my bike, though I feel a little dizzy and pray I can make the trip home. I also worry that the dawn breaking open the sky will make gettin' home before Mama wakes up an impossibility, which could mean a helluva lotta trouble headed my way. She promised to punish me in a big way if she ever caught me comin' in late again.

"Wait a minute," he says.

I ignore him, but he gets my attention when he tears himself from the tree as if I wasn't really holdin' him there at all. Was I not? Was he . . . fakin' it? There's so much I don't understand. My head's spinning.

Before I can get my full weight into the pedals, he blocks me and the bike. His iron grip squeezing my hands over the handlebars. He's stronger than he looks.

"Here's how it is," he begins. "I like you, Evalene. I always have. Believe it or not, you're the reason I came back to this shit town. My dumbfuck uncle thinks it's to take over his business when he croaks. It's not. And I won't.

"Lotsa folks aren't gonna understand us, but I don't much care for lotsa folks. Jim Crow is a pointless, intellectually hollow, and ultimately self-sabotaging model for a so-called civilization. It's an embarrassment. You see? I'm on your side. I'm no dummy."

His words surprise and confuse me. I don't know how to classify him in my mind, he's so unpredictable. I do all I can to hide my thoughts from him. He doesn't need any more weapons.

"I'm not asking for much. Just spend some time with me. Don't be scared of me. Nothin' serious." He smiles. I hate his smile.

"And your—uh—boyfriend? You're gonna have to end that."

I attempt to pull my hands away, but his grip tightens.

"I'm tryin' to be nice about this. I'm a nice person. But I'll warn you now: When I want somethin'? I get it. If you just accept that, there won't be any problems."

"Why can't you just leave me alone?"

He backs up, letting go of my hands, but still blocking me.

"I don't know. But I can't," he says. "You have to rearrange the way you think about me. This might surprise you, but a lot of young ladies would kill to trade places with you."

I reach, reach, and I just barely touch that bright red-orange, and I feel a wave of somethin' pass through me. It shoulda worked, but it didn't. It's like a dud when you expect a firecracker.

I give up on tryna use my powers, so I pedal straight ahead. He tries to leap outta the way, but I roll over one of his feet. He cries out like a li'l kid cuz I hurt him, but as I peel away, flying down that hill, I can hear him. Laughin' and hollerin'. "You won't forget me now, will ya? Virgil Hampton! That's my name! Virgil! Hampton!

14

Unspeakable

B Y SOME MIRACLE, I MANAGE TO MAKE
it home in time. More or less. I get inside and run
by the closed bathroom door with the light peek-
ing out under it just in time for Mama to come out
and see me standing in my bedroom doorway.

"Evvie, you scared the heck outta me. What're you doin'
up so early?" she asks, and takes a few steps closer to me. I try
to back up without her noticing.

"Are you—*dirty*?"

"Uh, yeah. A li'l bit."

"Why?"

Now I gotta come up with something quick when
there ain't a single reason I can think of for me to be

outside in the dirt at six in the morning.

"I had a nightmare. Dreamed somebody took my bike. So I woke up and went out to make sure it was still here, but then I fell."

"Backward?" she asks, examining the back of my pants.

I nod innocently.

She eyeballs me like she's trying to crack a code.

"Clean yourself up. Come down to the kitchen."

She doesn't sound mad, exactly. Not happy, but not mad. Could go either way.

When I get out of the tub, I can hear the twins in their room singing "Miss Mary Mack." Up and singin' and it ain't even seven o'clock yet.

I go downstairs in my robe without bothering to find my slippers. She's making coffee on the stove, fiddling with the newspaper, but not reading it. She gestures to a chair, so I sit.

"I won't suffer lyin', and I won't suffer sneakin'. I will not put up with it, Evalene."

"Lyin'?"

The water starts to boil, so she gets up to pour herself a cup.

"So you gonna stand by that stupid story you just told me?"

Okay. That was a lie.

"Sorry. That wasn't how I got dirty."

"I don't like this. You spendin' every free second with that boy and stayin' out all night? You think you grown now?"

"But I wasn't with Clay last night."

"Stop lyin'!"

I'm so tired, I almost laugh. Of all the times I have been

out misbehavin' with Clay—and there have been quite a few—last night was not one of them.

"That's the truth."

"Do I look like a fool to you?"

I massage my temples. *How do I handle this?*

"No. I wasn't out with Clay last night cuz I rode my bike up to the lookout to see the meteor showers, and I didn't tell you cuz I knew you'd say I couldn't be out that late, but it was important to me, so I—"

"And you just got home half an hour ago? You expect me to believe that?"

Something rumbles within me. I don't know what it is, but it drops down way past this petty argument and makes me think of this morning and how I felt and how I was confused and scared. . . .

"Who is Virgil Hampton?"

Her face drops. The air in the room shifts.

"Where did you hear that name?"

I try to read my mother's face to see if she's already answered my question without using words, but she's got a wall up, keepin' me out.

"He's been botherin' me," I tell her. "That's why it took me so long to get back home."

She's pale as a cadaver and frozen still. If it wasn't for the slightest rise and fall of her shoulders, I'd think she'd stopped breathing altogether. I'm now very sorry I asked, cuz I don't want to know the answer.

"You've seen him?" she asks, her voice raspy in her

throat. Her eyes. They're full of so much sadness. She looks like she's aged in just the last few seconds.

"Why does he know me?"

"You two used to play," she says, defeated. "When I did the cleanin' at the Hadleys. He was—is—one a their relations. He was older than you. Old enough to know right from wrong. He was a kid, but you were a baby."

The Hadleys. I remember going over there sometimes, especially in the summer. I can't place this Hampton person, though.

"I don't remember him."

"*Good,*" she says. "He wasn't a person. He was a pestilence."

"What did he do?"

Mama seems to think about taking a sip of coffee but then changes her mind. The twins come racing down the stairs.

"Mama, can we have cinnamon toast? We want cinnamon toast," they say in unison. Creepy when they do that. Mama starts to get up, but I stop her.

"I'll make it, Mama," I say. I get out the bread and place the slices in the toaster. Then I make Coralene and Doralene sit down, keeping my attention on Mama to see if she will tell me anything without using words. She does that every now and then. Sometimes on purpose, sometimes not. But she's somewhere else right now.

"Evvie, why you up so early?"

"You gotta go to work early today?"

I shake my head and spread the butter and cinnamon

and sugar on their toast slices and hand them the plate. Lucky for us they get quiet when they're eating something they like.

"What did he do?" I ask again.

"Who?" Coralene and Doralene say with their mouths full.

With shaking hands, Mama tries to take a sip again but instead throws the cup against the wall, smashing it and sending the caramel-colored liquid flying everywhere. The twins freeze in terror. I'm frightened too.

"He hurt you. In an unspeakable way. And there wasn't a goddamn thing I could do about it."

I don't say anything. I can't say anything. I just stand shaking in my kimono, not knowing what to do.

Then Coralene and Doralene start crying. I pull a hanky from the drawer and tend to their tears, but I'm surprised when Mama joins 'em, cuz she is not a crier. Now I got *three* girls crying!

"Mama! Don't," I say as gently as I can. I bring the damp hanky over to her, too. She just shakes her head.

"I'm sorry," she says, breathy and full of sorrow. "I tried— all they did was fire me. They threatened to do worse to both of us if I ever said anything again."

I caress her arm, feeling helpless. "You did the best you could. That's all any of us can do." What else can I say? I'm not upset with her. I feel so mixed up and shocked, I don't know if I can really get upset at all. Not right now. In a way, I'm relieved. At least now some things make sense.

Someday I might ask her exactly what he did. Though I can guess. Someday maybe I'll remember it for myself. It's amazing that my mind could hide something like that from me all these years. Maybe it was takin' care a me.

"Everybody stop cryin' right now. I mean it," I say.

"But I'm sad and Mama's sad and she broke the coffee," Doralene blubbers.

Out of ideas, I start singin' "Dedicated to the One I Love" by the Shirelles. First they look at me like I lost my mind, which I might have, but then they all stop crying and they have to sing. That's just the way it is. I mean, it's the *Shirelles*!

Before we know it, we're all laughin' like nothing bad ever happened to any of us. Somewhere, deep down, some small part of me returns to the thought of Virgil Hampton. His name alone had the power to break my mother in a way I've never seen, and she's strong as anybody. I get a chill and try to put him out of mind. Whatever happens, I won't let him break me.

15

Jubilation

I AM NO LONGER NEEDED IN THE KITCHEN. I just like to help if I can, but I think I was annoying Mrs. Alexander, cuz I was carryin' the green beans to the table, and she took 'em from me and said I should go visit in the livin' room. Whatever "visit" means.

This house is crawlin' with folks. I squeeze into a corner of a window seat in an attempt to stay out of the way. I've only met Clay's parents a few times before, and I probably won't see 'em much in this crowd tonight. It's too bad, but I guess I'll get to know them sooner or later.

"Hello, sugar. Are you Li'l Dottie's daughter?" an oldish woman asks me.

"No, ma'am. I'm here with Clay."

"What did ya say?"

"I'm with Clay," I say louder.

"Oh, that's nice. You are gettin' so tall and pretty! Is Li'l Dottie here?"

It's pointless to argue.

"No, ma'am. She didn't make it out this evening," I tell her.

"Aw, I haven't seen her in ages. You give her my love, ya hear?"

"I will, ma'am."

She dodders off. A couple small kids seem to be playin' chase, runnin' through all these bodies, bumpin' 'em, knockin' over shit. They been warned. I heard it. Only a matter a time before somebody's mama starts screamin' and the whuppin' begins.

From my perch by the window, I spot Clay across the room, surrounded by relatives. I had no idea this party was going to be *this* big. For all I know, maybe he never gets to see these people. I'm beginnin' to wonder why he wanted me here so badly. It's nice to be invited and all, but I woulda understood if he just wanted to spend time with family.

Now I'm seein' people holdin' plates, so I guess all the food's been laid out, but I don't feel like eatin'. Not in this crowd. I don't care for pushin' and shovin' and gettin' pushed and shoved just to get a plate a food. Rarely am I that hungry. I'd rather just sit here quietly like a ghost. It ain't half-bad actually. Peace, in the midst of chaos.

Them shrimp and grits sure do smell good, though.

That's all right. I don't mind. Maybe supper'll calm the brats down at least.

I bet there's two hundred people here. Could be more. Clay's house is much bigger than ours. His father owns his own business, as his father before him did. I don't think that means they're rich, but I think they're doing pretty well. They got a dining room separate from the kitchen and *two* bathrooms! I haven't gotten a tour, so I don't know what the upstairs looks like, but I think they also got an attic and a basement. All these rooms and all this space and Clay's an only child. I'm a tad envious, but I wonder if he ever gets lonely.

The front door opens again (I can't see it from where I'm sitting, but I immediately feel the energy shift out in the front hallway), and this time it gets kinda quiet out there. Because the sudden hush is so unexpected, I sit forward and strain to hear what's goin' on or if somethin' happened. I can't make out anything specific, but the hush seems to move like a bubble around one woman. The guest of honor. A woman who looks like she might be in her sixties pushes the wheel-chaired guest to the center of the living room. The quiet that follows her is either out of respect or awe. Or fear, possibly.

The woman in the chair is Miss Corinthia Tuttle, Clay's great-great-aunt, and today is her one-hundredth birthday.

Once she's in the room, the conversation picks up again, and several people gather around Miss Corinthia to pay their respects. I'm curious myself but don't feel like I have a right to bother her, since I'm not family. I've never met a one-hundred-year-old person before. I expected her to look like an unwrapped mummy, but she doesn't. I can tell that her hearing isn't too great, cuz people keep leanin' in close to talk to her. She mostly sorta nods. Not talking much herself, if at all. Her hair is thin and silver and pinned out of her face. I realize now that it might be a wig. If I'd met her in church or somethin', I'd probably think she was in her seventies or eighties.

Somebody awkwardly places a gift-wrapped box in her lap. She looks down at it without any interest, and that's when I notice the gnarled stiffness of her hands. There's no way she could open that box on her own.

"Here, Grandmama. I got it," says the woman who wheeled her in, and she puts it on an end table.

I get up to use the bathroom. I don't have to go, but I need to stretch my legs, and it'll give me an excuse to get a closer look at Miss Corinthia.

"Lord, you look like you're in better shape than *I* am," some lady jokes. I have a feelin' she's heard that one before. Miss Corinthia just smiles up at her. It's a strained smile, like a mask. Or it could be that she can't control the muscles in her face the way she used to. I slip by the entourage and down the hall to the bathroom, which is occupied, of course. I don't even know where the other one is. I lean against the wall. I'd rather wait than fight my way back through the crowd.

I feel a light weight on my side.

"Can you imagine how terrible it would be if one day we found out we were cousins?"

I turn my head enough to see Clayton with his chin resting on my shoulder. I giggle.

"Well? It wouldn't be great," I reply.

"I think we'd get over it eventually."

"You are so goofy!" I tell him. The door opens, and it's Clay's father.

"Oh, Evvie! I haven't seen you all evening!"

"Hi, Mr. Alexander. Thank you for inviting me. It's a lovely party," I say in my good-girl voice.

"Well, just know you're welcome here anytime, sweetheart," he says to me warmly right before shooting Clay the iciest glare I think I've ever seen. Clay's eyes stay on his, but the hostility only comes from one direction. Mr. Alexander leaves us, and I turn to Clay.

"It's okay, Evvie," he says before I can say anything. He nods his head toward the bathroom, and I go in.

I really don't have to use the toilet, so I'm in here for no reason. On the back of the door there's a cardboard growth chart with a cartoon cat on it and a few pencil marks where I guess they measured Clay when he was a little boy. They stop at a certain point. I try to measure myself. Assuming my hand didn't slip, I'm five seven. Now I know how tall I am if anyone ever asks.

I pretend to wash my hands by runnin' water for a few seconds. Selfishly, I think about that cold stare Clay's dad just gave him and hope that Clay didn't get himself into some kinda trouble that'll make it hard for me to see him.

When I come out, a girl about eleven or twelve pushes

her way in, suckin' her teeth. Maybe I took too long pretendin' to go.

Back in the sea of people, I notice that my seat of choice is now filled by a heavyset light-skinned man. I start to look for a new spot when Clay takes my hand and pulls me to a corner.

"It's too many damn people in here," Clay complains. He glances around, holds up his index finger to me, somehow squeezes around a couple guests, and comes back with a little collapsible chair for me.

"Oh, I don't need to sit. You sit," I tell him, even though I do feel like sitting.

"Okay then." Clay sits down. I did not expect him to do that. He looks up at me and bats his eyelashes, all coy. I give him a little shove, and he pulls me down so I'm sittin' in his lap! Feels weird bein' this close to him with hundreds of his relatives in the same room.

Then all at once the party breaks into "Happy Birthday to You." Mrs. Alexander and one of Clay's aunts bring the huge, glowing cake over to a small table now set up in front of Miss Corinthia. I join in the singing and watch Miss Corinthia's face to see what she thinks of all this. Her lips are tight, and her cheek spasms. Is she tryna smile? To cry?

When we finish singing, everyone applauds, and then it gets quiet as the flames continue to melt wax all over the cake. After a few more seconds, it becomes clear that Miss Corinthia ain't even gonna try to blow that mess out, so Mrs. Alexander, her sister, and Miss Corinthia's granddaughter bend down and blow them out for her. Some claps follow this. To keep the moment from becoming awkward, Clay's mother immediately begins to cut the cake.

"Aunt Corinthia," Clay's father bellows from the other side of the room.

Making his way over to her he says, "Is there anything you'd like to say? Any wisdom or advice for all us infants?"

This gets a giant laugh. Miss Corinthia's facial expression hasn't changed since the song. I wonder if she heard him. I wonder how aware she is of anything right now.

With great effort, she raises her right hand as though she's wavin' a fly out of her face, and everyone waits patiently.

"Nephew," she begins. Her voice sounds scratchy and tired. And old. Old like somethin' dug up from miles beneath the earth.

"I thank you. For this party. It is mighty. Kind. Of you. And. And Beatrice. To host." She pauses constantly, so just sayin' them two sentences took her about a month. That's okay. You can take a month to say your sentences when you a hundred.

When she hesitates long enough for everyone to think she's finished, there is light applause. Until she puts up one crooked, shaky finger to quiet the room again.

"However. You should not. Remind. Old. People. Of. How. Old. They are," she finally says, and everyone laughs and claps. For some reason, everybody enjoys a crotchety old person.

"You want some cake?" Clay speaks into my back. Chills. The good kind.

"Yes. Yes I do." It's funny that I say that, because I was totally plannin' on politely refusin' cake. Some ladylike nonsense.

We get in the long cake line.

The lady I briefly spoke to earlier passes us with a slice. She taps me on the shoulder.

"They got this from Stewart's! Delicious! You be sure to take a piece home to Li'l Dottie."

"I will, ma'am," I say.

She beams and keeps movin'.

"What was that?" Clay asks.

"Don't worry about it. She's just my new best friend."

Clay nods. "Yeah. I can see the two a you stayin' up late, paintin' each other's toenails."

I raise both eyebrows at him. "Is that really what you think girls do when no guys are around?"

"Psh! No," he scoffs, sounding completely unsure of himself.

"Well, hello there," someone says from behind me. "We haven't met yet. You havin' a nice time?"

I turn to see a smiling man. He's maybe about twenty. He has a nice haircut, but his unfortunate choice to use cologne on top of aftershave is makin' my eyes water.

"Oh, yes," I politely reply, blinking my eyes. "It's a lovely party." Back in good-girl mode.

"Jerome? This is Evalene. My *girlfriend*," Clay says. "Evalene, this is my cousin Jerome."

"Pleasure to meet you," I say, all peaches and cream.

"Yeah. Pleasure," he grumbles. Funny how fast he lost interest in meeting me as soon as Clay said the word "girlfriend."

"Let me get a cut," he mutters.

"No."

"Come on man, gimme a cut."

"No! Nigga, you want cake? Stand in line like the rest of us," Clay snaps.

Jerome walks away mumbling expletives. Clay rolls his eyes. I bite the insides of my cheeks to keep from laughin'.

We get to the table, and Clay hands me a slice of cake before taking one for himself, gentleman that he is.

And just like that.

Something's not right.

My breath starts comin' too quick for me, my heart pounds faster, and my hands start to shake. I don't understand what's happenin' right now. I put my other hand out to reach for Clay, but he's already moved a few steps away from me to talk to some people.

"Excuse me? Evvie? Dear? You holdin' up the line," Mrs. Alexander says to me and I know she's right and I want to move, but I can't. I feel a frequency near me. Not like a haint. This feels different. I look up to see Miss Corinthia starin' directly at me with razor-sharp focus.

It's her. I'm scared to address her, but my mind is blank. I can't think of no other options.

"Miss Corinthia? Ma'am? Can I go please?" I timidly ask. She smiles with complete ease—no facial tension or tics. I can move again, and as I turn to quickly get away, I stumble into Clay.

"What's the matter?" Clay asks me.

I try to speak, but then I almost fall cuz I'm dizzy, and he catches me.

"She all right?" somebody asks. Mrs. Alexander watches all this, arms crossed. I don't think I'm makin' such a good impression on her tonight.

"I'm fine," I say, but Clay ain't convinced.

"Can we go outside for a minute?" I whisper, and I hardly get the words out before he's got my hand and he's pullin' me past the hordes to the back door and out on the porch.

Hallelujah! I can breathe again. And I managed to hold on to my plate!

"Oh god. Thank you," I say with a laugh. His face is full of worry.

"Do you feel like you're gonna be sick to your stomach?"

"No," I assure him. "Not at all. Think I was just startin' to feel . . . suffocated."

He nods. I flash him an *everything's okay* smile, and then I eat my cake in silence.

"Why did you ask Aunt Corinthia if you could go?"

I didn't realize he'd heard me say that. I wish he hadn't.

I slowly take a bite and try to think of an explanation that he might accept. All I can come up with is the truth.

I need to sit, so I plop onto the porch swing. Clay joins me, and our knees touch. He searches my face.

"It's not this huge thing, and it's nothing you should worry about," I start. Then I stop to take a breath. I've been nervous about havin' this conversation with him. Some part of me hoped I'd never have to. I don't want him to think I'm a freak, but whatever I am, I'm no liar.

"What is it, Evvie?"

"I have . . . certain unusual abilities. One of 'em is—well—" I laugh anxiously. "I just learned that one of 'em is bein' able to sense others like me when I'm in their presence. Your aunt Corinthia is like me," I say. It's vague as hell, but I'd be delighted if Clay could just be satisfied with this answer without follow-up questions.

"What do you mean by 'abilities'?"

Goddamn follow-up questions. Guess I can't hide who I am forever.

"Sometimes, mostly when I'm feeling emotional in some way, I can make things move, manipulate things, and I can also . . . sometimes read peoples' thoughts. I can often feel things that are goin' on far away from me. They call that bein' two-headed. And every now and then, I get visions and see haints. I think that's all of it, but I don't know for sure. Feels like I'm learnin' new things I can do all the time." I must sound like a bona fide lunatic right now. Regardless, I decide to say nothin' more until he speaks.

I try to read his face, but it's impenetrable. The good thing is he doesn't look scared. He looks like he's in geometry class workin' on a complex theorem.

"You know all this. For sure?" he asks carefully.

I nod. "My grandmother calls it Jubilation, which makes no sense if ya ask me. I don't know if she made that up or if it was taught to her. She's been helpin' me figure it all out. Kinda like tutoring me."

"Miss Athena Deschamps? You been spendin' time with her?"

Oh yeah. Crazy ol' Athena Deschamps. I'd almost forgotten about all the folks who think my grandmother's bonkers. It's understandable, if unfair. Maybe it's cuz she doesn't care what anybody thinks of her that I forget about her reputation.

"Yes. There's nothing wrong with her," I tell him.

"I ain't sayin' there is, but hasn't she like . . . hurt people?" he asks.

"Who hasn't?" I reply. She's put the hurtin' on some people, rarely, though. In fact, I don't know of anybody that's been hurt as a direct result of Grammie Atti's practical magic. Gossip and rumors.

Clay lightly rocks the swing back and forth, starin' off into the distance.

"What are you thinking?" I ask, though I'm not sure I wanna know.

He turns to me and holds my gaze for a second, but he doesn't say anything.

"You're not gonna tell me?"

"I did. I wanted to see if you could read my mind," he says.

"Stop it. I'm not doin' that."

"Have you read my thoughts before?" he asks, and he's so quiet his words almost fly away on the wind before reachin' me.

"No. I never have."

He doesn't ask again, but his eyes do. They plead with me for honesty.

"It's true, Clay. I've never even tried. I wouldn't do that. I wouldn't—violate you."

He sighs and looks away, but our knees are still touching.

"So, what? Are you a witch?"

I swallow. "Are you makin' fun?"

"No. It's just—ya know—a lot," he explains. "I mean, havin' psychical and magical powers ain't exactly—" He stops himself. I know what he was gonna say. He was gonna say it ain't normal. I'm glad he didn't say it.

"Ain't it possible that some a the strange things that have happened mighta been coincidences?" he asks. I sink back into the swing. It's not like I expected him to immediately believe everything. Still. I hadn't pegged Clay as a doubtin' Thomas.

"The first time you took me to the colored children's library. Remember the rainbow?"

He does, but he shakes his head.

"You said that was a natural wonder."

"I lied."

He raises an eyebrow, but I can see he's still unconvinced.

"Clay? Do you remember the day you had Sunday dinner at my house? And we were out walkin' and we saw those leaves on the ground?"

His whole demeanor changes. He's seeing those words on the ground again. Those perfectly formed letters. "HAPPY HAPPY." He believes me now.

"How is that possible?" he asks.

I shrug. "No idea. But when you find out, will you let me know?"

He almost smiles. Not quite, but almost.

We sit without saying anything for a few minutes. I can tell he's really thinkin' about all this. He looks at me with an expression—quizzical, but not too serious.

"I swear I'm not makin' fun, but *are* you—like—a witch?"

"I honestly don't know. Guess I'll ask Grammie Atti."

He nods.

"Does it bother you?" I ask him, afraid of his answer.

He scratches the back of his neck, and he looks down at his cake slice, untouched.

"I don't think so," he says. "It's not like this is all you are or anything."

I wish he didn't sound so uncertain. I wanna keep talkin' about this, I wanna do whatever I can to put his mind at ease, but I don't get the chance, cuz the back door clatters open and Mr. Alexander is here.

"Your mama could use your help," he says to Clay, and somehow he made that statement positively cruel.

"Yeah, Pop. I'm comin'."

I see the briefest internal battle Mr. Alexander's fightin' with himself. He wants to continue punishing Clay, but he wants to be nice to me. He goes back in without either side winning.

"What's going on with him?" I ask.

"He fired me."

"He did *what*? Why?"

"For mouthin' off to a couple crackers who weren't willin' to pay full price for a tune-up." He shrugs it off. "I also mighta drained some fluid from their transmission. Like . . . a lotta fluid."

"Clay!"

"So what?" His hands tighten into fists, and his eyes darken with rage. "Fuck them peckerwoods! I am sick of it! SICK OF IT!"

"I know," I say, as docile as I can. "But you can't just take risks like that. You know how dangerous they are."

He shuts his eyes. "They take everything from us, Evvie. I can't just roll over and let 'em. I can't do that and be a man."

I touch his hand, and it relaxes a bit. I pick it up and kiss it.

"You are a man," I tell him. "Please don't do anything like that again," I say. "For me?"

Clay opens his eyes and looks at me like he could cry. I brush my cheek against his fingertips, and his mischievous grin returns.

"Girl, you turnin' me into a damn marshmallow."

16

Two-Headed

LATER, AFTER MOST A THE GUESTS have gone home, I try to help out with the cleanin' up. Clay's aunts and cousins seem to like me. They say "Thank you, baby" or "Don't you have good manners?" It's different with Clay's mother. She thanks me, but it's outta obligation.

"Thank you, Evalene," she says with a crisp formality. "Don't you think it's gettin' late?"

It's not even half past nine, but I nod, since she clearly wants me to leave.

"Yes, ma'am. I'm just gonna find Clay and say good-bye."

He's not hard to find. As soon as I enter the living room, I see him there, perched on the arm of a couch,

173

talkin' to Miss Corinthia. It looks like they're havin' a serious conversation.

"Excuse me?"

They both look up at me.

"I don't think you two met properly. Aunt Corinthia, this is Evalene. My girlfriend," Clay says to her.

"Very pleased to meet you, ma'am," I say. I'm doin' my best to ignore the jittery feeling I get when she looks into my eyes. "Happy birthday."

"Birthday. Yes. It might be today. Mighta been yesterday. Mighta been. A week ago. They decided. This would be. The day."

"She didn't get a birth certificate, so her family had to estimate when she was born," Clay translates. "Everybody seems certain that it was 1862 and summertime. They just don't know which day."

"A hundred years. Long time," she says. She still pauses every few words to catch her breath, but she doesn't seem to take as long to do it now as she did earlier.

"It certainly is," I agree.

Her eyes twinkle. "Two-headed women. Will always. Spot. Each other."

"Two-headed," Clay repeats, and looks at me, adding things up in his head.

"I was a baby. When. Emancipation came," she begins. "I don't remember. I was too small. To be. Much use. But I was born. In bondage."

I concentrate on listening to her. I push the nervous

energy away. This moment is too important for my own screwy jubin' to mess it up.

"It's a tool. What we. Have. Evalene. Survival. Tool. My mother. She—" Miss Corinthia stops suddenly.

"Miss Corinthia? Are you all right?" I ask her.

"Lemme get you some water." Clay dashes off to the kitchen.

Miss Corinthia reaches her weakened, deformed hand over to mine. I attempt to hold her hand, cuz I think that's what she wants, but she draws back from that. She places it on top of mine, and, with the one finger she can maneuver, she strokes the skin covering my knuckles.

"She told me. Magic. Saved. Her life. And mine. When I was. Just born." She stops to take a few breaths, but I don't breathe. This is far more talking than I've seen her do all night, and I don't wanna break our connection.

"Her labor. Was long. Violent. I faced. The wrong way. Overseer was told. Cut her throat. Drown the baby. In the sea."

I gasp and shiver, but Miss Corinthia continues stroking my hand, which calms me.

"Master thought. I'd be born. Broken or dead. He thought. My mother. Would be too. Weak to work. Useless. But. Magic. Inside her. Knocked the overseer. Into the wall. Knocked him out. She birthed me. We survived."

I feel like telling her not to say any more, to rest, but I'm too captivated to speak.

"We can. Save. Lives. We can. Move. Worlds," she says. "Do not tell. Any. Man. How much. Power. You got. They.

Can't. Handle it," she explains. I feel like I need to take her advice, and I hope I haven't already told Clay too much. As that thought crosses my mind, he rejoins us with a glass of water that Miss Corinthia ignores.

"I thought. We wouldn't. Need. Our. Kinda magic. By the time. I reached. This age."

"Aunt Corinthia?"

"Shh!" I shush Clay. She needs to say her piece.

"But I see. What is. Happening. We. Still do. I hope. By. Your one. Hundredth. Birthday. We won't. Need. Our. Kinda magic. Anymore," she says. She then settles back into her chair. Her hand, still on mine, trembles, and I notice a tiny bead of sweat form at the top of her forehead. I feel tired from just listening to her. She must be exhausted right now.

"Grandmama, you need anything?" Her granddaughter enters the room, cheerful, but lookin' fatigued.

"No, Noni. Thank you," Miss Corinthia says quietly.

"This has been nice, but it's a li'l overwhelming for her," Noni confides to us. "I should be gettin' her home and in bed."

"Miss Corinthia?" I venture. "Do you know why we have this and other people don't?"

"Why do. Some folks. Sing. Like. Angels? Why do. Some folks. Put pencil. To paper. And draw. Masterpieces?"

"Okay, Grandmama. Why don't you take it easy?"

"Why do. Some folks. Find cures. For. Diseases? Everybody. Has some. Kind. Of magic. Ain't. Just. Us."

Miss Corinthia is incredible. I want to follow her around and just listen to her talk for the rest of my life. Well. The rest of hers.

The granddaughter—Noni—steps in with a tight smile and starts to wheel her toward the kitchen and away from me forever.

"Good-bye, Miss Corinthia. Thank you," I call after them. It seems strange to thank her, but I feel so grateful that we met.

Noni rolls her along, but then they stop in their tracks, and I see the poor woman raise her head to the heavens and heave a sigh. She then turns to me.

"Honey? I'm sorry, I don't know your name, but she wants you for a minute," Noni says to me. I go over to Miss Corinthia's chair. I stoop down beside her so she won't have to speak loudly.

"Be. A good. Girl. Try. To. Save. Lives," she whispers so only I can hear.

"I will, ma'am. I promise."

"And when. You can't. End them."

I try to nod as my limbs go numb.

"All right now. I think somebody desperately needs some rest," Noni laughs. Under her breath, she adds, "And that somebody is me." Then she wheels her away.

"Wow. Jesus," Clay muses, a little dazed.

I shake my head at him. "It ain't Jesus."

* * *

Clay opens the door for me, and I appreciate his chivalry, as always, but it's hard for me to enjoy it right at this second.

He gets in on his side and backs the car outta their gravel driveway. We start down the road, and we're quiet. Bad quiet. After a minute, he turns on the radio. "Any Day Now" by Chuck Jackson plays. Clay sings along, and it is a great song. But I simply can't hold it in anymore, so I turn it off.

"Hey! What gives?"

"Why does your mother hate me?"

"What?" He tries hard to sound shocked, but it's so obvious he's faking it.

"I heard her, Clayton. She did *not* want you to take me home. She wanted me to walk! All alone at night. And I'm wearin' heels!"

Clay rolls down his window and rests his hand on the side-view mirror. Suspiciously silent.

"What did I do wrong?" I ask. My voice breaks a bit, and I swallow hard, cuz I do not want to cry.

"Nothin', Evvie. She doesn't hate you," Clay says.

"Okay. Why does she really strongly dislike me?"

Clay pulls the car over to the side of the road. I think he has trouble arguin' and drivin' at the same time.

"Was she like this to your other girlfriends?"

He draws back, face all scrunched up. "You're the only one she's ever met."

I don't have enough space in my mind right now to find that flattering. Maybe I will later.

"She's crazy. Okay? She's seriously cracked. She's got it

in her head that you're the reason I wanna move to Chicago, when the truth is she just wants me to stay with her till she's cold in the ground."

"Wait. What? That doesn't even make sense!"

"This is what I'm tryna tell ya."

"Ain't that what you always wanted to do?"

"Yeah," he says hesitantly. "It is, but I hadn't told her about it. Not till this summer."

"Why didn't you tell her before?"

He runs his fingers over the grooves in the steerin' wheel. Then, outta nowhere, he leans over and kisses me. It's nice—I'm not gonna lie. 'Specially since I haven't for-real kissed him in hours, but we are having a conversation!

I push him away. "Quit distractin' me. I'm tryna talk to you!"

He groans and slumps down in his seat.

"So she don't like me cuz she thinks I'm the one pushin' you to go to Chicago?"

"Yeah."

"Maybe I should tell her that I truly don't care where you live as long as you're happy."

"I don't think so."

"Why not? If this whole Chicago thing is why she hates me, why can't I set the record straight?"

He looks over at me all apologetic.

"She doesn't understand you," he mumbles.

"What's not to understand?"

"Evvie, let's not do this."

"I don't even know what we're doing!"

Clay slumps farther down in his seat. Feels like any minute now he's gonna open the door and slink away.

"Clay, you can tell me whatever it is," I tell him.

"Not this."

"If you don't tell me, I'm gonna assume all the worst imaginable things," I threaten. He just stares straight ahead.

"Fine. Don't tell me. But I don't know if I can trust you anymore if you can't trust me with this," I say.

"Oh Jesus," he sighs, and pulls himself upright in his seat. "You're not who she would like me to be with, okay?"

"Oh." I don't know why I'm surprised, but I am. "Is there—another girl?"

Clay shakes his head. "Why can't you leave this alone?"

"Put yourself in my shoes for a second. If my mother had some mysterious problem with you, wouldn't you wanna know what it was?"

"She doesn't think you're a nice girl, Evvie," he finally says. I try my best to grasp this new piece of information. But I can't, cuz it don't make sense. I am a nice girl. She's wrong!

"Remember: you made me tell you!"

"*That* is your mother's big issue with me? That's so stupid! I'm so nice! I'm nice to everyone!" Even as I'm professing my innocence, I'm asking myself, *Am* I nice to everyone?

"That's not what I mean." He looks at me hard now, his eyes still sorry, but communicating something else.

I catch on at last. Wow. Clay's mother thinks I'm a whore.

Now it's my turn to slump down in my seat. She thinks I'm impure. She wants a girl for Clay whose first time will be her wedding night. Well, there's nothin' I can do about that. I am not that girl.

"For what it's worth, I think she's an old-fashioned harpy," Clay offers.

I don't say anything.

"This is why I didn't wanna tell you."

"It's better that I know."

"*How?*"

I fiddle with the door handle, ignoring his question.

"I also kinda made the mistake a tellin' her when I go . . . I'm takin' you with me," he says.

Hmm. This is news to me. We've never discussed our future plans at all. I'm of two minds about it—being two-headed, this is not uncommon. On one hand, I don't like him assuming I'll just do anything he tells me to without asking me first. But on the other, I'm elated that he wants me to stay in his world. I can't even imagine mine without him now.

"She's all up in arms over it, and it don't matter that I told her it ain't happenin' for a while yet. She's too attached to me anyways. We gotta cut the umbilical cord eventually," Clay mutters. I know I need to say somethin', but I can't think of what that is. This is a lot to digest.

"But? I never asked you what you want. You might not wanna do that," he says finally.

"I just hadn't thought about it before," I say.

"Oh." He goes back to playin' with the grooves on the steering wheel.

Shit. I think I just hurt his feelings.

"To be honest? I don't think about our future cuz it scares me," I admit. "I just like thinkin' about now cuz we're together and happy."

"You don't think we can be together and happy in the future?"

"No, I do. I mean. I hope so."

Clay slides his arm around me and pulls me into him. I rest my head near his chest.

"I have a question for ya," he says, and his voice vibrates through my skull.

"Then ask."

"Would you like to move to Chica—?"

"Yes."

"Just like that?"

I raise my head up to look at him.

"I'm assumin' you don't mean tomorrow?"

He chuckles. "No. I don't mean tomorrow."

"Okay then. In the future, I will move to Chicago with you. Or anywhere else," I say.

He kisses me again, and I don't push him away this time. And we kiss and kiss until I become aware that we're on a public road.

"Um, Clay?"

"Huh?" he says breathless in my ear before givin' it a lick.

"We can't do this here."

Instantly he stops. Pulls himself off me and back into the driver's seat. I straighten out my skirt and blouse and sit upright.

"You are right. Good to know one of us has some brains."

I snicker as he starts the engine. I accidentally notice the difficulty he's havin' over there adjusting his pants so he can comfortably drive. I know I shouldn't be starin', but . . .

"Quit lookin' at it, Evvie," he says, and I can't help but crack up. He isn't laughin', but he's got a big smile on his face.

"I'm kiddin'. Keep lookin' at it."

Now he's got me laughin' so hard I'm scared I might piss myself! I can't imagine talkin' like this with anybody else but him. If things with the trumpet don't pan out, he could certainly go into comedy.

We pull back out onto the road, and as my laughter subsides, I remember how this whole thing got started.

"None a this will get your mother to like me any better."

"Please don't worry about her. She'll come around."

"How d'ya know?"

"If she ever wants her son to come home to visit, she will learn to love his lady," Clay informs me.

I grin, and I'm glad it's dark enough that he can't see me blushin' like a cartoon character. Not totally dark, though. Lights. Behind us.

"Did you see that car before?" I ask him.

He checks the rearview mirror. A black Chevy pickup is right on our tail, and I think it's been there since we started movin' again.

"No," he says. "I'm gonna do somethin'."

At the next traffic light, he takes a sharp right. The truck stays behind us. We pick up speed and then take a sudden left. I grab on to the dashboard to hold myself steady as we take an immediate right. And then another left. All the while, the truck stays with us, and, of course, I know who it is. I knew who it was the second I saw the truck.

Without realizing it, Clay's taken us in a circle, and we still end up on my street, but he speeds by my house.

"It don't matter, Clay. He knows where I live."

Clay turns to me now. "You still don't know who this psycho is?"

I sigh. He remembers Virgil from the night at the lookout and knows he's become a nuisance, but I haven't been entirely honest with Clay.

"I do know now," I say. "Virgil Hampton. He . . . um . . . hurt me a long time ago." I can't say more. I bite my lip and hold back my tears. Just thinkin' about it fills me with shame, and I didn't do anything wrong.

And even without tellin' him every detail, he's red with rage, and my pulse starts racing.

Clay hits the brakes in the middle of the street, and they screech in my ears. The truck does the same, but as it wasn't prepared, it does hit Clay's bumper before backing up. It's not enough to cause real damage, but enough to scare us. Me anyway. Clay, on the other hand, swings the door open.

"Clay! No!"

He gets out and slams it shut. We're now idling in the middle of a residential street, and Clay's finna confront a deranged white man!

I get out in time to hear Clay yell, "That's what you want? Come on then."

He's standin' in front of his bumper, darin' Virgil to hit him.

"Right? That's what this is? Come on, you so goddamn brave!"

Virgil revs the engine, and I run to Clay's side.

"Evvie, go! I know what I'm doin'."

"So do I." I stand my ground and shield my eyes from Virgil's high beams.

"If you wanna hit him? You gotta hit me, too!" I shout.

"NO, Evvie!"

I dig my fingernails into Clay's hand to make him shut up and let me do this.

"Hey! Hey, Hampton?" I call. I get closer and bang on his hood. I feel outrageously bold right now.

"You want me? COME GET ME!"

A new car comes down the street toward us. Shit.

"Evvie?" Clay sounds helpless, and I got him in my grasp so he can't move. The car comes up behind Virgil and honks.

Clay and I look at each other. We know what's to be done.

He hops up onto his trunk, reaches out for me, and I do the same. We sit, hands interlaced together, legs danglin' over the edge, watching Virgil. We ain't goin' nowhere.

Virgil revs his engine again. I hold my breath. Clay squeezes my hand. The truck starts backing up. The driver behind him lays on his horn and curses all of us but has no choice but to back up too. Virgil backs all the way to the end of the street. Where he halts.

I dip down into that deep, pulsing, anger place for strength. I seize it, and it's mine. I feel it and I understand. I am not afraid.

Virgil revs that engine again.

"Hey, Evvie?"

"Yeah, Clay?"

We both hold our breath.

"I love you."

Virgil slams on the gas.

"I love you more," I cry, and hold him and hold me with everything I have and there's no time left to run, to scream, to do anything but be here. The red-orange fire burning in my belly tingles my insides with a terrible joy, and within the blink of an eye, Virgil loses control of the truck. It jumps the sidewalk and smashes into a fire hydrant, sending water blasting up into the air.

We run, and we're back in the car before Virgil can come to his senses. Clay starts driving, tearin' down the road way too fast. And I can feel the band's potency fadin'. Normal Evalene thoughts are coming back to me. Like where are we goin'? What are we doin'?

"Stop the car!" I plead.

"Where?"

"Anywhere!"

He swings us into an empty lot. We're both gasping for air, words, thoughts, anything.

And then I start to laugh. Low at first, but it gets louder.

Clay shakes his head in disbelief. We both finally start

to catch our breath. To use our lungs like functioning humans again.

"I don't know what the hell you think's so funny."

"It ain't," I laugh. "I know it ain't funny." I stop laughing. I have to stop because I am so tired. "I just felt really good there for a second."

"Adrenaline," he says, starin' straight ahead.

"No. It was more than that." *Happy-happy, Evalene.* I shiver. I heard it. Clear as tap water. I look around, but I don't see anybody or anything. Clay didn't hear it. He woulda said somethin' if he had.

We sit for another few breaths. I can't hear our breathing without straining my ears now. All is quiet. No otherworldly beings tryna start a conversation. Good.

"Evvie? You did that?"

I've calmed down. I'm calm enough to feel a li'l self-conscious now that reality's settin' in.

"Yes. Are you scared?"

Clay nods. "Uh-huh," he says. "I am."

We coulda died tonight, if I hadn't used my abilities right. Could be the level of fear, or the adrenaline Clay mentioned, or I don't know what, but Clay grabs me, and let me tell you: we have no trouble workin' off any excess energy we might have left. Right there in that lot. Not carin' who might see.

17

Haunted

NOT TOO HOT OUT. LEAST THERE'S that.

I follow Grammie Atti out in the woods behind her shack. When you get out far enough, you end up in what people call the General's Woods. I hate it. They love honorin' their generals. They lost the damn war, but you'd never know it around here.

If I'm being honest, I do think I've gotten better at controllin' my jubin', and that's mostly cuz a her, but damn if she don't get on my last nerve. We been at this shit for two hours already, and now she wants to take a field trip.

"Quit walkin' so slow," she calls back at me. "Slower you walk, longer this'll take," she warns.

I pick up the pace, rolling my eyes at her back. I wouldn't dare do that if she was lookin' at me. She probably knows I did it anyway.

The light gets dimmer deep in the woods, just able to peek through here and there. Big, ol' black moss trees tower over us. Imposing. The more time you spend in the forest, the more alive the trees seem to be.

At one such tree, Grammie Atti stops. She inspects its trunk and stares way up into its thick branches above. I watch her but don't say anything. Grammie Atti places a hand on the trunk and closes her eyes. She moves her lips but makes no sound.

"Grammie Atti?"

She opens her eyes, looks up into the branches again like she's searching for something and then, reluctantly, takes her hand from the trunk. Without sayin' a word, she starts trudgin' again, so I trudge behind her.

We get to a small clearing near Bottomless Pit. Which isn't a pit but a pond; that's just what folks call it. I've also heard it called Bottomless Shit, because apparently it was once used for that. It ain't too big across, but supposedly if you get out in the middle of it, there is no bottom. Mama said when she was in school, one of her classmates went for a swim in Bottomless Pit and was never seen again.

Anyway, if you can ignore the fact that there's possibly raw sewage and a decaying corpse deep in the water somewhere, it's a really pretty pond.

"Okay," she says, her sharp voice at odds with this tranquil scene. I turn to her. More sunlight has found us in this spot, and the moss on the ground feels soft as carpet under our feet.

"You gonna change what we see and what we feel," she announces. "In times of strife, it may be necessary for you to alter the atmosphere you're in. So. Go ahead and do it."

I wait for her to say more, because surely there's more to say. She just looks at me. Not even botherin' to have an expression right now.

"Can you be—I don't know—more specific?"

"Yes," she says. She takes out her pipe and lights it. After her first exhale, I realize she has nothing more to add.

"Change the atmosphere," I sigh.

"That's what I said," she affirms. "Just the one right here. The one that we're in."

I glance around me. Why would I change somethin' that's already beautiful? But I guess that's not the point. I plant myself and dig down deep. I'm not angry, nor do I have any reason to be, so I'm not sure how I can possibly do something this big.

I turn to see what Grammie Atti's doin'. She's sittin' on a rock, starin' out at the water and smokin' her pipe. She ain't in no hurry.

Another gentle breeze blows, and some love grass brushes against my ankles and I smile. I imagine bringin' Clay here sometime, if I could do it without Grammie Atti knowing . . . and then I feel tickles and I feel the giggles comin', and I ain't in the mood to get hollered at, so I push 'em down. Down, down, down . . .

To another place. There's something else down here, and it pulses too. I can almost hear the giggles I shoved down here. Are these the giggles of haints? Ain't sure, but if they are, they don't bother me down here. I think I know what to do. I internally search for every bit of giggle or happy I'm feelin' right now and gather 'em all up. I bring 'em on down to this other pulsing, and wouldn't you know it? I have another band now. This one is greenish-yellow, and it makes me feel how I imagine drinkin' champagne must feel. I'm giddy and bubbly and silly, and I can't help it! My whole body erupts in a giant burst of joyful laughter.

"Get it under control," Grammie Atti calls from her rock.

I'm bent over laughin' so hard I'm cryin'. She's right: I gotta get this under control. There can be too much of a good thing.

I leap up from down inside my new greenish-yellow band and focus on the present moment. And then . . .

I shiver in my short sleeves. It's cold. Why is it so cold? I look up, and the sun has clouded over and lace droplets fall from the sky onto my hands, onto my eyelashes. Snow. I am seeing . . . snow. Falling from the sky, covering the ground, the surface of the water, and me and Grammie Atti.

It's astonishing. It's an astonishing modern miracle that I can never tell anyone about. It's too impossible to conceive. I've never seen snow before. Is it supposed to look like somethin' from a fairy tale?

"Grammie? Do you feel it?"

"Uh-huh. You did good," she says, not particularly interested in the island of storybook winter I just created. "Was it intentional or accidental?"

I watch the dainty crystals melt in the palm of my hand.

"Intentional," I tell her. It was. I thought it would be fun if I could make it snow. I think about that rainbow I made for Clay and me on our first real date. The laughin' kids in church. Those things just happened, but if I can do this kinda thing on purpose?

Damn! That is somethin' else. I feel like a character from a Greek myth.

"Do you know how you did it?" she asks.

"I think so."

"Revert it."

"Already? But we just—"

"Revert it. All this is temporary. You can't be toyin' with the planet's real ecosystem. Do it. Now."

I wanna cross my arms and tell her no, I should be able to spend more time with my first snow, but I'm not brave enough.

"Evalene! If you don't do what I tell you right this minute—"

It's simple. I release my hold on my new greenish-yellow band, and it gently dissipates. And winter is gone. All gone. The sun is back. The ground is dry. My body just as warm as it was before. Like nothing ever happened. This time, she is impressed and can't hide it.

"Okay. You gettin' good at this, ya know?"

I nod. "Thank you."

I sniff the air, searching for traces of the snow scent, but all I smell is the warm summer dirt.

"What am I not doin' right yet?" I ask her.

She frowns. "Hard to say. You catch on fast, but got this li'l girl in you that wants to throw tantrums way too often. She's impatient as hell. You gotta watch out for her," she warns. Then, quite uncharacteristically, she smiles, and it's a warm, almost grandmotherly smile.

"Come. Sit by me," she says. I sit on a patch of sunbaked grass and look up at her perched on her rock.

"Grammie Atti? How come we can do these things? Do you know?"

She glances down at me; then she sighs, still smiling, but now more wistfully than grandmotherly. "Well. I don't know how it began, but I know some a your foremothers used it when the masters' and mistresses' wickedness became too much to bear. I imagine their foremothers used it too. Somethin' in our particular DNA is determined to live and to fight. It's an advantage we're fortunate to have. You gotta remember that," she explains.

"Mama sure don't see it that way."

"Your mother made a choice. She's a full-grown woman, and she has to do what she thinks is best."

This is the most compassion I've ever heard Grammie Atti express toward Mama. I wish Mama could've heard it for herself. I doubt she'd believe me if I told her.

"Why do only some people have it?"

She coughs hard, and it takes her a minute to recover.

She probably shouldn't be smokin' her pipe so much. When the coughin' fit passes, she acts like it didn't happen. She covers the pipe's chamber with her palm, snuffing out the flame.

"How do you think the world would work if everybody could jube? Like anything else in the spirit realm, the select few are cherry-picked to protect the masses. No use cryin' about it. Just the way it is."

"Are we . . . witches?" I ask her.

She stares at me for a second before chuckling. "Who knows? Some people think witches ain't human. If that's the case, then you can't call us witches. Most often, though, when you hear people cryin' 'witch,' it's just an excuse to hurt or kill somebody they're scared of. Or somebody that just lives life differently. And these somebodies bein' accused tend to have cooches."

"God, Grammie Atti!"

"It's the truth. Don't matter what people call ya. They'll decide who you are regardless of any label you might choose."

The one thing I know for certain about Jubilation is that there will always be more for me to learn about Jubilation. I take in what she's sayin'. It's all useful, but it don't answer the one question that's been haunting me since my first run-in with Virgil and his flunkies. "How come I can't jube when I'm scared?"

She sighs. She seems more tired today than usual. "You can. You just can't in his presence. Yet," she says.

So she already knows about him.

"Why?"

"He's your malcreant. It's what we call an opposing entity that's found your Achilles' heel and exploits it."

She looks down at me and takes my chin in her hand. Her eyes are sad.

"You mighta given him somethin' dear to you without even knowing it. Whatever it is, it's a crucial piece a who you are. As long as he's got it, the malcreant has the upper hand," she says.

That feeling of dread returns, pooling in my abdomen, and I'm reminded of what my mother said about him. She said he was a "pestilence" and that what he did to me was "unspeakable." He does have something of mine, but I didn't give it to him. He took it.

Grammie Atti lets go of my chin and stares up into the trees again. I watch ripples form on Bottomless Pit's surface.

"What do I do?" I ask.

When she doesn't reply after a minute, I look up at her face. Her mouth is set in a hard line, her eyes ablaze. I think she's angry *for* me.

"Sankofa. You heard that before?"

I shake my head.

"It's a symbol from an old African proverb. It means 'go back and get it,'" she says.

"Get it?"

"He took something from you. So take it back."

I let that settle in my mind. No task has ever sounded so impossible.

"You seen it, though. You just didn't know what it was. Sankofa symbol is a bird with her feet pointed in the direction she's going. But her head is looking backward as she holds a li'l egg in her mouth. You can look back without gettin' stuck there, and you can take what belongs to you. No matter how delicate."

Grammie Atti's backward cuckoo bird. I've always thought that deformed bird was a mistake, but maybe it wasn't.

A swift breeze catches some loose strands of her gray hair, and I hear something so soft, but it's there. It sounds like all the voices of a choir holding on to one, long note. Maybe I don't hear it so much as I *feel* it.

"Do you hear that?" I ask her.

"Just spirits in the air. They always around. You probably just couldn't hear 'em before."

Spirits. Haints. Guess they could be anybody. I've never thought much about who they were when they were alive. Regardless, I don't feel scared. It feels nice to have them with us.

Grammie Atti reaches into one of the many odd pockets she sews on the dresses she makes and pulls out a cinnamon candy, which she offers to me. I take it and pop it in my mouth. Probably got lint and dust on it from her pocket, but I don't really care.

She sucks on one too, and we both just stare out at the pond.

"My mother didn't teach me, either," she says unexpectedly. "Never had the chance. My grandmother was long gone by the time it hit. Had to teach myself."

"What . . . was your mother like?" I ask. I hope I'm not

bein' too nosy. This is the first time my grandmother has ever talked to me about anything personal. Today she's in a quiet mood, open to talking. But I don't wanna push her too far. If I do, she might never open up again.

"Oh, so many things," she says. "She worked a lot. She wept a lot. She was a churchgoer. Like *your* mother," she says with a small laugh. "It's amazing how rigid the patterns of our blood can be."

I have no idea what that means, but I wanna know more about my great-grandmother.

"Were you . . . close?"

"I'd say so." She takes her tobacco pouch from her pocket and shakes more into her pipe. "I was with her when she died."

This I did not know. What I've heard about my great-grandmother is spotty and vague. My mother never talks about her. All I know about her death is that it was too soon.

"Was she sick a long time?" I ask.

Grammie Atti narrows her eyes at me, and I know I misspoke.

"Who told you that?"

"Told me what?"

"That she was sick?"

For a split second I can't remember how I came to know that. Then it dawns on me that I never heard that. Because no one ever told me what had happened to her, I just pictured her dyin' young of somethin' like consumption. Like *Camille*. And at some point, that picture became my idea of the truth.

"I don't know. I'm sorry," I say.

Grammie Atti's expression softens, and she relights the pipe. She goes into herself momentarily, but seconds later she's back.

"I don't believe she was sick," she says, as though this is still a mystery to her.

"She was haunted, Evalene. You and me, we can see things in other worlds, make big things happen. Lotsa folks can. It ain't always a picnic, but you can live with it." She inhales deeply. "My mother was haunted in a different way. Nobody paid her any mind. They just thought she was a li'l flighty. Her haints scared her to death." Grammie Atti rubs her forehead. She looks up into the trees again, like there's somethin' up there she lost. "She believed they would kill her. So she wanted to kill them first. She got a heavy knife, the kind used for cleanin' fish, and she stabbed 'em. She said. For days, she carried that knife around with her everywhere, stabbin' into the air whenever she felt the need. She wasn't sleepin' anymore by then. It got to be too many of 'em at once. That's what she told me. They chased her up the stairs and into the back bedroom. I chased her up there too, cuz I was scared, ya know?"

"How old were you?"

She makes a funny sound, like she was tryna laugh, but a groan caught her in the act.

"Ten."

She pauses to puff on the pipe.

"She was stabbin' at every inch of air and space in that

room and screamin'. I tried to tell her that she got 'em all, but she wouldn't stop. She saw one on the other side a the window, and she reached out to stab it and fell through the glass. They didn't make 'em so sturdy in them days. I didn't see her body land. But I heard it."

I'm speechless. This might be the worst story I've ever heard. And she had to live it. At age ten.

"When I come out this far, I keep on the lookout. Sometimes she stops by. Usually up in the trees. She always liked high places."

"I'm sorry that happened to your mama, Grammie Atti."

She laughs dryly. "Don't go gettin' sentimental, girl. Everybody's life's hard. I ain't special."

When she first told me she wanted to bring me out here for "field work," I was grumpy as all hell and couldn't wait for it to be over. But for the first time that I can remember, I don't mind bein' with my grandmother.

We sit lookin' out at the water sayin' nothing more. Passin' the time until the sunset turns the sky pink.

18

Love

IT'S LATE. I AM EXHAUSTED. AND I HAVE to look after that brat tomorrow, but I can't sleep. Thoughts and images keep crowdin' in on me, and I can't get 'em to stop or slow down enough for me to relax. And then even if I do get to sleep, who knows what's waitin' for me in dreamland?

There's a knock at the door, which is surprising, since nobody knocks in this house.

Mama slowly opens it and comes in.

"Somethin' wrong, Mama?"

She sits on the side of my bed.

"We need to talk about things," she begins. I sit up, attentive. I don't know what she wants to talk about, but I sure hope it ain't Virgil Hampton.

"You and Clayton. You're real tight, huh?"

Oh. *This* conversation. Maybe it won't be so bad. Maybe Mama can see that I'm growin' up. "Yeah. I really like him, Mama. A lot."

"Uh-huh. I think you more than like him," she says. I don't say anything. She seems to already know, so why do I need to confirm it for her?

"You know you too young to be havin' sex, Evvie."

I drop my eyes to the orchids on my bedspread. I don't wanna talk about this, either. She shakes her head and lets out a deep sigh. Then she hands me a small paper bag. I look at her, confused. She turns it upside down, and a box of condoms falls in my lap.

I don't touch it. If I touch it, it means I'm fine with what's happening.

"Please tell me he has had the decency to wear rubbers," she says. It's not a question.

I fiddle with my hair, which I'd put in two thick plaits cuz I was too tired to use the rollers. I don't think my mother has ever even used the word "sex" in a sentence before. At least not with *me*. I feel uncomfortable, and when I feel uncomfortable with Mama, I slip into good-girl mode. So my impulse is to deny everything.

"But we're not doin' . . . I mean, we haven't done anything."

"Funny that your impulse with me is to deny everything, and with your grandmother, you didn't bother denyin' a thing. I was there. Remember?"

Oh, yeah. I hadn't thought about that lie too carefully.

"Answer me. Does he use rubbers?"

"Sometimes."

"Excuse me?"

"Sometimes. He hasn't . . . every time."

She looks so hurt. Maybe it's the plurality of what I said that's upset her. Maybe I'm makin' it sound like we've done it a whole lotta times. We haven't really. Compared to some. Oh lord, I shoulda just taken my chances and kept on lyin'. This is awful.

"And what about the other occasions?" Through her hurt, she is deadly serious. I have to behave like an adult for this conversation.

"There's a trick to it. He doesn't believe me. That's why he uses 'em sometimes."

"A *trick?*"

Damn. I can't believe she's gonna make me describe this.

"You know how if you concentrate, you can locate your eggs inside? Well, when he's ready to . . . when it's time? I relax 'em, and they don't let nothin' stick. So? No baby." Saying it out loud, I must sound like some crazy country woman. I probably sound a lot like Grammie Atti.

Mama just stares at me with this strange look on her face that I can't read. Shock? Disgust? Confusion? I don't know how I know how to do it. Nobody taught me. All I know is when he entered me for the first time, it just came to me and it worked, and it's been working ever since.

"Ain't that a trick lotsa girls use?" I ask.

"No! And don't you tell none of 'em about it either."

"So you know what I'm talkin' about?"

She purses her lips. "It's a jube thing. Not everybody can do it," she explains. "And it don't always work," she warns.

"It has for me."

"It don't always work. Don't make me tell you again."

How would you know? I think it, but she heard it.

"If ya don't believe me, go ask Coralene and Doralene. When you're done with them, ask your own damn reflection," she retorts.

I swallow. "Oh."

"Don't misunderstand me: I wouldn't trade any a y'all for anything. But what you are doin' is risky, and I ain't raisin' no grandkids."

I nod, cuz I get it, but why she been lookin' at me like I'm a weirdo when she's done the same thing?

"And you know what else it can't do? Keep the clap away."

"Mama! Eww!"

"Damn right *eww.* You think life's fun when you crawlin' with coochie diseases? No, it ain't!"

I feel like I might throw up. Mama takes out a cigarette and lights it.

"You have got to be more careful, Evalene. You wanna do adult things, but they got adult consequences."

"Okay, Mama. I promise you I will be more careful. I'll . . . make sure he uses 'em."

She takes a deep inhale, and her leg starts bouncing, a nervous signal. "Love can make a normal person act stupid, but it's a whole other thing with people like us. Has your grandmother talked to you about love and Jubilation?"

"*Love?* Definitely not."

"Yeah, that's what I figured. You know how if you're fryin' somethin' and a grease fire starts, the worst thing you can do is throw water on it?"

I nod.

"If love was a grease fire, Jubilation would be a kettle of water thrown on top."

"But everybody feels love. I love you and you love me. Are you sayin' that's bad?"

"Not that kinda love, baby. It's the kind you feel for a man that gets us in trouble. The things we can do require clear judgment. Love muddies the waters."

"Well, what can I do? I can't just never feel love," I say.

Her leg starts bouncin' faster.

"No. But you can see Clay less often."

Before I have a second to think on that, I'm already shaking my head no. My body won't even give me the chance to lie. The last thing I wanna do in this life is see less of Clay. If I could be with him twenty-four hours a day, I bet I'd want twenty-five.

She studies me for a minute. She's tryna speak, to say things she can't out loud. She's not doin' such a great job, since she rarely uses her skills, but I hear her. She's pleadin' with me. She wants me to let Clay go. She thinks we'll both be better off.

I answer her back, and I ain't defiant about it at all. I'm sorry about it. I know she wants what's best for me, but I love him too much to let him go.

Tears fill her eyes. "You're as stubborn as I am. We are

all the same. Why do we keep on makin' the same damn mistakes?"

I don't know what she means by that, but I refuse to believe that lovin' Clay is a mistake.

In any case, all I want right now is to put her mind at ease. I know she'll worry about me no matter what, but I need her to know that I'm not a walking time bomb. So I reach out and hold her hand.

"I'm fine, Mama," I say. "Grammie Atti says I'm gettin' good at jubin'. She's taught me a lot. Trust me: I know what I'm doin'. I swear I do." I say it with as much conviction as I can summon, so I can convince her and myself.

She dabs at the tears in her eyes and takes another long drag. The ash on her cigarette is growin' long, and I wanna find her an ashtray before it falls, but I feel like I can't move. Mama ain't lettin' me move.

"The next time you feel the urge to hurt someone or . . . worse? Do me a favor. Run as fast as you can and put your target out of your mind as fast as you can. No matter who they are or what they done. And then you pray. This is my prayer: 'I am a child of God. I am not ugly. I will do no harm.' Use it, or you can make up your own."

I squint, tryna picture this scenario. I wanna harm somebody so I run, try to put 'em outta my mind, and then I pray? This doesn't seem very practical to me.

"Doin' that works?" I ask.

She smiles sadly. "Doin' that *helps*."

I can't imagine runnin' off and prayin' the next time I see Virgil. It's weak.

"Have you ever wondered why me and your daddy ain't together no more?"

"Cuz he went to prison."

She sucks her teeth and waves me away. The ash misses my bedspread and drops to the hardwood floor. I watch it closely to be sure it holds no embers.

"Before that. Donchu know?"

I don't say anything. I *don't* know. I just thought they couldn't get along with each other.

"I sent him away for his own good. I loved that man like crazy. I still do."

Really? I would've never guessed in a million years that she still loved Daddy or ever loved him "like crazy."

"That love brought out the ugliest of urges from me. When I thought he wanted to leave me for my cousin, I took his voice away from him for seven days. He lost his job cuz a that stunt."

Damn. Mama didn't play around.

She finally notices the ashes and wanders off to find an ashtray, I guess. I still can't seem to move. Is she sayin' I could hurt Clay cuz I love him? What kinda sick shit is that?

She comes back into the room with an ashtray, looking as tired as I feel.

"I sent him away. He was scared a me, and he was right to be. I didn't like myself when I used my power to do such things. I didn't like myself too much at all in them days." She stubs out her cigarette. "That's why I started goin' to church. You may think it's funny, but I know it's what saved me."

"That's why you—why you don't jube no more?"

"I don't feel the need to no more."

I just nod. What do I do with all this information?

"You gotta fight the ugly, Evvie. You might not get a lotta time to do it either. That's why you run. That's why you ask God to intervene."

She kisses my forehead and leaves without saying another word.

I sit stewin' on everything Mama just dumped on me. Now that I'm startin' to understand my powers more, the idea a disownin' 'em outta fear just seems half-baked. If she feels better the way she is, that's fine. Honestly, though? Goin' against my nature to repress the jube sounds much worse than just livin' with it. I may be stubborn like her, but I'm different from Mama. In more ways than one. Nothing could make me send Clay away.

I turn off the light, and I still can't sleep. Curse my stupid family for stickin' me with this niggery witchy bullshit. Who needs it? What good does it do any of us really?

Then I think about Miss Corinthia and how it saved her and her mother's lives. I see how it's useful in an emergency. Unless you're me, and your emergency is Virgil Hampton.

I start to drift off finally as I imagine what it must be like to be born without weird powers. To have the choice to believe in God or religion or magic. To view these things as interesting concepts for an enlivening discussion, as opposed to knowing how real they can be. And how dangerous.

19

Normal

MY TWO-HEADEDNESS HAS BEEN workin' overtime lately. I'm way too attuned to what's going on around me. Just now, when I was readin' to Abigail, I got the sharpest feeling that somethin' was wrong with Anne Marie. It was so strong that I handed Abigail the book and stood up mid-sentence to go to the phone.

"Evalene, you can't stop before it's done. I'm ascared a the pale-green pants in the dark!"

She trails after me, draggin' the book that I've read a hundred times and that can't possibly scare her at this point.

I dial Anne Marie's number.

"Read the book first! You're bein' mean," Abigail hollers.

While it's still ringing, I lean down close to her. "If you be good and quiet, when the pale-green pants come to pay a visit, I'll tell 'em you don't live here no more so you'll be safe."

"The pale-green pants *knows where I live?*" In a panic, she runs into the living room cryin' and throws herself onto the couch. Dammit. Here I thought I was bein' nice.

"Hello?"

I'm not sure who it is that's picked up, but the voice doesn't sound so good.

"Hi, um, is Anne Marie at home?" I ask.

Silence on the other end. All I can hear is Abigail blubbering in the next room.

"Hello?"

"It's me, Evvie," Anne Marie says. I've never heard her voice sound like this before. Something awful has happened.

"What's wrong?" I ask.

"What is it you want?" she asks in a strange way.

"I had a feelin' . . . that somethin' was wrong. With you. So I got worried. That's why I called."

I hear her breath catch on the other end. Then more silence. All I hear is Abigail's cryin' fit, which has already dwindled to a few whimpers and hiccups.

"I can't—uh—I can't really talk right now," she says.

Hearing her like this hurts my heart. I don't know what to do. My instinct is to run out the door and find her. But I have three more hours of work left.

"Can you get out? You could come over again," I offer.

She sniffles. She's been cryin' for a while. "No. I can't do that."

"What about right after I get off at six? We can meet at the fountain?" There's a fountain in town that we once discovered is almost exactly halfway between our houses. It's a good rendezvous spot in an emergency.

"Could you meet me at church later?" she asks, her voice cracking.

"Yeah. Of course. It might take me about ten minutes, but I'll get over there as soon as I can."

"Okay," she whispers.

"Is—is there anything you can tell me now? Or anything I can do?"

"Yes," she says. "Please pray for me."

The second Miss Ethel opens the door, I fly out of it.

"See you tomorrow," I throw behind me as I reach the sidewalk.

I slow down so I don't draw attention to myself, but I move at a fast trot, wantin' to get to the church as quickly as I can. Dreadin' what I'll find when I get there.

Anne Marie's outside on the front steps.

"Hey," I say. "Tell me what's goin' on."

She's got her arms around her knees, and her head lays on 'em to one side. She hasn't made eye contact with me. She's hasn't acknowledged me.

I stoop down and try to get her to look at me.

"I wanna help, but I can't if I don't know what's wrong," I tell her.

She then tentatively lifts her head to look at me, and I swallow my urge to gasp. Her eye socket is red and badly bruised. By tomorrow, she'll have a black eye. I don't know if she has any other injuries, so I delicately lift her to her feet and walk her around to the back of the church, where there's benches and shade and some degree of privacy.

"Who did this to you?" I ask her once we're sitting.

"It doesn't matter, Evvie. There's nothing you can do." She sounds hopeless.

"Fine. Let's assume I can't do anything," I say. "Then what difference would tellin' me make?"

God she looks so defeated. I've never seen her in such a state.

"Uncle Roland," she whispers.

I knew it! I knew it was that bastard uncle that moved in with them!

"I don't care what he told you, you have got to tell your parents so they can kick his no-count ass outta there today!"

At first she nods a little bit, but then she bursts into tears, falling into herself, and I throw my arms around her.

"It's okay, Anne. You can cry or scream or yell. Nobody'll hear ya but me. And possibly the choir, cuz it's practice night, but they'll survive."

Usually when I try to toss a joke into a serious situation she laughs. Didn't work this time.

"Is this the first time he's hit you?" I ask.

She nods. "He threatened before. I never thought he'd really do it," she says.

"Why would he hurt you? You're the sweetest, most thoughtful person in the world! What kinda animal *is* he?"

Anne Marie leans away from me, sitting up straight. She tries to wipe a tear away from her discolored eye and winces.

"Do you want me to come home with you?" I ask. In an instant, I'm thinking about my red-orange band and the caliber of damage I could do to Roland with it.

She shakes her head violently. "No. That's not a good idea."

"I mean . . ." I try to put my revenge fantasies aside. "I could just be with you while you talk to your parents, if that makes you feel safer."

With shaking hands, she takes out a cigarette and lights it. I can faintly hear the choir singing from the church basement, since they got the window open.

"It's complicated, Evvie," she says, really looking at me. I feel a chill as I catch a flash of Anne Marie twenty years from now, sittin' on this same bench, smokin' and lookin' just as beaten down as she does right now. It comes and goes faster than an eye blink.

"Maybe if you say what happened out loud, it'll seem less complicated," I suggest.

"I have no privacy. Nothing that can just be mine," she says.

I wait for her to continue. I don't want to rattle her thoughts with my interruptions.

"Since the seventh grade, I been keepin' a diary. I started

it after we read *The Diary of Anne Frank* in English. Not that I ever expected to be locked up in an attic for two years or anything, but I thought it might be good to write my thoughts and feelings down." She stops and shakes her head, takin' another drag off her cigarette. "How wrong I was. I never much appreciated the sanctity of that diary. Till today. I went out to pick up groceries, but I had to come back cuz I forgot my change purse. Mama and Daddy were at work, so the only person that was home was Uncle Roland, which is not unusual. So I went up the stairs and saw that my bedroom door was shut, and I knew I didn't leave it that way. I only close it when I'm in my room. I opened the door, and there was Uncle Roland on my bed. Reading my diary and laughin'," she says.

"Does he have no shame?"

"Please. That man wouldn't recognize shame if it crawled up his leg and bit him on his lazy ass," Anne Marie replies.

Things are bad when Anne Marie curses without excusing herself.

"Then what happened?" I ask.

Her face changes. Righteous indignation replaced by fear.

"He tried to throw it across the room and deny he was readin' it. Like I hadn't just seen him with my own two eyes. I scream at him for bein' in my room and gettin' into my personal business. Then he pulls that 'don't raise your voice at me' crap, and I told him to drop dead. Next thing I knew, I was on the floor. Him standin' over me, like he was darin' me to get up."

As she's talkin', I'm listening to her and sympathizing, but part of me keeps on thinkin' of all the glorious harm I could do to this good-for-nothin' without lifting a finger. I try not to, though. Anne Marie's so virtuous, she'd probably end up hatin' me, too, if I took it upon myself to punish him.

"He sat down on my bed again, and he looked a little scared himself. I got up and promised him I'd tell Mama and Daddy everything. Then he quit lookin' scared. He's half smilin', and he says to me, 'No you won't.' I tell him there's nothin' he can do to stop me." She stops speaking then. She finally finishes that cigarette and drops it to the ground.

"That's true, ain't it?" I ask, confused. "I mean, there ain't nothin' he can do to stop you."

She turns to me, and I wanna hug her for my own sake. So I wouldn't see the profound pain in those eyes.

"He can tell my parents what he read," she says simply.

I hadn't thought of that. Mostly because Anne Marie's such a good girl. Smoking's her only vice, and she feels guilty about *that*. What could he possibly have found in her diary that would upset her like this?

"Well. He can," I begin, "but it's not like you're out runnin' around committin' crimes. And you'd be smart enough not to write about 'em in your diary if you were. Like it or not, you are a good girl. You have nothing to be ashamed of," I tell her with full confidence.

"Evvie," she says, "I like someone, and I wrote about it in my diary. I wrote a lot. Things that—if my parents saw some of the things I wrote, I'd wanna die. I'm not joking."

Jesus! She may not be joking, but I certainly hope she's exaggerating.

"They may not want to know these things about their little girl," I begin, imagining how Mama must've felt when she bought me that box of condoms. "But it's just life. Things everybody has felt, including them. They might be upset for a little while, but they'll recover. It's normal," I finish.

Anne just stares at the ground.

"Either way, the awkwardness you and your mama and daddy might feel won't last. It ain't worth lettin' some ogre knock you around," I add.

"It's normal," Anne repeats, and I can't tell if she's asking a question or making a statement.

"As normal as hoppin' John on New Year's Day," I say, giving her a warm smile.

"What if the person I wrote about is a girl?"

Oh. Wow. For all my two-headedness, I did not see that one coming. Shit. Oh shit. What do I say? What is she *talkin'* about?

"Really? Like? You like a girl the way you'd like a boy?" I ask. I just wanna make sure I understand.

"The way *you'd* like a boy, but yes," she replies.

I shrug. "I mean—I guess it's normal for you. Probably normal for a lotta people. Just cuz we don't know 'em don't mean it's not." I will admit: I can't quite picture two girls makin' out. It just sounds silly to me, but I am in no position to judge anybody. There's a good chance that Anne Marie likin' girls is still more normal than me jubin' all over the place.

She looks up at me, and I can see the beginnings of a little, teeny smile.

"You're a good friend, Evvie," she says, and I hear her voice cracking again. I don't know whether to leave her be or to embrace her again. Either could hasten the waterworks.

"That don't mean my parents would understand. And . . . it's against"—and she whispers—"God."

"Isn't everything?"

"Evvie, I'm serious. I've worked too hard to go to hell!"

"You're not goin' to hell! I'm sure they have a special room up in heaven all ready for ya when it's time."

"It's in the Bible. Leviticus 18:22. 'You shall not lie with a male as with a woman; it is an abomination,'" she recites mournfully. "They don't say a woman shall not lie with another woman, but it's implied."

"So? Bible's fulla ridiculous shit," I say.

"Wow. Right outside the church. You'll just say anything, woncha?"

I don't know if that's true, but I'm unnerved by how much I just sounded like my grandmother.

"I feel like Leviticus is one a those books of the Bible that was written by crazy people. You can't take it literally."

"I appreciate your willingness to blaspheme in order to make me feel better, but—"

"I'm not just tryna make you feel better. I honestly remember readin' stuff in that book that is positively crazy."

"Evvie . . ."

"Hold that thought!" I run inside through the back door

of the church, up into the hallway, and Reverend Henry's office door is open. I race in before I realize he's in there.

"Evalene! Surprised to see you here! What can I do for ya?" he asks, startled by my abrupt appearance.

"Um, can I borrow a Bible real quick? I'll bring it back, I promise."

He breaks into a huge smile. "Of course." He goes to his bookshelf and pulls down a small one. "This is a King James, but it's especially suited for young people who—"

I snatch it from his hands. "Thank you!" I run back out the way I came. Anne Marie's sittin' on the bench lookin' irritated, which is a healthy step up from despondent.

I quickly flip to Leviticus and start running my finger down each page.

"Is this really necessary?" she asks me.

"Yes," I answer.

She fidgets while I speed-read. Outta the corner of my eye, I see her check her watch.

"I should be gettin' home soon," she says. The despair's sneakin' back into her voice, and I won't have it.

"This," I exclaim. "I found it! Listen up. 'The Lord said to Moses, "Say to Aaron: 'For the generations to come none of your descendants who has a defect may come near to offer the food of his God. No man who has any defect may come near: no man who is blind or lame, disfigured or deformed; no man with a crippled foot or hand, or who is a hunchback or a dwarf, or who has any eye defect, or who has festering or running sores or damaged testicles.'"' This is sayin' that God wants nothin' to do with the crippled! That's insane! There. I have discredited the book of Leviticus for you. Your room is safe in heaven." I wink at her, disproportionately proud of what I've accomplished here.

And she smiles! A real smile, a joyful smile. Hallelujah!

"You always make me feel better," she says.

"Same here."

Despite her arguments, I walk her home before it gets dark. We get inside, and her mother's in the kitchen cookin'. She pops her head in from the doorway.

"Oh hi, Evalene. Nice to see you! Should I set another place?" she asks. I glance at Anne Marie, who's sittin' in the corner of the couch with her hair in her face, covering her eye injury.

"No thank you, ma'am, but d'ya mind if I use your phone?"

I call Clay, and he agrees to come pick me up and take me home. Before I hang up, Roland enters the room. Anne Marie stiffens. Her mother fries fish in the kitchen, unaware anything's amiss. I watch this man closely and take a deep breath.

"Anne?" I begin. "Remember that red checkered top you borrowed from me?"

She frowns in confusion.

"Yeah. Didn't I give it back to you?"

"Maybe. I just haven't been able to find it. Can you check your closet? Just in case?" I ask.

"I'll look, but I'm sure I gave it back to you," she says as she heads to her room.

Now it's just me and Roland.

He holds up a newspaper to block me from his view.

It's practically effortless. I look at him—as if flimsy news-print could protect him from me—and his stomach makes a terrible sound. He drops the paper and inhales sharply. He leaps off the chair and tries to run, but he can't. His stomach rumbles again, and again he tries to move, but he cannot. He chokes back a moan.

"You have to use the bathroom, doncha?" I ask softly. I don't want to disturb Miss Alice in the kitchen.

He nods. Helpless.

"It's real bad, ain't it?"

His eyes grow wide with fear.

"If you touch her again, I will make you suffer. If you violate her privacy again, I will ruin you. Do you understand what I'm sayin' to you?"

"What are you?" he whispers.

This time his insides roar like thunder, and tears stream down his face.

"I'm just playin' with you right now. Don't make me get serious with you. Do you understand?" I try to ignore it, but I feel just a taste of it again. A taste of the happy-happy.

He nods. I hear Anne Marie coming down the hall, so I release him. He races past her as she reenters. She glances at him and then just rolls her eyes.

"Evvie, I'm sorry, but I don't have your shirt. Did you lend it out to anybody else?"

"Oh, you know what? I think I might have. Sorry for wastin' your time," I tell her.

"That's all right," she says, starin' in the direction her uncle went.

"I wish he would just . . . leave," she says. She wanted to say worse, but she's too good for that.

"If he bothers you in any way again, you call me. I mean it."

"What are *you* gonna do?" she whispers.

I take her hand and give it a strong squeeze. I need to get through to her, and I want the jube to help me.

I look deep into her dark eyes, and she gasps. Something got through.

"You don't need to worry about him, Anne Marie. Ever again."

20

Destiny

SHE TOLD ME TO COME AT NIGHT. ON
top of that, she told me to come alone and to not
use any magic to help me. Not that I would've, but
I don't appreciate being told not to.

I have to use my flashlight. It's too wild back here. I
shine the light on the house, and it's dark as a crypt. Lord.
She better not be leadin' me into a trap.

I get to the door and walk in.

"Grammie Atti?" I call. No response. It's so quiet and
dark in here it feels like the place was abandoned long ago.

"Where you at?" Guided by my light, I creep through
the kitchen, into the sittin' room, and peer through the window that looks out onto her porch. She is *not* here, and her

home is scary enough as it is. I don't need to be wanderin' around here in the pitch blackness by myself.

That daggone cuckoo clock goes off, announcing that it is ten, and I scream my fool head off.

Stop that.

I do.

Calm down and turn off that goddamn flashlight.

I sigh and do what she says. I concentrate. If this is how we're gonna communicate this evening, I have to give it my full attention.

Where are you? I ask.

You tell me, she taunts.

I don't bother responding to that. I clearly don't know, and if I start guessin', she's just gonna holler at me.

What are you doin' right now? she asks me.

I shrug. *I'm just standin' here.*

How are you standin'? Describe and don't move.

Describe how I'm standin'? On my damn legs.

I clear my throat.

Quiet, she orders.

I'm not standin' up straight. I'm slouchin'.

Where is most of your weight? Do NOT move, Evalene.

On my right.

She stops speaking. The quiet gets loud.

Look inside, she says. *What is your heart doing?*

I take a second. I had a feelin' this was what she was gonna ask me next. I start to feel like I understand what she wants me to see, but I don't know why yet.

It's pumpin' blood through my veins.

Describe the blood.

Rusty red, viscous. Oxygen rich and warm, I say. Wow. I didn't know I had all those words just waitin' to come out.

Look outside. In which direction are you facin' right now?

North . . . east.

Keep lookin' outside. What's goin' on next door?

Next door? Now I'm stumped. I wasn't prepared for that. I think I'm doin' pretty well, but I don't wanna be a Peepin' Tom.

I don't know.

Unacceptable. Don't try to eavesdrop. Give the house one look and not with your eyes. Don't imagine what's in there. SEE it.

See it. How was I able to see inside my heart so easily? I can feel myself dropping down, down, down once again. But I'm in a brand-new space. I think this is a new band. I swallow and feel each individual molecule of saliva migrate down my esophagus to my stomach. This is a new feeling. It's not about focusing my anger or my giggles. It's about goin' quiet and gettin' clear. Finding perfect awareness. It's like all my senses are under a microscope. Time slows. Details expand. It's coming together for me. It's purple and silver, this band. It's powerful, but unlike the others, this one makes me anxious.

Answer, Evvie. Firm but not impatient. I answer her.

The Ellisons live next door. Mr. Ellison is worried they won't make the rent this month, because he lost his job at the paper mill. Mrs. Ellison is afraid to tell him she's pregnant again. Millie, the youngest, is asleep right now and dreaming about a car crashin' into a truck fulla chickens. Jake and Ritchie are sposeta be asleep, but Jake's the oldest and can sense his parents' stress. Ritchie's tellin' his big brother a story about the kid in his class that peed himself during assembly, but Jake's not payin' attention.

I stop. That's all I can see, and it feels like far too much. As soon as I see it all, it starts to fade away. My hands are jittery. The second the new band formed down in my special space, I could see everything as clearly as seeing my own likeness in a mirror. For some reason, it makes me almost feel like cryin'. Their lives are none a my business.

Do you understand how you did that? she asks me.

Not really.

Liar.

I take a deep breath and listen to the quiet. *All my distractions fell away, so suddenly things inside me and outside me were noticeable. And clear. I think.*

Break it.

What the hell does that mean?

Don't get smart!

Whoops. I only meant for me to hear that thought.

Break off a piece and toss it outside, she says.

This is so strange. I don't understand what she means, but I fiddle with my new band until it feels like a shard has come loose. A wobbly feeling. I try to throw it.

Like that? I ask her.

And I'm jolted with new knowledge that comes spewing out.

The ground out there. Full of death and pain. Old blood, bones, flesh, hair, teeth, decomposition deep underground. We walk on their graves.

I jolt back into myself and shake my head violently. Intentionally separating myself from what I've just seen. This house. This land. Horrors have taken place here.

Who died here? I ask.

If you hadn't stopped yourself, you'd know.

I don't wanna see. Tell me, I say.

Before she can respond, I hear a sound outside the back door. With the silence and my heightened senses, the sound has the impact of a rifle shot.

"Grammie Atti? Is that you out there?" I ask with my regular voice.

She says nothing, vocally or otherwise. Forget it. She can yell if she wants to, but I flip my flashlight back on and tiptoe toward the door and look out. I don't see anyone.

"Grammie Atti, if you're close, will you please come out now?" I beg. I hear a rustling out in the dark and throw open the screen door just in time to see a figure disappear behind the bushes. My heart drops. I don't believe this. That scumbag has followed me here.

I steady myself. I'm terrified, but I'm also angry. No more. It's time to end this.

I shout with all my strength, "Come out now!" I see movement, and, tryin' not to shake, I shine my flashlight behind the bushes.

"*Clay?*"

He shrugs, embarrassed. "Uh, hey, Evvie. What's goin' on?"

I'm just starin' at him, not knowing what to say. The kitchen light comes on inside the house.

"What you doin' out there?" Grammie Atti calls from inside.

"Nothin'. Just a second," I say to her.

"Clay," I whisper. "What're you doing here?"

"D'ya mind . . ." He points to the flashlight, which I now see is blinding him. I shut it off.

"I was just—checkin' up on ya."

"Since when?"

Grammie Atti comes through the door. She looks at us and then at me and smirks.

"Who are you?"

"Oh, I'm Clay. Clayton Alexander. Junior, ma'am."

"I ain't impressed by good manners, so don't waste your time."

"Grammie? Clay's my—"

"Yeah, I get it. Either leave or come in," she says, and turns back into the kitchen.

"Sorry, Evvie," he whispers. I gesture for him to follow me, and we join Grammie Atti in the house.

"I don't care for uninvited visitors, so—"

"Grammie Atti, please be nice."

She gives me a look but doesn't say anything else. She pulls her pipe out and lights it.

"I didn't mean to interrupt y'all. It's just—it's late. And I noticed you leavin' your house, and I didn't want anything to happen to you, so I followed."

"What you think's gonna happen to her?" Grammie Atti asks, and Clay glances at me like he's afraid to say any more.

"How'd you know I left?" I ask.

Clay lightly taps the table, guilty.

"Sounds like somebody's been spyin' on somebody else," Grammie Atti says. Then she laughs.

"I wasn't spyin'. I happened to be in your neighborhood, and I saw you. That's all. I mean it," he says. "And I'm sorry. I should leave."

"Why you afraid to admit you was spyin'? You know you were, and you know it wasn't the first time," Grammie Atti tells him. Clay gazes at the floor. He won't meet her eyes or mine. She's right.

"What is it you wanna know? Just ask," she says.

"Nothin'. I told you what I was—"

"He only wants to protect me. There are worse things," I say in his defense, but I have to say, I'm kinda siding with my grandmother on this one. Somethin' doesn't feel right. He's not telling the whole truth.

"So you her protector, huh?"

"Uh—I mean—yes," he stammers.

Grammie Atti howls with laughter, and my cheeks get hot. Clay will not be able to charm her, and right now he's not even trying. I can't recall ever seein' him so tongue-tied.

"You thirsty?" she asks him.

He takes a small breath before answering. "Yes, ma'am. A little."

"I know. Thirsty for knowledge. We ain't talkin' 'bout

soda pop. What do you wanna know? This is the last time I'm gonna ask you nicely," she warns.

Clay looks up at her with fear in his eyes, like he's terrified Grammie Atti's finna go outside, tear off a switch, and use it on his behind.

"I just . . ." He swallows. "I just wanted to know what it's like," he says.

"What *what* is like?" I ask.

Grammie Atti holds up her hand to shut me up. She's focused on Clay. "Does it scare you?"

He's still for several seconds, and I think he's ignorin' her. But after a while, he finally nods his head.

"Good. That means you're smart. You should be scared. It's not a bag a parlor tricks," she explains. I think I know why Clay's here now.

"You could sit and watch while I help Evvie figure out how to use her many gifts, but you wouldn't understand half of what we'd be doin'. It's not for spectators." Abruptly she turns to me.

"Why'd you tell him?"

I feel put on the spot. Was I not supposed to?

"He noticed somethin'. Didn't feel right to lie," I reply.

She inhales some more pipe smoke, turning back to Clay.

"You better be worth it, young man. The more folks that know about us, the less safe we are. The less safe *she* is."

"Is there anything I can do to—like—help her?" he asks. I smile a little to myself. He doesn't understand jubin' at all—how could he? But it doesn't matter. If he thinks I might be facing any kinda dilemma, he wants to fix it.

"It's not an illness. She was born with somethin' extra, and now she's figurin' it out. She doesn't need your help, and you wouldn't know how to give it if she did."

I glance at Clay, and he looks like a deflated balloon. I wanna comfort him, but I'm still irritated by the spyin'.

"You know what you *can* do, though?" Grammie Atti offers.

"What?"

"Trust her and stay out of her way," she says.

Clay sighs and nods.

"It's a vulnerable process. Imagine you tryna learn to play a new instrument. It's gonna sound like nothin' but noise for a while. What if she was hidin' in a closet, secretly watchin' you fumble around? That's an invasion of privacy."

"I think he understands, Grammie," I say. Does she know Clay's a musician? Does she know *every*thing?

"Are we sure he understands?" she asks, her eyes on Clay.

"Yes," he responds.

"Good. Anything else you wanna know?"

"Does it—does it hurt her?"

"Well that depends—"

"I can answer myself," I say. "It depends on what I'm doing, what I'm going through, and what the triggers are. Some things hurt and others don't. Like anything else," I tell him. I take ahold of his hand and speak to him without words.

Try not to worry.

I don't know if he heard me or not, but his face brightens a little.

"I'll walk you out," I say.

Clay rises, and I head for the door.

"Again, I'm sorry for causing any trouble, Miss Athena."

"I can't stand apologies, but I suppose I can accept yours. Come back on a Saturday. I'll give ya a special reading. Family friend discount," she says with a wink.

"Good night, ma'am," he says. I grab my flashlight, hold the door open for him and walk him down the steps.

"You mad?" he asks.

I shake my head. "No. But I don't like bein' spied on."

"I won't do it again."

We walk in silence for a moment. When we get to the gate, he stops and turns to me.

"Can you honestly blame me, though? Some maniac chases you all over town, and then you go out at night alone? That's insane!"

"No, it's not," I say, but he does have a point, and truth be told, I *didn't* want to go out by myself; that was Grammie Atti's idea.

"Promise me you won't do that again," he says.

"I don't know if I can promise that."

"Evvie, come on! Don't be stupid."

"Don't call me stupid!"

"I'm not calling you stupid! I'm just—I'm sayin' don't make a stupid choice."

We stare at each other. Neither of us willing to concede.

"I'm always careful, Clay. And you should know by now that I can take care of myself," I explain.

"You know? It doesn't make you weak to lean on somebody every now and then," he informs me.

I look out at the dark street. I flick the flashlight on and off. I turn around to look at Grammie Atti's. Her kitchen light's still on. Wasn't sure if she woulda just gone on to bed—she does that sometimes. But it looks like she's waitin' for me.

"I know that."

"I thought—I don't know. You said your grandmother's like your teacher. I was worried. I just wanted to make sure you were . . . safe."

So Clay still thinks Grammie Atti is a fruitcake. Great.

"There is nothing wrong with my grandmother," I tell him. "She has no intention of hurting me. I don't wanna discuss this again."

"What about—" He stops himself.

"What?"

"Your grandfather. Didn't she hurt him?"

I freeze. I have no idea what he's talking about.

"Clay, are you an old church lady now? This is nothin' but gossip! She never hurt nobody. She loved my grandfather, and he was taken too soon." That is literally *all* I know about my grandfather. The exact same thing I know about my great-grandmother. Nobody in my family talks to me about our history. Once someone's dead, they disappear.

He lets out a big bear of a sigh.

"All right. If you are sure that she ain't touched in the head and you feel safe with her . . . then I'll have to trust you."

"Didn't you tell me once that in every rumor there's a ounce of truth? Not a pound?"

He stares at me, eyes full of worry and maybe some anger, but the longer we look at each other, the calmer he seems.

"Yeah. I did," he finally says.

"Go home, Clay. I'll talk to you tomorrow."

I turn and head back up Grammie Atti's walk. When I get to the door, he stops me again.

"I'll wait. I'll take you home."

Somehow accepting this offer feels like I'm losing something (what it is, I don't know), but I'd rather not walk home in the dark.

I nod, and he goes back to his car, parked across the street.

"He's somethin' else, ain't he?" Grammie Atti appears again at the open door, makin' me jump.

"He's a good one. I can tell. Not like the drunks and troublemakers your mother used to mess around with," she says. I say nothing and make no movement to agree or disagree. One of those "troublemakers" she's referring to is my father, and I don't appreciate her insulting him.

"Sexy, too. That never hurts. He reminds me a little bit of . . ." She waves her hand away, as if what she has to say isn't worth it.

"Who?" I push. Now I'm curious.

"Your grandfather. Roy. I was pretty smitten with him when I was your age. He was smart and handsome, and he could make me laugh like nobody else." She laughs for a second, but then her smile fades.

"How did he die?"

She raises both eyebrows at me, taken aback by the question; then she sucks her teeth.

"Ah hell. Is that rumor goin' around again? People are so damn stupid. He got hit by a train. It was a tragedy. And I had nothin' to do with it. End of story."

So Clay didn't hear a rumor that she "hurt" him. He heard she *killed* him.

"Why am I just now hearin' all this? Why didn't I know what happened to your mama or my grandfather before this summer? Why do we keep so many goddamn secrets? Is he the one buried out here?" I blurt. I think I went too far. I didn't mean to be disrespectful. I just feel so frustrated. I hate that if I don't come out and ask about a thing, I may never have the whole story or any part of the story at all.

Her mouth tightens, and I think she's about to read me the riot act. Or worse. She side-eyes me, but that's it. Her scowl relaxes, and now she seems more sad than mad.

"Death ain't somethin' we like to talk about, Evalene. We've seen a lot of it. A lotta horrors. We do what our foremothers did: we keep goin' forward, and we only look back when push comes to shove."

"But why do we keep all these secrets?"

"We don't. We have our own ways of sharin'. You're just startin' to learn. It's not so mysterious."

"Who . . . who is buried out here?"

"Lotsa folks. Some by choice, some not. Ain't nothin' to cry about. We will all be feedin' worms at some point," she chuckles. "Once somebody's dead, there ain't nothin' to fear no more."

That's a helluva way to think about death, but I guess it's true.

"I'm sorry for gettin' snippy. Just tired, I guess."

"You look after that boy as best you can," she says. "We can't prevent destiny once it's been writ, but we can do our damndest to influence it. A little goes a long way."

That statement is too complex for my mind to unravel right now.

"Time for you to get home," she says, and then she goes inside and closes the door. Done for the night.

As I walk down the path, I think about the word "destiny." I've never cared for it. I hate the idea that our lives have been etched in stone someplace we can't touch or see, and we're all just players in a drama that already has an ending unbeknownst to us.

When I open the gate, Clay turns on his engine. I will look after him—even when he annoys me like tonight. I will look after Anne Marie, Mama, and the twins. And me. Though my malcreant has been absent lately, until I get rid of him myself, I won't feel safe.

I believe I have the strength to take care of myself and the people I love. I will keep my eyes and my heart directed at them, so that if destiny tries to harm any of 'em, it will have to go through me.

21

Acquainted

"EVALENE! TELL HER WHAT I DID AFTER lunch! Tell her about my art!" Abigail demands. It's the end of the day, and all I want to do is go, but Miss Ethel won't stop talkin'. Sometimes she gets chatty with me when she gets home just before I leave. Whenever this happens, it's cuz she feels the need to remind me that she's the boss.

"Wait a minute, sugar," Miss Ethel tells Abigail, sweet as honey cake. She turns back to me with considerably less sweetness. It's already five minutes past six, but she enjoys wasting my time. "Now, Evalene, you didn't let her eat any Mary Janes, did you?"

"No, ma'am."

"Because I told you, she cannot have any more candy before her dentist appointment on Monday, and I mean that."

"I understand, ma'am. She had no Mary Janes."

She looks at me doubtfully. Maybe she hopes she can catch me lyin'. Maybe she gets her jollies that way.

"Evalene! Evalene! Evalene! Show her my art! Show it to her!"

I indicate the paper stuck to the fridge with an old "Peace and Prosperity" vote-for-Ike magnet. It is the most pitiful rendering of a baby and her dog I have ever seen, but Abigail is proud of her "art," so I dutifully point it out.

"My, how pretty," Miss Ethel lies. She then pays me with a tight smile and advises me to get enough sleep so I won't be late in the morning. Bitch.

I pedal home quickly. Keeping an eye out in case somebody's followin' me. Again.

When I get home, I'm granted the honor of bathing the twins, cuz I'm doomed to take care of little girls endlessly, it seems. I can't figure out how they get so dirty. Tonight they looked like they'd been workin' all day on a damn farm.

I get in bed later, and I'm antsy. I wonder what Clay's doing right at the very same moment. What he's thinking. I check the clock. Ten till eleven ain't so late.

I tiptoe down to the kitchen and quietly dial the phone. I decide if he doesn't pick up by the third ring, I'll hang up.

It rings once. Twice.

"Hello?" It's his mother, and she does not sound happy.

I panic and hang up. I go back up to my room and look

for something to read. I pull out my old standby, *The Golden Book of Astronomy*, and leaf through the worn pages.

I feel more relaxed and sleepy as I read. I don't know if anything is as calming for me as the stars and the night sky. What would it be like to travel out into space? If it ever becomes possible for regular people, I wanna go.

Something jolts me awake. I don't know what time it is, but it feels late, and my book has fallen to the floor. I fluff my pillow, and I am about to lie back down when I see Coralene standing stone still in my doorway.

"What are you doin'? You scared me," I whisper.

She just stands there, staring.

"What's wrong? It's late."

"I can't sleep," she says.

I sigh and beckon her over to me. "Bad dreams?" She shakes her head no, but something has frightened her. I check to see if she's wet herself, but she doesn't smell or feel damp. I try to blink myself more awake when Doralene's little face appears in the doorway.

"What is going on?" I whisper-shout.

"Evvie? Can you make that man go away?"

I am wide awake now. "What man? Are you dreaming?"

"The man in our room," they both say in unison.

Before I can think, I'm up and runnin' down the hall, and there he is, illuminated by their strawberry night-light, without a drop of shame. The blood drains from my face to see him here. In my home. This close to me and my sisters.

He has a thick bandage on the side of his head, and his face is bruised. The accident. I did that to him. Too bad he wasn't hurt worse.

"Hello, Evalene," he says to me as if I invited him.

I can't speak.

He smiles. Then he picks up a doll and, for no reason I can imagine, pops its head off and pockets it.

His dirty white fingers around the doll's neck. Somethin' familiar about that. I'm seeing red. And black. That coal-black hair. Those ocean-blue eyes.

I'm remembering now. I'm remembering fragments of Virgil Hampton. Oh god, I remember him, the smell of him, the feel of him, the pain of him. I want to disappear, to go unconscious, but none of that can happen. I can't let him see the terror I feel, and I have to protect my sisters.

"You get the hell outta here now." I try to make my voice steady. Cold and steady.

"You caused serious damage to my truck with that little game of yours." I'm noticing now that his voice has an odd dulcet quality. Like a Svengali. Everything about him is vulgar.

"If youda left me alone, none of it woulda happened," I say through my dry throat. I know I'm angry. The very thought of this fucker fills me with fury. But I cannot activate my anger band. I try to remember what Grammie Atti said. Take back what he took from me. It's inconceivable.

"A spiteful man would make you pay dearly for what you've done, but I'm not a spiteful man. I didn't come here to fight. I came for a truce."

I almost wish one a the bad headaches would come to me now and I could at least make myself puke on him. But I think I mighta grew out of 'em. Lucky me.

"I'm going to give you one more chance. Let me escort you home from your job. That's all. During that time, we can get reacquainted and put an end to this frivolous power struggle before somebody gets killed."

"You do realize if you stopped bothering me, it would be over, don't you?" I'm starting to feel stronger.

"Why do you need to make this so hard?"

"Why do you want what you can't have?" It slipped out before I could think about it. If I had, I probably wouldn't have said it.

He doesn't seem angry, though. He leans against the pink-and-green mini dresser. It's not meant to support the weight of a grown man. He better not break it.

"If you got to know me, you wouldn't be so defensive all the time," he says.

The twins have crept down the hallway in total silence. I didn't know they could be that quiet. I glance at them and, with a gesture, warn them to freeze where they are. I wanna pick 'em both up and run to Mama's room, but I remember how she crumbled just upon hearing Virgil Hampton's name. I remember feeling like I had to take care of *her* in that moment.

Then a more ominous thought crosses my mind: she couldn't protect me back then. Why would she be able to now?

"I'm really not that hard to get along with, you know?

I have no intention of disruptin' your life," he continues. "That said, you are *going* to drop your Negro auto mechanic. It has to happen. It's non-negotiable."

The little dresser creaks, and Virgil springs away from it. I think this is the first time I've seen him genuinely startled by somethin', and it was nothin' at all.

"Seems like he has a high opinion of himself," he says. "Good for him, I guess. He'll get over the hurt. But you gotta do it, Evvie."

I'm seething. He has the gall to call me Evvie? Like we're friends? *Who the fuck does he think he is?*

"I get that it's hard, but I want him outta the picture. It'll happen one way or another."

I cannot have him threatenin' Clay. No, ma'am! He scares me, but I don't care. I stretch myself up to my full height, spreadin' out like a cobra. Time for him to see that he is not the only predator in this room.

"Virgil Hampton. I will be blunt so there is no confusion. I do not like you. I have no interest in getting acquainted with you. Leave my house and do not come back."

His eyes sparkle. I hate him, and he *likes* it.

"I'm not asking for much," he says, "and I'm tryin' to make it a fair arrangement. Course you can make it hard if you want to. Hard can be fun. In the meantime . . . Coralene and Doralene, right? That's cute. They sure are pretty, aren't they? Just like big sister. They can call me Uncle Virggie. I can teach 'em some games."

My heart throbs in my throat, in my head, my guts. And

I still can't make the power I been relyin' on work. He's too strong, and he knows where I'm weak. I gotta do somethin' now. So I just use my brain.

"Non-negotiable you say? This is not how a negotiation works. What do *I* get?"

He looks surprised; then he laughs. "You're right. What do you want?"

Shit. I want him to shrivel up and die, but I don't think that applies in this situation.

"I want you to stop following me. I want you to stay out of my home—"

"That's two things."

"Quiet," I say. He listens.

"I want you to keep my sisters' names out of your mouth and out of your mind. *That* is non-negotiable. Do you understand me?"

"I do. Funny. I thought you were gonna ask for money," he quips.

I take the deepest of deep breaths. He's complying. I am making a risky decision, and I can only pray it's the right one. The time has come for an everyday hex.

"Fine," I say.

"Fine?"

I try to sound as civil as I possibly can. "What you are asking for is fine. As long as you bring me straight home."

He perks up. "At first. That'll give you time to get used to me. Yeah. I can agree to that."

I swallow bile and nod. "Good." I know it's now or never.

I have to sell the lie. I move toward him. I don't take in his nauseating scent. I close my eyes and tilt my head up to him. His face collides into mine, violent and clumsy and wet. I hold back the vomit in my stomach with all my strength, and then I reach up to that coal-black hair of his and caress the oily tresses before ripping out a fistful.

"Jesus!" he cries, stumbling backward. The twins run in the room, and I think I can hear Mama stirring now.

"I'm sorry," I say quietly. "Got carried away."

Though he rubs his head in pain, he grins, proud of himself. "I'll see you tomorrow." He reaches for the doorknob, but I stop him.

"Virgil?"

He turns to me, and his eyes actually seem to have life in them tonight. "I like hearing you say my name."

I cringe, my insides shudder, but I continue. "The other night at the lookout, you said you came back to this town cuz a me. Why now?" I ask.

He leans in the door frame. Looks like he's really thinkin'.

"My aunt keeps up with everything in this shit town. She remembered you and I used to be playmates not so long ago. So she thought I'd get a kick outta that story in the paper. You savin' that family from the fallin' tree."

God. Dammit.

"And she was right. I did. Made me realize how precious life is. One minute you're here; the next . . . We don't have that much time on this planet. You find what makes you happy? You gotta take it."

He regards me for a long second, waitin' for me to say somethin' maybe, but I got nothin' else to say. Abruptly he vanishes down the hall. I strain my ears, but I don't hear another peep from him. I have no idea how he got in or out of my house. Gone like a ghost.

"Get into bed," I whisper to the twins. "Everything's okay now."

"You gonna see that man tomorrow?" one of 'em asks.

"No. And don't tell Mama about any of this. It'll just worry her."

"What if she finds out by accident?"

"I mean it! Do not tell her, or you will be in real trouble. Trouble you don't even know about yet," I threaten. Then I kiss them both on the cheek and turn out the light.

In my room I look around for a suitable place to store the clump of hair in my fist. I grab the bag with the condoms from Mama, and I'm caught off guard by its weight. I look inside, and the condoms are gone. Replaced with a black-varnished wooden box.

I take it out. The top and sides are decorated with colorful Chinese-looking houses and trees and fireworks. It's a jewelry box. The lid is fastened to the body of the box with a golden latch. I flip it open, and a lullaby starts to play. The interior is lined with bright red velvet except for the inside of the lid, which displays several rectangular mirrors of diminishing sizes. At the back, just in front of the mirrors and atop what must be the music box, a ballerina spins to the music. The mirrors make it look like a whole line of ballerinas getting smaller and smaller. And this ballerina. She wears all white, including her fluffy tutu. And her skin. Looks like mine. She's my shade of brown. She could be a miniature version of me.

I feel a lump in my throat. I've never seen anything like this. I never thought anybody would make something like this. When you see a reflection of yourself from out in the world and it's not meant to hurt or shame you? When it's there to show you that you're beautiful and loved? It just fills you up with warmth and something like grace.

There's a tiny red envelope in the bottom that I almost didn't see because it matches the lining. I open it and remove a thin sheet of paper that's been folded many times.

**I know you don't remember me, but you will
in time.
You always remember your first.
~V.H.**

I slide down to the floor. Still clutching his hair, the lullaby playing over and over. How could this exquisite jewelry box have come from him?

I'm cold. I'm hollow. I mourn what Virgil took from me all those years ago. I'm too shaken to cry. To breathe. To anything.

I'm haunted by the living.

22

Brave

I T'S EARLY. I'M NOT DUE AT WORK FOR AN
hour yet.

I go up the path, and when I get to the back porch,
I hear voices. She gets clients before a lotta folks wake
up. A bird lands in one of the shorter trees and takes up res-
idence behind an empty blue bottle. The glass magnifies
the bird's image to absurd dimensions. I can't make out the
bird's species from here. Blue feathers? Or is that the reflection of the bottle? Could it be a blue jay this late in the year?
Blue jays bring good luck. I think.

The bird flies over to another tree on my left, and I
get a better look at it. I don't think it's a blue jay. Too big.
A blue falcon, maybe? I don't know if they're good luck or

not. If there's any point in believin' in luck at all.

I'm about to knock when the door swings open and R. J. nearly knocks me over.

"Oh shit! You all right?" he asks.

"Yeah, I'm fine. R. J. Why are you here?"

He shrugs, embarrassed. "Miss Athena done a favor for my aunt Mabel, so Aunt Mabel made a peach cobbler to thank her. I was just the deliveryman."

I nod, looking past him to see if any other visitors are inside.

"Well, I gotta go, so . . ." I go through the screen door into the dim kitchen, leaving him behind me.

She's sittin' at the table with a cup of tea and barely looks up when I enter. "What you doin' here so damn early?"

"Hi, Grammie Atti."

"Whatcha mean 'hi'? What's wrong with you today?"

"He's botherin' me. My—what did you say it's called?"

"Malcreant."

"Yeah. Him. Last night he got into the house. He threatened to hurt the twins and Clay. Mama doesn't know about this, and I need it to stop and I can't do it myself. Whenever he's around, I'm powerless."

She leans back, thinking. "What did I tell you to do?"

I plop down in the chair opposite her.

"I know he took somethin' from me, and I know what it was, but I have no earthly idea of how to take it back, and this is an emergency. I need *practical* magic now. Please! Pretend I'm just a client. What would tell me to do?"

Grammie adds some tobacco to her pipe and lights it. She studies me.

"You want him to stop botherin' you? Or you want him stopped?"

I pick at my fingernails, and I really think about it. I know what she's asking. Honestly, I'd be happy if he just left us alone, but would that mean he'd go after somebody else? I'm not sure. Still, I'm not ready to sign off on what she's implying.

"I want the pain he's been causing me to boomerang back to him."

"Good. That was a test. No way in hell you ready for a death hex," she says. She goes into the other room. I look around at her spirit cards, voodoo dolls, statues, poppets, bottles, and a mess a novelty salt and pepper shakers. She never talks to me about her trinkets. Her "tools." I ponder all the thousands of stories Grammie Atti must've collected over the years and the hand she's played in the destinies of others.

When she returns, she has two prayer candles: one white and one black.

"You have something personal a his?"

"I got some of his hair."

"Which hair?"

"Which . . . ? From his *head*!" I don't wanna think about how I'd get any of his other hair.

She wrinkles her nose, unimpressed. "Nothin' else?"

Dammit! I thought that'd be enough. Then I remember that I do have more.

"I have a note written in his hand," I say. She smiles and nods when she hears this.

"Use the note with the hair. On the right day, just before twilight, light the candles. Speak what you want done, and in your mind, *see* it done. You know how to see now. Speak it and see it until you've done it enough." She cracks her back in a way that gives me the shivers.

"How do I know when it's enough?"

"You'll know. Now if you don't mind, I have some real clients comin'. The *payin'* kind."

"But wait a minute. The right day? How will I know it's the right day?"

She sighs like I'm her idiot child she hides in the basement when company comes over.

"It's the day when you can't blow the flames out. That's instinctual. You should know that."

"Sorry, Grammie Atti."

She pounds the table with her fist. "Quit it with the sorries! It's weak. Don't be sorry. Do better," she lectures.

She hands me the candles, and I inspect them. They're dusty and cracked, even though the wicks look like they ain't been lit yet. These candles are old. So old, I'm worried they might not work.

"That's all. I will see you later," she says, pointing at that ugly cuckoo clock.

I mumble a thank-you and leave the way I came in. I'm walking back down the path to the street, and I see R. J. again.

"You still out here?" I ask him.

"Um." He quickly stamps out his cigarette. "Yeah. Thought I could walk you to work."

I sigh. "That's okay. I can get there by myself."

"Haven't seen you hardly at all in weeks. Feels like months."

"Just been busy," I say, quickening my pace.

"Do you hate me?"

I stop. I really don't have time for R. J. and his feelings. Especially now.

"Of course I don't, R. J. I just have to get to work is all."

"I've only ever been nice to you, and you treat me . . ." He shakes his head and looks around, like he's searching for the right word. "Like I have no value," he finishes.

Oh man. I didn't know I made him feel so bad. I guess I didn't think about how he was feelin' at all, which is pretty unkind. "I don't mean to be like that," I say.

"Then why are you?"

I don't know what to say. He doesn't want to hear the truth. Nobody wants to hear it when it hurts.

"You can walk with me. If you want," I concede. He does, and we don't speak for several uncomfortable moments.

"So?"

"So, what?" I ask as if I have no idea what he's talking about.

"So why can't you be nice to me?"

"I guess—I was worried."

"About what?"

"I just . . . I didn't want to give you false hope." I wish I could've found a better way to put that.

His pace doesn't decrease, but his shoulders sink a bit.

This is why I didn't wanna talk about it. I don't always know how to say things right. I meant for that to be gentle, but it didn't come out that way.

"Those are my feelings. What you do or don't do isn't gonna change 'em," he replies.

"I'm sorry, R. J. That I haven't treated you so nicely," I say.

"Thanks for sayin' that."

I expect him to walk away after my apology, but he doesn't. I don't know what else to say, so I ask him about his folks. They're fine, he says, but he accuses them of bein' too overprotective. He wants to join the actions the Student Nonviolent Coordinating Committee has taken around the South, but he has to wait until he graduates, cuz his parents won't let him go now. He thinks they treat him like a child.

All this catches me off guard. I didn't know R. J. had it in him. Demonstrators get spit on, called nigger and every other name in the book, beaten, and thrown in jail. I hope not, but I wouldn't be surprised if some of 'em disappear. And if that happens, they won't be comin' back. I'd be terrified to join up—with or without the jube.

I never realized how brave he was. Where was *this* R. J. all the times he was gettin' on my last nerve? Then again, maybe I just wasn't payin' attention. By the time we get to the Heywoods', I'm glad we ran into each other.

"Don't be a stranger," he says to me as I open the gate.

"Same goes for you," I tell him.

We stand there for a second just kinda smilin' at each other.

"Well? Bye," I say.

"Hold on, Evvie."

"Yeah?"

He rubs the back of his head then looks up to the sky. "If there wasn't no Clayton Alexander Jr., would I have—uh— would I have had a chance? With you?"

Speaking of bravery, that's a damn brave question. If he'd asked me this a month ago, I might've run away screaming, but I feel differently now. With me off-limits, he was able to talk to me like I was a friend, and as a result I learned more about him in the last ten minutes than in all the years we've known each other.

I smile again and nod. For some reason, this seems to fill him with complete joy. He beams and practically skips away.

R. J.'s a good guy. I wouldn't mind spending more time with him. I wouldn't mind it at all. Sometime. Like when I'm all done hexin' my malcreant.

23

Safe

FOR THE FIRST TIME EVER, I LEGITIMATELY dread leaving work. My "escort" isn't here yet, so that's fortunate, but I can feel him closing in.

Miss Ethel and Abigail fuss in the kitchen, so they don't notice that I'm still here, hoverin' in the foyer. I'd really hoped that Grammie Atti would've given me somethin' more fast acting this morning. I was prepared to grin and bear his presence for one day, but with her vague instructions, who knows how many days it'll take to get rid of him? Just the thought of allowin' him to "escort" me home from work turns my stomach inside out.

I crouch below the front window and dive down, reachin' for my joy band. Quickly I think about the last time Clay had me laughin.' Oh lord! The other night he had me dyin'! He was doin' an impression of Marlon Brando in A *Streetcar Named Desire*, but instead of "Stella," he was hollerin' "Evvie" at the top of his lungs! I gather it all up and pull it down into my guts. I gotta save the laughin' I wanna let out so badly for the task at hand.

There it is. My pulsing, giggling, greenish-yellow joy band. I like this one. I hope this one will work.

I breathe deep and close my eyes and feel the short and sweet temporary setting I need right now. A whole new environment . . . just for a while.

"Jiminy Cricket," Miss Ethel suddenly cries out. "What is goin' on?"

I open my eyes with relief and a bit of pride. The sky is now black, even though it's only minutes past six. It worked.

I slip out the door into the night. Fog accumulates, makin' it hard to see anything farther than a foot ahead of me. Seeing is harder still, since the power in this neighborhood has just been knocked out. By me. No sun, no lights, just dark.

I worked it out in my head this afternoon. All I need is fifteen seconds at full sprint. Damn, I wish I had on my sneakers! I close my eyes and picture the route I'll take so I can make it. I mentally count fifteen Mississippis, and then I revert it all. The low sun is back, the fog gone, and electricity restored. Everything is restored.

I slow down right before gettin' home, smilin' to myself. As far as I know, the atmosphere change didn't affect my neighborhood at all. Grammie Atti's right: I'm gettin' good at this.

I come in the front, and I can hear Mama out on the back porch playin' with the girls. Good. They're all occupied. I go to my room and shut the door. I take out my candles, and I pull the cast-iron pan out from under my bed (this ain't my first attempt at a hex, but I sure hope this one works). I take it to the bathroom to run some cool water in it, and I bring it back to my room. I remove the candles from their glass holders, and using a hatpin, I carve the word "Virgil" into the side of the white one and "Hampton" into the black one. It's hard to do and takes longer than I expect. It's a sloppy job, and the loopy letters are a mess, but I imagine the spirits will know who I'm talking about. I put the candles back into their holders.

Now it's time to find out if today's the day. I need it to be today. This has to end. I light the candles, and when they've got a good, strong flame goin', I blow. Lightly, because she didn't say I had to blow *hard*.

I blow a couple more times, and they stay lit. They're still going strong after my fifth try, and I decide this is the day.

I take the music box with his note and his hair, and I grip them tightly while watching the small flames.

"All the evil you do
Can't touch my loved ones.
It bounces back to you.
All the evil you do
Can't touch my loved ones.
It bounces back to you."

I mumble-chant the words faster and faster until it all

starts to sound like one long word. My tongue and lips move with a speed beyond my own efforts. As though I'm possessed.

And then it's dark. And I see them. They're outside, huddled around a bonfire. Hummin'? I think they're hummin'. My haints. And that weird girl I met before that looks like me is there too. Still wearin' them sneakers, denims, and her purple poetry shirt.

Now I'm outside with 'em. The haints are all hunched over. Eatin'. Eatin' and hummin'. Makin' all kinda strange noises. This time they look like blurry shadows. Maybe they're always in a state of motion.

The weird girl turns and sees me. She steps away from the circle and joins me. I wait for her to say somethin', but she doesn't speak this time. Her eyes stay on mine as she opens my hands and places two small objects in my palms. I flinch at first because they're wet, and I wasn't expecting that. They kinda look like oblong rubber balls, slit down their middles.

Then the slits start to move. Coarse, tiny hairs sprout out along the slits' edges. They begin to open, and dirty water comes flowing out of them into my hands, spilling onto the ground. The slits peel back to reveal two familiar eyes. Ocean-blue eyes starin' up at me.

I stifle a scream. I sit straight up. Back in my room. The hummin' of the haints morphs into the eerie lullaby that my colored ballerina can't stop twirlin' to. I run into the bathroom and throw up in the commode. It's always awful to puke, no matter what, but at least this time it's quick, and I feel somewhat better once it's done.

I hear voices in the kitchen, so I know I have to wrap this up fast. I go back into my room and tear his handwritten note into strips. I torch several of his hairs along with some of the note strips. Once every letter I'm holding has been touched by flame, I drop what's left of the scorched debris into the pot, and it sizzles out. I want to burn it all right this minute, but what if I need to redo this later? I save what I have left and hide it back in the music box, closing the lid and silencing the lullaby.

I admire my restraint. Because I *badly* want to burn all of it.

Doralene barges into my room.

"What stinks in here?"

I douse the flames.

"Just some candles," I say to her.

"Why?"

"Cuz I felt like it." I wait for the barrage of *whys*, but her face changes.

"It's for that man, ain't it?" she asks.

"SHHH!"

She whispers, "I won't tell, Evvie. Will them candles keep him from comin' back?"

Wow. She's way more perceptive than I realized.

"I hope so."

"Me too," she says. "I heard him say he wants to play with me and Coralene, but I don't wanna play with him."

I'm sorry she heard that. I guess they both did.

"Don't worry. I won't let him," I assure her.

She sits down next to me on the floor.

"I dreamed that he came back and he took your smile away. Mama and Grammie Atti tried to get it back for you, but they couldn't."

I pull her onto my lap and try to stay coolheaded. I don't wanna scare her any more than she already is.

"Nobody can take my smile away. Yours either. We're gonna make sure a that right now. Open your hands."

She does. I smile like a demented clown and she starts laughin'. I pretend to peel my smile off, leaving my lips in a boring straight line. This makes her laugh harder.

"Here." I hand her my "smile." "You put it somewhere where nobody can ever take it, okay?"

"Okay. You take mine." Doralene imitates my actions to a T and hands me her "smile."

"Let's make a deal to always keep our smiles in a nice, safe place. Sound good?" I ask.

She nods and puts out her hand, and we shake on it.

Then Mama hollers at us to come down for supper. Doralene races outta the room, her worries forgotten. It's silly, but I take *The Golden Book of Astronomy* down from the shelf, open it up and place my sister's "smile" inside it.

Nobody's gonna take it.

24

Faith

IT'S THUNDERING AND RAINING OUTSIDE. We're on the floor in the old colored children's library. I could stay here all night and be completely happy. I think Clay's gettin' bored, though.

"Maybe we could find a broom. Clean up the cobwebs and mouse shit," he suggests, looking around.

I groan. "I don't wanna clean!"

"We could get this place lookin' nice again. Maybe the town would open it back up."

I stare at the cobwebs on the ceiling, not mindin' 'em so much. I know his heart's in the right place, but not only do I have no interest in cleaning—under any circumstances—at best, if we did make the place look presentable again, somebody would notice and take it over, and it wouldn't be our secret spot no more. At worst, our work would make someone realize all this space has been going to waste, and then they'd just tear it down to build somethin' else.

"I don't know, Clay. Might be best to leave things the way they are."

"I disagree," he says.

The door clatters and I gasp but quickly see that it was just the wind, and it's an old rickety door.

"Did that scare you?"

"Nah, I'm fine," I say, but the truth is the thought of Virgil out there somewhere keeps me on edge. I'm jittery these days, and I never used to be.

"Nasty," he says, running his finger along a table, makin' dust bunnies. Apparently my brief scare didn't make much of an impression.

"Okay. You can sweep if you want. While you do that, Imma take a nap," I inform him.

He glances at me.

"Could you—like—clean this place up with your mind?" he asks.

Before I answer, I check him to see if he's makin' fun. Doesn't look like he is.

"I don't know. Maybe. I don't want you to think I'm some freak of nature, Clay," I tell him.

"I don't, Evvie." He says the words, but he seems doubtful. "It makes sense that you'd have powers science can't explain," he reasons.

"Why do you say that?"

"Cuz you're special," he says. He doesn't stop talking long enough for me to swoon. "The only thing is . . . What if we got in a fight, or you just got real mad at me? You could hurt me. Badly." He doesn't meet my eyes.

He's afraid. Unfortunately, Grammie Atti's pep talk didn't put his fears to rest. It's like what Mama said about Jubilation bein' dangerous to the ones we love. But I know in my heart I am incapable of hurting him. How can I make him believe that?

"I'm not sure I can say much except that I'd never do anything to hurt you. The scary stuff? It's only for worst-case scenarios. When I'm in real danger. Or someone I love is. So, if you never attack me with your fists or any other weapons, you got nothin' to worry about." It's the best I can offer, and I hope it's enough. I don't think I could bear to lose Clay. I need him to trust me.

He gives me a crooked smile. "You are somethin' else, you know that?"

"Yes." I grin back, relieved. He seems to trust me for now. He goes back to judging the dirtiness of the library, and I think his fears have melted away.

"You sure you don't wanna whip this place into shape with your unique gifts?"

"Yeah, I'm sure," I laugh. "Why are you so obsessed with fixin' it up? It's fine as it is."

He shrugs. "I get restless. Always get like this when it rains real hard." Then his face lights up; he has an idea.

"Be right back," he says.

"You ain't goin' out in that mess," I tell him. As I say it, lightning illuminates the whole room for an instant.

And he just runs out in it like a looney tune! I shout after him, but my voice gets lost in the clatter of the downpour. I don't feel like usin' magic right now, but I don't want him to catch a cold, either. Cuz if he's gettin' a cold, *I'm* gettin' a cold! I sigh and try to focus, but before I can do anything, he bursts back in soaking wet.

"Look atcha! Why'd you do that?" I say to him.

"No big thing. Ain't made a sugar," he says.

"Clay!" He's taken his shirt off. Out in the pourin' rain in twilight hours with no shirt. "Have you lost your *mind*?"

He sets down the thing he's cradling in his arms. What he used his shirt to cover. His trumpet case. A bit damp, but mostly protected by his sopping-wet shirt.

"You could catch pneumonia," I tell him, wiping a few raindrops from his forehead.

"Not with you takin' care a me, m'lady."

I can't help but smile at that.

He opens the case and assembles his instrument. This is a rare occasion, cuz he's never played it around me before. Wait a minute. . . .

"Clay? How come you ain't never played for me before?"

"Haven't I?"

"No, you haven't."

He glances up at me, and now *he's* blushin'.

"Mighta been nervous."

"Cuz a *me*?"

"Yeah, cuz a you. I also was—well—I been workin' on somethin', and it's takin' me a while to get it right. I should probably keep on practicin' before givin' you a concert, but what the hell?" He clears his throat. "When I'm done, can you tell me what you think of it?"

"Uh-huh," I say. I must admit: it is not the easiest thing in the world to talk to Clay and listen to him when he's standing before me, naked down to his waist, skin glistening from the rain. I wanna grab him right now, but I know how important his music is to him. I do my best to focus.

He begins to play. A simple melody. A few simple notes in a minor key. And then it gets more complicated, surprising, but still gentle. This is a sad piece. Not quite funeral sad, but sad. The sad you feel when you get old and you look around yourself and realize you haven't lived the life you longed to live. How could I know what that's like? How could Clay? I can't say, but it's right here in his music.

A warm tear slips down my nose. I try to hide it. There's something I can't explain or avoid in this piece of music. A beauty that none of us can ever hold on to.

He finishes it and stares at me without saying anything. My tears keep coming. I give up tryna hide 'em.

"It's beautiful, Clay," I tell him. I don't know what else to say. I don't know how to tell him what this piece has made me feel.

"Didn't mean to make you cry," he says. He wipes some of my tears away.

"No. It's a gorgeous piece. What's it called?"

"'Evalene,'" he says, as if I should've guessed.

"Wait a minute. Clay? You *wrote* it?"

He nods bashfully, his cheeks gettin' rosy again.

"Clay! You have so much talent! I knew you were the best trumpet player around, but if you can write music like that . . . you could go all over the world!"

He snickers. "I don't know about all that."

"I DO know!" That music he just made is better than anything I've heard on any radio station. Why is he still here when he could be out makin' himself famous?

"Have you played it for anybody else?"

"No. I wanted to know what you thought first."

I grab his face and kiss it. "I think you're brilliant."

"You think I'd make it up in Chicago?"

"What'd I just say? Of course you could make it in Chicago! Or New York or—Clay!—you could go play in Paris! The one in France!"

A slight shiver ripples through him. Oh yeah, he's probably gotten chilly without a shirt. I have a little sweater that I try to wrap him in, which barely covers any of him. Then I hug him, rubbing his arms to get the warmth back in them. There's a loud clap of thunder, and a bolt of lightning strikes something in the near distance.

"So? You ready to conquer the world?" I ask.

"Nah. I think that's your job."

Us huggin' turns into us kissin' turns into our slow merge into each other. Always the gentleman, after the rubber's on, he eases inside me as carefully as possible, and I love him for it, I do. But today I feel such a need for him that I can't wait for his politeness. I roll over on top of him, rushing the process.

"Damn, Evvie," he laughs. But then he closes his eyes, and the pleasure he's feeling is obvious. Evening darkens the sky, and the storm ain't helpin'. Soon we're movin' through each other almost in complete darkness with occasional lightning guiding us. I know him well now, and this is usually his moment, so I brace for it.

But not yet. He sits up and kisses my half-covered breasts and looks into my eyes, still rockin' slowly. And now I can feel *my* moment coming, and he joins me. I don't know how, but he does, and it's all said and done at the exact same time.

He falls backward on the floor, and I kiss his cheek and lay my head on his chest. I know it's undignified to talk about the sex you just had, but I really wanna tell somebody about this one!

We rest a bit. I mean, we kinda have to.

"When are you going to Chicago?" I ask after a while.

He plays with my hair, wrapping it around his fingers.

"I don't know," he says. "We'll figure it out eventually."

I bite my lip, afraid of what I'm about to say.

"You should go soon."

"Why?"

"So you don't miss your chance."

"I won't," he says softly.

We listen to the rain. The thunder is faint now.

"If you did decide to go now . . . I'd go with you," I tell him.

The steady up and down of his chest under me stops.

"No, you wouldn't," he says.

"Yes, I would."

He raises himself up so I have to move. "No, you wouldn't, because I wouldn't let you."

"*Why?* What difference would it make?"

"A helluva difference!"

"No, it wouldn't."

"Stop it, Evvie. You're finishin' school and gettin' your diploma."

"Don't tell me what to do!"

I cross my arms and come perilously close to throwin' a tantrum. Shit. Grammie Atti's right: I do have a li'l impatient girl inside me with a bad temper.

I hate this. Yeah, I want to get my diploma, and yeah, I might even dream about college someday. But not like this. If he stays in town because of me, he's liable to vegetate, and he'll probably wind up hatin' me. If he goes now without me, I'll wanna die every day I have to spend without him. Might sound like I'm bein' dramatic, but I'm not.

"Evvie? Don't worry about it, okay? Baby? We'll work it out."

By now it's too dark to see each other's face, so he lights some candles. I look at him, and the smile on his face is so sad that I immediately think about his song. "Evalene." The piece he named after me. And then I understand that this is what it's about. Having this extraordinary talent and urge to go and feeling stuck all because of . . .

I get up. I pull on my top and my skirt.

"Please don't get upset," he says to me.

"I can't help it! You might be the next Miles Davis and, what? You're just gonna stay in this stupid town like a bum cuz your stupid girl has another year a high school left? I don't wanna hold you back."

He grabs my face hard and kisses me. I try to pull free to keep arguing, but he just kisses me again.

"Quit it, Clay."

"I want you to have the best chance you can in life, and that means gettin' an education."

"But if it wasn't for me, you'd go tomorrow, wouldn't you?"

"Well . . ." He clears his throat before continuing. "It's hard to say. I mean—who knows? I might already be there," he mumbles.

A painful thought slaps me across my face.

"Maybe you really wanna go on your own anyway. I'm sure they got some swell girls up in Chicago."

Clay cuts his eyes at me.

"Don't you do that," he snaps. "Don't make me prove I love you when you know I do. That's beneath you."

I feel like I just got scolded by a teacher. I walk over to the window. I can't always think straight when I'm too close to him.

"First you wanna take me to Chicago. Now you want me to stay in school. But if you could be, you'd be in Chicago right now. Forgive me, but all I'm hearin' are contradictions."

"Sorry I'm not perfect," he spits.

"Me too!"

We stare at each other for a second, and I think he wants to laugh, but I look away. Not in the mood.

"Why are you so worked up about this?" he asks.

I stare out the window at the rain as it tapers off. I can almost hear Mama callin' me right now. Silently sayin' *Let him go, Evvie. Let him go.*

"A year is a long time," I say. "It ain't forever, though. You should go. Without me. Then—" I pause to choke back my tears. "If you still want me to come up after I graduate, I'll come then. We'll write letters. It'll be like you're overseas in a war. We'll keep in touch, and if you need to move on? I'll understand," I finish.

I remove my eyes from the rain and turn to Clay. He looks at me like I just tore his heart out. I run over and snuggle next to him.

"I know we can do it. Stay together. We'd just have to be strong, I think," I say.

"I don't think I'd survive up there without you."

"So . . . ? Do you wanna—I don't know—marry me eventually?"

He lifts my chin to force me to make eye contact with him.

"Are you proposing to me?"

I sigh and shrug. "I guess."

"My heavens, this is so sudden," he says in the high-pitched voice of a southern belle, teasing me.

"Stop makin' jokes. I'm being serious."

He drops the silliness. "You know my answer."

I lean against him, and he wraps his arm around me. "Well. You said it. In a way. So we got a spoken agreement now. Don't forget it."

"Never," he says, and he kisses my forehead, and without any warning, I start to cry. Harder than I've cried in a long time. I'm like a wild bawlin' animal. Clay immediately pulls me into him, rests his chin on my head, and rocks me.

"Please don't be so sad, Evvie," he whispers, and I feel a few warm drops fall onto my scalp.

He tries to chuckle. "Remember when I told you you might be the smartest person I know?"

"Uh-huh," I sniffle into his chest.

"This right here? This is one a the problems with bein' so damn smart. You think too much. You just thought yourself into the saddest future imaginable, and I promise you: it ain't gonna be like that. We're connected, you and me. I think we always have been."

I sit up and try to pull away. He doesn't let me at first, but he does when he sees that I'm lookin' for somethin' to wipe my nose on. I give up and use the bottom of my shirt.

"Why you think we always been connected?" I ask, the sobs dyin' out.

"I bet it sounds strange, but when we were young, even though we weren't friends, I was always happy when you were around. A game of hide-and-go-seek could be fun, but it was always better when you were there. Bossy as you was."

"I was not! Was I?"

He grins at me. "You were kinda like the sun. The sun goes away sometimes, but you know it'll always come back. And it'll always make you smile."

He sure can say some pretty things.

"We weren't friends, cuz I did my best to avoid you," I tell him.

"*Why?*"

"Cuz I always had a crush on you, dummy! When we were really little, it wasn't a big deal, but by about age nine, I got too self-conscious. I didn't want you to think I was a dodo, so I just avoided you." I've never told anyone that. I don't think I even admitted it to myself before.

"But you are a dodo," he says.

I kiss his chin.

"I wish life didn't have to be so complicated," I muse.

He kisses both my cheeks. Then both my hands.

"We can't worry about all that. All we can do is have faith. Love each other. And believe we'll make it work," he declares.

We hold each other for a long time. As long as we can.

25

Kin

I'S A SATURDAY, AND I DON'T HAVE TO work today. No work for the next couple a days; the Heywoods went to the shore to get some beach time before fall gets here.

It's a gorgeous day. A hair cooler than usual for deep August, but sunny, with big fluffy clouds. I can't enjoy it the way I'd like, cuz I can't stop lookin' over my shoulder. Every time I go outside alone now, I keep waitin' for Virgil to show up and make me pay for going back on our "deal," or for the damage to his car and his face. Or for just not wantin' a thing to do with him. He's been so scarce that for a minute, I was relieved. I thought maybe my hex had worked and he'd left town, but I know better. My cursed two-headed self knows better. The hex flopped. He's still here. He wants to punish me, so he's waiting. He likes keeping me in a state of dull fear.

Worryin' about this piece a shit is nothin' new. Today should be no different, but if I was an insect with antennae, they'd be sittin' straight up right this second. Somethin' feels off. I hope my grandmother will know what it is. And will be willin' to tell me.

I clock her shack on my way up the path like I got X-ray eyes. She ain't busy and she ain't got no one in there, so she can't try some excuse. I open the door without botherin' to knock or use my hands.

"Imma make you start payin' rent," she says with her back to me. She's got something small in one hand, and the other picks at it with a dainty carving knife. She's giving this thing her full concentration, glasses on the end of her nose.

"As soon as I woke up, I could feel somethin' was wrong. Whatever you got left to teach me, you think we could try to cram it all in today? I got a strange feeling—" I stop myself and consider ending the thought there. But that ain't the end of the thought.

"Grammie Atti," I say, "I got a strange feeling that I'm runnin' outta time."

She nods in the direction of a plate. She still hasn't looked at me.

"Want a cookie? Chocolate chip," she offers.

"No. Thanks." Cookies? What the hell's goin' on?

"Huh. Boy in the Marines made 'em for me cuz he

couldn't pay. They taste like shit if you like cookies, but I hate cookies, so they taste fine to me."

I stand across from her, tryna force her to look at me.

"You heard what I said, right?"

"Uh-uh," she says. "I don't have nothin' more to teach."

"Please don't tease me, Grammie Atti. This is urgent."

Finally, she stops what she's doing and looks up at me. She points to a chair, and I sit in it.

"I ain't teasin' you, girl. I taught you what you needed to learn. The rest is on you."

I shake my head. "But—" And I grab one of her spirit cards. "What about this stuff? You didn't teach me anything about that. You have all these tools to protect yourself, and I don't!" I cry.

She snatches the card back from me. "Touch 'em again and Imma crack your knuckles with my switch," she warns, and I know she means it.

"Why don't you want me to know what you know?"

"All this 'stuff,' as you call it, ain't Jubilation. It has little to do with it, in fact. This is my livelihood. I made a choice to direct some a my energy toward spiritualism. I was not asked to give you that kinda apprenticeship. I was asked to help you control the gifts you've always had, and that is what I did."

I cross my arms and stare at the floor. I hear what she's sayin', but it just don't feel like enough to me.

"You have all you need, Evalene. Except patience and confidence. That's why you're upset, and it's why everything feels off. You are so close to bein' unified in who you are, but you afraid to trust it."

"Can you feel what I'm feelin'?" I ask helplessly.

"Don't matter if I can or not. Ain't my battle."

"I'm scared."

She nods. "If you believe in your power one hundred percent and wait for it to have the effect it needs to have, you'll be fine."

"How do I know when it's had the effect I need?"

"By not asking questions like that." She sighs. "It's like when you go on a trip, and the more you ask 'Are we there yet?' the further from your destination you seem to be. Stop questioning so much. Stop worryin' about what ain't workin' or don't feel right." She leans closer to me, and she does something that stuns me: she touches my cheek with actual affection, and she looks at me with love and deep, deep sadness. "No matter what happens, you gotta have faith that you *will* survive and you *will* become the whole person you're meant to be. This I know," she finishes. Then she sits back in her seat and starts carvin' again, her face back to its normal state somewhere between skeptical and indifferent.

Her intensity hasn't exactly calmed my fears. And after tellin' me I need to be patient, I decide I'd better not ask if she knows if my hex on Virgil is working. Patience. How am I sposeta just wait for shit to happen when I can be doin' other things to solve my problems?

"Okay," I say.

"Okay," she says.

She examines the tiny object, blows on it, and nods. Meticulously, she threads a hole in its body with a long string of buckskin.

"Come 'ere," she orders. I walk over to her, and she stands.

"Turn around," she says.

I do, and she lifts the stringed trinket over my head and ties it in the back. This is a necklace.

"What's this for?"

"Don't get excited. It's not a magical talisman, if that's what you're hopin'. No. This is just a reminder."

A *reminder*? I examine the delicate charm she just carved for me. It's a small wooden bird with its feet planted on imaginary ground. Looking backward. Sankofa. And unlike the cuckoo clock version, this one's delicate and pretty.

"You just now made this. You knew I was comin' over today?" I ask.

Without answering, my grandmother turns me around to face her. She probes me with her eyes, like she's looking at me and *in* me at the same time. Just like that, we're jubin'. And she has something to tell me.

Go back and get what's yours.

I have another dream-vision. I don't walk through an empty field this time, but I end up on that same hill overlooking my town dressed up as a city I don't recognize, with booming bass music blasting outta large, fast cars, and the billboard of the gorgeous jet-black Negro woman, and that Popeyes place.

I sit in the grass, and as I expected, the weird girl appears and sits next to me. We both stare down into the busy street. She's still wearin' those white things in her ears, and now I hear sounds comin' out of 'em like maybe they're very small headphones that you stick in your ears instead of wear on your head. Yikes. I would not like that!

"Why are we here?" I ask.

She keeps starin' like she can't hear me. I gently tug on the wires connected to the things in her ears, and she turns to me now.

"I just asked why are we here," I say.

She touches the little box the wires are plugged into.

"It's interesting that you'd ask me that," she remarks, "because I was gonna ask you the same question."

This does not bode well.

"Why would you ask me?"

"You're the one that keeps pullin' me into these visions," she informs me.

"*Me?* No! There's no way I'm doin' it," I tell her.

"You are, though," she says, her voice emotionless.

At this point, nothing should surprise me.

"Are you sure it's me?"

"Positive. You're better at jubin' than I am," she says. "For now, anyway."

"Who are you?"

She lies down in the grass, shielding her eyes from the sun. "Oh, I thought you knew. I'm Atti."

"Atti? No, no you're not."

"Yes I am."

"Your name is Atti? Like my grandmother? I don't think so. That's too much of a coincidence."

"It's not a coincidence at all. I'm named after her," she says evenly.

I turn to this girl, who looks a lot like me except for her terrible taste in clothes and her hairdo. She's got it in tiny plaits all over her head. It's a look I'd gladly leave to Buckwheat, but somehow it looks cute on her.

"Who named you that?" I ask, tryna sound calm and casual.

She sits up on her elbows and gives me a confused look.

"Wow. You really have no idea who I am. How are you calling me if you don't know what's going on?" she asks.

"Can you just tell me please?"

She sighs. "My mother. Violet. Your daughter."

Lord Jesus, can I ever just have a regular, boring day? Just one? And—HEY! Why the hell didn't she name that kid after *me*? What a bitch!

"I have a daughter. Named Violet. Great," I say.

"I'm startin' to get why you don't know this stuff. You look like you're about my age right now. So this is all still far off for you," she reasons.

"Why didn't I call *her*? My . . . daughter? If I'm doin' all this callin'?" I ask.

Atti snorts. "Yeah. You and Mom don't get along so well, so that part makes perfect sense to me."

So sometime in the future I will give birth to a girl, and we won't get along. Figures.

"If you don't know why you called me," Atti begins, "why don't you tell me what it is you want, and then I can tell you if there's any way I can help with that?"

I frown at her. "I just want me and the people I love to be safe. That's all," I say.

She stares at me. Does she have any idea what I'm talking about?

"What if you woke up tomorrow, and all of you were under a safe dome."

"A what?"

"Safe dome. It's like a big half globe that would protect you all from anything dangerous. Let's say the dome covers every house in your neighborhood. You just have to get all your loved ones there. You'd have plenty of oxygen, water, and enough to eat. You'd no longer be in any danger. But you'd have to stay under it for the rest of your lives. Would you be happy with that?"

This girl is so weird.

"No."

"Why not?"

"Cuz! We need to be able to interact with all kinds a people, to go to work, and go to school. We could never have a normal life if we lived like that."

"But! You'd be safe. And you said that's *all* you want," she points out.

"Are you tryna confuse me?" I ask her.

"No! I'm trying to find out what you REALLY want."

"Well, I do really want us to be safe, but not the way you suggested."

"So what you want has qualifications?"

This girl is exasperating! "Well, maybe—"

"Like what, specifically?"

"I don't know! I—"

"Sure you do! You know you don't wanna live in a safe dome, so what's the opposite of that?"

"WILL YOU SHUT UP?" I scream. I did not intend to snap like that, but she is drivin' me outta my mind. Goddamn, I hope I don't have to babysit her!

She doesn't seem shaken or upset that I yelled at her. In fact, she smirks.

"Wow. You're kinda impatient, aren't you?" she asks.

I tighten my lips and stare down at the street again. The next person to call me impatient is gonna regret it.

"You'll be different later. After I'm born. The contrast is mind-blowing."

"I'm glad this is entertaining for you."

Her smirk morphs into a quizzical expression.

"What if you're scared of the thing you really want?"

"That makes no sense to me."

"Miss Corinthia told you to save lives, and if you can't—"

"I know what she said."

"Maybe deep down, you wanna do more than protect. What if you wanna also . . . destroy?"

I don't like this. I don't like what she's saying to me. I

don't like what she's making me think and feel. She's crazy. I'm a good person, mostly. I just want my life to go back to normal. Before I knew anything about Virgil and before I was dangerous.

"Wow. That shut you up quick."

"Hasn't anyone ever told you to respect your elders?"

"Right now you're the same age as me."

"Right now isn't real."

"Who's to say what's real and what isn't?" Atti squints into the distance.

Next to us, a patch of grass ignites into flames for no reason. It burns with the steadiness of a fire in a wood stove.

"Do I have any sons?" I ask her.

She shakes her head. "Two girls."

"*Two*? What's the other one's name?"

"Indigo."

After Mama. Oh no. Is Mama already—gone?

"Did—did you ever meet your great-grandmother?"

She spins around to face me, suddenly angry.

"Why are you asking these questions? None of these things matter!"

I'm so caught off guard by her reaction, I don't know how to respond. At the same time, I don't feel like I asked anything inappropriate, so I will not apologize.

Then she surprises me yet again. She flashes me the sweetest smile.

"I think I understand. Family, loved ones. Your people mean everything to you. You called me because you don't want to go through it alone. You need someone with you," my future granddaughter informs me.

I'm tired. I think this Atti girl is makin' me tired.

"Go through what?"

Her smile fades. "What's coming."

I close my eyes, wishing I could ferry myself away from her and this strange place. Unfortunately, that's not a skill I have.

"What about the others I've seen you with?" I ask her.

"Oh. They're different," she says. She sits up, glancing around, wide-eyed and nervous. "They're not of this world anymore. They scare me," she admits. "They want us to be like them."

"Like them how?" I ask.

"Dead."

I turn back to the street below. So much life down there. They have no idea of the terrors livin' in the air that they breathe daily. I'm tired of thinking, feeling, sensing, and anything else that ends with an "ing."

"You look sleepy."

I shrug.

"Why don't you take a nap?" she asks me.

"Here?"

"Yeah, why not? I promise to stay awake and keep watch over you. I promise I'll stay with you when it gets bad, even though you might not be able to see me."

Without intending to, I start to lie back, the sun of this beautiful day shinin' down on me, but it's not too hot and it's not too bright. The fire beside us calms me with its crackling.

"Why is that there?" I ask her, referring to the fire.

"Don't worry about that now. It's just a figment. When you're putting the pieces together, some are gonna be out of order," she explains.

"I don't think I can sleep out here," I say, though my eyes are getting heavy.

"You can. This might relax you," she says, and she holds up the little box her white wires were attached to so I can see it. It has a little tiny screen! Like a baby TV set! It's so cute! She taps the screen, and I see stars and planets. This is a show about the universe, and she has it trapped in this tiny box. A man's soothing voice speaks to us. "A tiny blue dot set in a sunbeam. Here it is. That's where we live. That's home," he says. I'm both overjoyed and disheartened, because I'd love to watch this show, but I don't think I'll be able to find it on our regular big fat TV at home.

She's right about it relaxing me. Though I'd like to see the whole program, after only a few minutes, my eyes close, and I fall into a deep sleep with my future granddaughter watching over me.

26

Clear

"EVVIE, WHERE YOU GOIN'?" CORALENE asks. She keeps hoppin' around on one foot.

"Movies. Like I said the other three times you asked."

She hops in a circle. Doralene stares at *Beany and Cecil* on the TV, oblivious to everything around her. Coralene hops directly in her view a few times, and Doralene just leans over until she can see again, ignorin' her.

"But you went to the movies last week," Coralene protests.

"That is true. And now I'm goin' again."

"Why can't we come?"

"Because."

"Because why?"

"Because you're too little."

"It's not fair. You get to go wherever you want alla time, and I ain't never been to no movies!"

"Gotta wait till you're older," I mutter, and check the clock. I thought Mama woulda been home by now. If she ain't here when Clay comes, I won't be goin' anywhere.

Coralene crosses her arms and tries to stomp with her hoppin' foot. She loses her balance and topples over and it's hilarious, but I don't laugh. Her face instantly scrunches up like she's about to wail, but then she just sticks out her bottom lip and stays on the floor.

"Ain't fair," she whines.

I wanna tease her; she's funny and cute right now, but something stops me. As she mumbles to herself about never getting to go anyplace fun, she grabs a headless doll from the floor. She takes one look at it and slams it back on the floor. This doll once had a head. Until Virgil pilfered it during his late-night visit.

Doralene's had nightmares about him. Coralene just looked at that doll with a rage in her eyes I've never seen. He's crept into our lives, and that is unforgivable. I clutch my sankofa necklace. This cannot continue.

I'm lost in thought when I hear the screen door in back swing open and slam shut.

"Hey, y'all. Sorry it took me so long. Sister Greta," Mama grumbles, setting her purse down and kickin' off her shoes. From time to time, Mama volunteers at the church on Saturday evenings, preparin' meals for the old and sick or settin' up if there's to be an event on Sunday, like communion or somethin'. One a the folks that she volunteers with, Sister Greta, practically lives at the church and is never short on words. Mama's so polite, she just lets the woman talk without interrupting her, but if you never interrupt Sister Greta, you could wind up stuck with her for all of eternity.

"You know how she normally is. Well, today was worse, cuz she got a bunion on her toe and now she's convinced her whole foot's gonna have to be amputated! I told her all she needs to do is rest it some and wear comfortable shoes, but she didn't wanna hear that. Just kept goin' on and on about how she won't be able to get up the steps or take care of herself after her foot's gone. Damn near had to run outta there. Poor Vicky May. She probably *still* standin' there. Sayin' 'uh-huh' and noddin'.'" Mama chuckles and sits on the couch.

"They eat?" she asks me.

"Tuna!" Coralene complains. We oughta invest in a couple a muzzles.

"So what? Nothin' wrong with tuna," Mama tells her. "Did you have enough?"

"Yes," Coralene answers through her clenched jaw.

"Did it taste okay?"

"I guess," she says.

"Then quit whinin' about it," Mama finishes. "And what the heck are y'all watchin'? Almost time for Jackie Gleason." Mama and Doralene get into it about turnin' the station, and I check my watch. Quarter past seven. It's only fifteen minutes, but Clay's never late.

Mama wins the argument and turns to channel nine, even though *The Jackie Gleason Show* don't come on till seven thirty, when Doralene's cartoon woulda surely been over anyway. She whimpers in the corner, and Mama warns her to stop cryin' or she'll give her somethin' to cry about.

Twenty past seven.

I start to feel an itch I can't scratch. *Lolita* starts in ten minutes. The Orpheum ain't far, but this ain't like him. I feel Mama glancin' over at me and tryna decide if she should say anything.

"What you say y'all gonna see? *The Music Man?*"

"Yeah," I lie.

"Is it at eight?"

"Mama? I'm gonna go," I announce.

"Well, ain't he pickin' ya up?"

I sigh. "His dad ain't lettin' him use the car right now, so he's walkin' over. He's runnin' late, so Imma just see if I can catch him on the way. So we don't miss the beginning," I say.

She gives me a long, serious look.

"You sure it wouldn't be better just to wait?"

I think about it for a second. I think about all the reasons he mighta gotten held up. And reasons why I should wait. What if he had to do somethin' I don't know about before meeting me and will be comin' from the opposite direction, and we miss each other? What if there's an emergency and he tries to call the house and I'm gone? There is a logic to waiting.

"No. I can't wait no more," I tell her, and step out onto

the front porch and down the steps. The street is quiet except for the crickets. I look in both directions and don't see a soul. The Orpheum is between Clay's house and mine, so it's possible that I'll find him on his way to me.

Other things are possible too. But I can't let my mind go there.

"I am a child of God. I am not ugly. I will do no harm," I say aloud, just in case. I wish somebody else was on the street right now. Anybody. Where is everybody? Usually kids are still out playin' at this hour.

I stop in the middle a the sidewalk. I know somethin' ain't right. Ain't been right all day. I just don't know what that somethin' is. I walk a bit farther, and I stop again and look around me. I reach for my purple-silver band of energy: awareness. I reach and reach and know I've found it when a fly lands on my arm, and I see its bulging eyes and know it's thinking about where it'll go next, its wings beating, the blue veins on its wings pumping blood.

Time slows. Everything is perfectly clear. I know what this band allows me to do, but I need to figure out how I can use it to . . .

Slow-motion crunching sound behind me, musky sour air invades my lungs, hot breath bounces off my neck and—

Darkness now. I'm in a new place of nothing.

Nothing is here. A deep nothingness. I hear nothing. I

see nothing. I feel nothing. The only thing here is nothing.

I try to remember. There was a crash in my head like lightning. I heard it and saw it and felt it. Then I heard ringing. And now nothing.

My thoughts.

My thoughts are somethings. My thoughts tell me that I am alive. I'm not part of the nothing. I am Evalene Claudette Deschamps. I am sixteen years old, and I am alive. I'm here, wherever here may be. I am something.

My thoughts tell me that this nothingness is not real. My thoughts tell me my life is not real. My thoughts tell me to seek help. My thoughts tell me to trust no one. My thoughts confuse me.

Then I hear a sound. The dial tone of a phone before you make a call. It gets louder and softer and louder again. That sound is something. I hold on to it.

Then I see a face, a body. Her again.

Young Atti carries our kitchen wall phone awkwardly, like she doesn't know what to do with it.

"Why is this phone so big? Why's there a wire attached to it, and why is the wire so curly?" She laughs, fiddling with the beige spiral cord. "And what d'ya do with this thing?" She tries to balance the handset on her head like a hat, which fails and only makes her laugh more. I don't have time to worry about the simplemindedness of my granddaughter-to-be.

I open my mouth to speak. I wanna ask her what's happening, but I can't make a sound. I push hard, but it doesn't work.

She stops laughing. She hangs up the phone, and the dial tone vanishes.

"The phone is a joke," she says. "I brought it cuz you keep callin' me. I thought it would be funny." Despite her desire to joke, her face is grave now. Not even a smile.

"I came to be with you," she says. "Like I promised."

I open my mouth again to speak. More nothing.

"I'd protect you if I could." Her voice cracks and reaches a new octave.

I blink hard. Good. I can feel my eyes, my lashes, the muscles in my face. All of these are somethings. Although my voice isn't working, my mouth opening and closing is something. I look into this future granddaughter of mine and know that she's every bit as two-headed as I am. Jubilation is in her. I feel it, and it's more powerful than mine.

We lock eyes.

How did I get here? What is going on? I ask.

This is the night that you'll try to forget. I'm so sorry. She says this to me, and she starts to cry, her eyes still locked on mine. But for reasons I can't explain, my fear takes a rest when she tells me this. I feel like I've been awaitin' doom for quite a while now. It's almost a relief to know it's finally here.

How close is it? I just want it done, I say.

She takes my face in her hands and touches her forehead to mine.

I will stay with you as long as I can, she says.

Can you tell me what to expect? Just so I can prepare myself?

"There's only one thing I can say to you right now. It's

not enough, but I hope it gives you some comfort," she says in her regular voice.

Atti releases my face and walks backward, never taking her eyes off mine. Her steps make no sound cuz we're still in the nothingness. When she's a short distance away, she turns her back to me. The darkness around us transforms into the night sky.

And we're among the stars. Real stars.

I see Orion, the Seven Sisters and rare sights like Corona Borealis, Scorpius, and Hercules. They're all too close together to be accurate, but I don't mind. I see star clusters and nebulae. I see a *supernova*!

I look at Atti, her back still facing me.

How are you doing this? It isn't me, I say.

She doesn't answer. Instead she spirals around in a queer way and says, "While I'm far away from you . . ." She's waiting for me to say something. The tears steadily stream down her face.

"I know it's hard for you," she cries out.

I try to sing *My baby,* but it comes out in a squeak.

"'Because it's hard for me, my baby,

And the darkest hour is just before dawn,'" she sings for me.

She continues singing the song, and eventually other voices join hers, but I can't see who they belong to. I can feel myself smiling, and I want Atti to smile too. You gotta be happy if you gonna sing the Shirelles! I try to sing once more, and I cough. I figure out the problem: somethin's stuck in my throat. That must be why I can't speak. I cough and cough, tryna force it out of me. Atti's now doing a dance routine, but she still looks so sad. Poor thing. I cough some more and hold a finger out to her, cuz I can feel that I've almost dislodged it, and soon we can sing and dance together.

"No," she cries. "Just ignore it." And she goes right back to singing.

I can't. It's still in there, but loose now. Loose and wiggly.

"NO! Don't leave! Stay here with me," she wails.

I'm not leaving! I just want to get this thing out of my mouth, I tell her.

She runs toward me, reaching her arms out to grab me. As though I were about to fall.

27

Daughters

I BLINK SEVERAL TIMES. SLOWLY. FUTURE Atti's gone. A dim light must be shining somewhere, cuz now I can see things. I'm outta the darkness and away from my beloved stars.

My eyes begin to adjust, and I'm pressed down flat, my head turned to the side, facing a wall of wood paneling. Something's under me. A mattress, I think. Its cover is scratchy and irritates my skin. I try to cough again, and it gets stuck again, which is when I become aware of my mouth and what's in it.

Musty-tasting skin, sharp edges cutting into my soft palate. I scream and try to move, but someone is holding me down, crushing me.

"Hurry up, man," I hear a voice say, miles above me.

My head throbs, but I have to get clear right now. I bite down on the fingers in my mouth as hard as I can and hear a yelp. Two voices are here. Down, down into the shimmer of purple and silver. At the bottom of my gut. It's pulsing with activity. I feel everything now. Everything. Purple-silver clarity meet red-orange rage.

I open my mouth and release a savage howl and blast Virgil away from me, sending him slamming into the opposite wall of this dingy room. The other one scurries to his side like a scared mouse and tries to drag Virgil to the door, but Virgil doesn't move. I don't even have to hold him there. He just stares at me. His pants are undone and halfway between his knees and ankles. I don't need to look down to know what he's done, what he was *doing,* to me. Somebody was lookin' out for me, though. Maybe it was my granddaughter. Cuz he didn't finish what he started.

I keep my sharpened focus on him while I pull up my underwear and torn capris. The other one starts for the door, but I knock him right back where he was and hold him there easily.

I learn something new. In the purple-silver band, all things become clear. All enigmas have explanations. Riddles suddenly have obvious solutions. A long time ago, Virgil took my innocence. I can't take it back from him, because I no longer need it. And I don't want it. No. His conviction of supremacy over me is what I must take from him. I can't believe it's taken me this long to understand that.

I need Virgil to feel absolute fear. I want to be his nightmare. I want him to curse the day he met me. I don't give a shit about destiny. I will get what I want.

"You crazy bitch," he says to me, baffled. After everything that's happened, he's surprised by my reaction. He's a li'l scared, cuz he's smart. But not scared enough. What can I do to truly terrify this man?

"I tried to be sweet to you, but you just wouldn't listen. You brought this on yourself," he says.

If I were Virgil, I'd never want to be alone, in the quiet of the night, with my thoughts. I'd be scared to face who I really was. I know what to do.

"I'm gonna show you your soul," I inform him. Like my grandmother taught me, I sever a shard of energy with my razor-sharp clarity band, and I fling it at his redheaded crony. The crony transforms into a freakishly tall and thin man. He cries out at first, but his own terror silences him. His face blanches into a white unnatural to human beings. Paper white. Whatever expression he was wearing moments ago has been wiped clean and replaced by emptiness. His eyes become black mirrors. No scleras, no pupils, no corneas. Nothing. All the hair vanishes from his head. All lines, blemishes, moles—the things that make a person look like a person—they're all gone.

Virgil stares at the creature that has replaced his friend, speechless and ashen. I'm startled too. At my power and at this sight. I would've thought Virgil's soul would be a hideous monster from a horror story. This is far more chilling.

"That's your soul," I begin, "if your soul wore clothes. Take them off." The crony disrobes. With each piece of clothing he removes, more of the truth can be seen: nothing. A shapeless void of dark nothing remains where the clothes once were. He finally pulls off the white face, revealing it to be a mask. A tall blob of infinite darkness stands before us.

"What kinda voodoo hypnotism is this?" Virgil asks, his voice trembling. I think I can actually hear his teeth chattering.

I just stare at him. I consider showing Virgil more, but that isn't necessary. This is enough.

"You are so much more trouble than you're worth," he sneers, carefully pulling his pants up and fastening them with jittery hands.

Everything remains sharp. My mind could carve intricate etchings in glass.

He's backed himself flat against the wall, as far away from me as he can get, tryna stand steady and strong, but he's not foolin' anybody. "Enough of this sick shit," he spits, his voice jagged and raw. No dulcet tones tonight. He takes a moment, like he's puttin' himself back in control, but he just sounds desperate. "Change Teddy back."

Instead of changing Teddy back, I slide him closer to Virgil, who screams. Terrified of his own soul.

"Goddamnit! Change him back," he screeches.

"Tell me where we are," I demand.

"Teddy's place." He's visibly shaking, and he looks so small. But I will not gloat. I was raised better than that.

"How far are we from my house?"

He shrugs. "I don't know. Ten minutes."

I swallow hard and think. I don't know if I should try to find home or Clay or call Mama for help.

"Change him back," Virgil repeats. This time he's begging. I don't want to give Virgil anything he wants, but I can't think of a good reason to keep a walking void around that could accidentally swallow anything it touches, so I change him back, a reverse of how I changed him in the first place, only faster this time. It only takes a few seconds, and Teddy's back. Shell-shocked.

I check my watch. Five past eight. Feels much later, but that's good. I haven't lost too much time.

I stand to go and try to think of how to handle these two. I bind their hands behind their backs with restraints that can't be seen, and I'm not gentle about it. Teddy moans.

"I'm leaving," I say. "When I close this door, count back from one hundred. I'll do it too. When I get to one, I will release you both. If I ever see you again, I will not be so kind." I turn to go.

"Evalene?" he calls, and all the hair on the back of my neck and the bottom of my scalp stand at attention. His slimy confidence is back, and I can't imagine why or how. He should be scared out of his wits.

"There's a question you should be asking me, and you haven't asked it yet," he taunts.

How dare *he speak to me!*

"Haven't you wondered where lover boy is?"

My body goes cold. Since fallin' into the nothing darkness, I'd only been worryin' about my safety. Not Clay's.

"I might know," he says.

"What have you done?"

"Me? I haven't done anything. I've been here with you. My friends on the other hand . . . I told 'em he's just some dumb kid, but they're not like me. They don't much appreciate him having a big house and a nice car. They also don't like him playin' little tricks on his father's customers just cuz they happen to be white. They think he's gotten too big for his britches."

I remove a shard from my purple-silver band, and instead of stabbin' Virgil with it, I use it to slow everything down. To stay calm and focused and absorb every detail.

"Where is he, Virgil?"

Virgil shrugs. "Now I said I *might* know. But who knows anything for certain?"

To hell with stayin' calm and cool. With a breath, I hurl Virgil up into the air, and his hard head bangs into the ceiling. I hold him. He ain't goin' nowhere.

"Jesus Christ," Teddy hollers.

"Tell me, or I'll show you what your intestines look like," I say in a voice three octaves lower than I knew I could go.

The bastard tries to laugh, but he's almost there. He's almost attained absolute fear.

"Try the General's Woods," he finally says. I release him, and he falls to the floor with a thud. I bolt out into the street.

The General's Woods. Not too too far, but I can't possibly run there. I see a car comin' and I try to flag it down, but it just zips past me. Seconds later, more headlights. This time, using all the strength I can muster, I force this one to pull over to me, and I hop in the front seat.

"What are you doin'? Get outta ma car!" an old lady yells at me.

"Sorry, ma'am, but this is an emergency. Don't resist." We speed away from the curb, her fussin', not understandin' why the car she's driving no longer seems to be under her control.

Aches of all kinds, not just my head, are startin' to talk to me from the far reaches of my body. I can't listen to what they say. I can't think. I can't think about what just happened to me and how I am lucky to be alive. Can't think.

I can feel, though, and I'm in pain and feel terror like I've never known, so I go back to my old neutralizin' game to give my mind a task. Dashboard. Vinyl blend. Maroon. Glove compartment. I'm neutralizin', which keeps me steady and blocks out the old lady bitchin' next to me, and in this state, I have an unusual thought.

The General's Woods. I'm pretty sure that the general to which that name refers is Wade Hampton III.

Virgil Hampton. Why didn't I put it together before? They're related. His ancestor was a wealthy slaveholder, Confederate general, and early KKK financial backer. As well as famous South Carolinian (these are our celebrities). We—*all* of us—just keep fightin' the same battles in new eras with new faces each time. It's never ending. Until the world changes in an unfathomable way, our kinda Jubilation ain't never gonna die out.

When we're close enough, I make her stop the car in the middle of the road, and I jump out and race off, down into the thick forest. I run, managin' to keep myself from stumblin' or rammin' into a giant trunk. I run until I hear voices ahead.

I slow down so they don't hear my steps, but I keep pushing toward them, and I see a flickering light through the trees. I follow the light and sounds down a steep incline and practically come tumbling down the hill to a clearing. Where there is a large bonfire. And next to it are five crackers, jokin', drinkin', and takin' turns beatin' Clay.

"NO!" I shout. They briefly go silent, and I need to focus on these fiends, but my eyes and heart go right to Clay and his swollen features, one eye shut, the other starin' at me as his bleedin' mouth forms the word "Evvie."

Once their shock wears off, they laugh.

"And what *you* gonna do about it, li'l girl?" one of 'em asks me. "Flap them big lips?"

"I got somethin' she can flap 'em on," another one says. Him I throw straight up into a tree. The first one I just knock over with a thought, and the others go down like squirmin' dominoes as I run to Clay.

I cradle him in my arms. "It's gonna be okay," I say, rockin' him as the men holler and curse and try to resist my hold on 'em.

"Nigger witch!" one of 'em spits.

I'm dippin' down low into my red-orange space, but I can't hold 'em all. Not all at the same time. I don't have enough strength, and my anger is compromised by my heartache for Clay.

I can't do this. And more are comin'. I hear 'em on their way down the hill. This is a party. A real event.

"Evvie," Clay whispers.

"Shhh, baby, it's okay," I whisper back, tryna sound calm.

"Leave," he says. "Just get outta here."

I rock him faster as I think about all the tools I have and try to figure out what to do.

"I am a child of God I am not ugly I will do no . . . ," I say as I rock. "I am a child of God I am not ugly I will do no . . ."
I can't say it. I *want* to do them harm. I *want* to pierce every nerve in their bodies. Atti was right: I want to destroy them.

I'm doin' my best to hold 'em, but they're gettin' loose. Gettin' loose and gettin' close, drinkin' more beer and conspirin'. They wanna punish me for my trespasses.

I look around wildly and see it. Just yards away from me and Clay—Bottomless Pit. On the other side of it was where I made it snow. That means Grammie Atti is only yards, the width of the pond, and a mile or so away.

More noise, more nasty laughter, more beer cans. About a dozen are here now, and I'll be damned if Virgil ain't one of 'em. I thought I still had him and Teddy bound, but I'm startin' to see I don't have as much control as I thought.

I call to Grammie Atti. I call hard. I cannot do this on my own.

"Grab her," one of 'em says. Another two put their hands on me, and I dip into red-orange and repel them off me with electric shocks. They yelp and cuss me.

"Fuck this bitch! I ain't touchin' her!"

In that brief instant, others pounce on Clay, and they kick him in his ribs, and somebody, sweet Jesus, somebody steps on his fingers, and I hear the catastrophic crunch.

"*Leave him alone*," I scream! He can barely move!

"Looks like I win again," Miss Athena—Atti only to her near and dear—cackles at her associates around the card table, which she's moved into the sittin' room for Saturday night pinochle.

"You cheat," Miss Mary Margaret complains.

Miss Athena relishes her triumph, collects her winnings, and then she stops as if suspended in time. The other women talk among themselves and don't notice that Miss Athena has stopped moving. Stopped breathing.

"I'll be back," she announces, and rises.

This is unusual. She never skips out on pinochle early.

"Are you gonna keep playin' or not?"

"Deal me out," she says.

She walks through her back door, out into the night. It's a good mile to get to her destination, and she's gotta move fast. Her granddaughter has called on her for help. Evvie has never done this before. She can't ignore this call.

Miss Athena sees and hears them long before she's in their midst and has to pause to catch her breath. She places a hand out to lean on a tree for support.

I didn't see her land. But I heard it.

Any thoughts of her mother she must let go. She shakes them from her head. Any thoughts of her Roy left on the train tracks way back when she was Evalene's age she must let go. She mustn't be clouded by grief tonight. She gathers all her wits about her.

I'm tryna fight 'em off and protect Clay at the same time, and I'm not succeeding. We're in a sinking ship, Clay and me. Every time I plug one hole, another leak springs up.

I'm runnin' on empty in red-orange cuz I'm gettin' too tired to feel properly angry. I can't figure out how to change the atmosphere without gettin' happy first, and I am about as far away from happy as I can be. And clarity? I can't locate a clear thought in my head right now. One of 'em throws a punch that catches my jaw and knocks me sideways till I topple over. Immediately I roll onto my stomach, spit out blood, and start crawlin' back to Clay despite the pain. My sankofa necklace scrapes the ground under me, still clinging around my neck. As I crawl, Virgil punches the guy who punched me, about six times in a row. Guess he's the only one allowed to hurt me.

And that gives me an idea. I can't hold them all, but I

can steer one. I make Virgil my puppet and use him to sock, kick, and bite any of 'em that's on Clay.

"Stop it, you fucking—" He tries to insult me, but I lock his lips to shut him up. He can't stop me and I ain't stoppin'. I'm gettin' weaker, though, and Clay. Oh, Clay. What have they done to you?

"*Clay!*"

He's left on the ground as a few of the others try to restrain Virgil. His breathing is comin' slow now. I reach out to touch him, but as I get near, he's moving away. They're right back on him and pullin' him away from me. I grab for him, but its no use.

Where is my puppet? I don't see Virgil anywhere now, and it's gettin' hard to see anything at all cuz there's smoke in my eyes. Smoke blowin' all around in giant billowy puffs makin' me cough and choke.

It's too late, baby. My mother said that. Where is she?

You gotta run now! You gotta let him go! she says.

Mama, help us! Please!

You are a child of God! You are not ugly—

"SHUT UP," I scream at her, wherever she is. I need more than a prayer! I am losin' oxygen fast.

The glow of the fire is fadin' from me and I'm fadin' from everything and I'm startin' to feel relief. Just to be able to rest . . .

NO! I cannot give up. With the last strain of power I can feel, I reach into my gut. I can't think. I don't know what to do. So I combine red-orange, greenish-yellow, and purple-silver into one giant undulating rainbow.

My head hits the ground. The smoke thickens. The

rainbow vibrates and glows, and it ain't peaceful like the first one I made. This one smells like electricity and moves like a twister. I try and fail to lift my head. My hand absently clutches at my necklace. *Go back and get it. Go back and get it.* Reach back into the past . . . *take what's yours.* The words float in my brain, barely makin' sense anymore. My eyes start to close for good, but they spy somethin' unbelievable. Something even more extraordinary than my volcanic rainbow.

I see a miracle.

The haze all around me ain't just smoke. It's them. My haints. The blurry, giggling, and frightening shadows lurking at the corners of my life since before I can remember. Here and now, I can finally see their forms and their faces clearly. These women—all women, all family—in flowing, transparent gowns tinted with violet and lavender and indigo. So many colors. My rainbow acts like a vibrant highway for them—a bridge between their world and ours.

I feel a bit of energy come back, and I'm able to dip into the clarity belt for a moment. And when I do, I see them as they left this world. The one in front has deep bruises and strangulation marks on her neck. Heavy welts across her chest. Another has burns all over her body and part of her face has melted. The one behind her shrinks in size to become a flesh-covered skeleton. She must've starved. They rebelled in their lives, and their rebellion scared someone so much, they tortured each of them to death. I wonder what I'll look like when I join them. I don't intend to find out tonight.

In defiance of their mutilated bodies, they all smile at me, and I think I smile back. This is my family, and they're beautiful and terrifying all at the same time. Like me.

I almost laugh; I must be in some kinda delirium. And then I hear a cry come outta Clay that chills my blood.

"HELP US!" I wail. Please, God, let them help us.

Miss Athena reaches the pond, holding her chest and breathing hard. On the other side of the water there is a massive bonfire and a lynch mob dragging the boy away. Her granddaughter lies on the ground, losing consciousness.

Miss Athena would never make it across the pond in time. But she sees them too. An unending chain of haints hovering above all their heads.

I'm here, she calls to her granddaughter, who's too weak to reply.

Miss Athena must attempt something dangerous. Something no living soul should ever do.

Opening her arms wide, she roars into the atmosphere:
"SistersMothers,
DaughtersOthers,
We have been kin since our time began.
We will be kin after our time ends.
Your youngest daughter has called upon you.
Yo sperrit am our bress.[1]
'E wantuh, needuh hunnuh. **Yuh.**[2]

---

[1]   "Your spirit is our blessing" in Gullah language.
[2]   "She wants, needs you. Here" in Gullah language.

As your loyal daughter
I grant you permission
To transform your condition.
Come down
To the world you left.
Come down.
You needn't feel bereft.
Come down,
Guide us,
Abide us,
If you must,
Crawl inside us.
Do what you need
To make them bleed!"

Miss Athena can't catch her breath. She fears she's about to faint when someone approaches. She turns and searches the night until she sees a familiar face right next to her. She's surprised but shouldn't be. Miss Indigo grabs her mother's hand, and they both cry:

"SistersMothers,
DaughtersOthers,
Come down.
Come down.
Come down.
COME DOWN!"

Miss Athena falls back against a tree, spent. Miss Indigo strokes her mother's back.

The floating haints crash to earth. Miss Athena, her

God-fearing daughter, and her granddaughter have helped them return to the human versions of themselves. This is their moment.

The white men scream and scatter, tripping over their own feet and empty beer cans. The haints laugh at the comedy of it. Their laughter is too loud, too screechy, too otherworldly to be mortal.

One of the men, who was just torturing Evvie's boyfriend, tries to escape, but they catch him. He falls over in his tracks, and they drag him back to the fire without laying a hand on him. He cries and pleads for mercy. They huddle around him, listening to his pleas, but they quickly tire of him, and one sinks her finger low into his forehead, penetrating his skull.

From across the pond, Miss Indigo watches in horror, sickened but unable to turn away. Miss Athena watches, fascinated. She didn't know what the haints would do if she invited them down and lent them some flesh and blood. So far, she isn't disappointed.

They're here. For real. I can't see much. I pull myself up from the ground to try to make out what's happening. The crackers yell and scatter, bumpin' into themselves like clowns. The haints laugh their eerie laugh like this is the funniest show they've ever seen. Most of the fools get away, and that's fine with me, since they just had the fright of their lives.

One of 'em comes out from behind the trees where they had Clay and he tries to run, but he doesn't make it. He falls over mid-run like a sack a potatas, and they yank him backward at breakneck speed, his useless body leaving a deep trail in the earth. He cries and begs. They huddle over him, but they ain't about mercy. One of 'em digs her long finger into his face, and he goes unconscious.

They laugh some more—they're beyond giggling. The party is now theirs.

It looked like alla the men were gone, but a new one emerges from the trees, pale and quivering. He tries to quietly make his escape while the haints huddle around their first catch.

My energy's returning. Just in time. I latch on to him and hold him where he is as panic fills his entire being. Then I send a huge ball of flame into the air, causing the whole fire to rise and roar.

The haints whip around to see the victim I've caught for them, and they cheer. By the time they dance over to him, his Levi's are urine-soaked and he's too petrified to speak. They barely look at him, and he falls limp at their feet. They strip him naked and carry him over to the blaze, where he will meet the same fate as the other unfortunate soul.

And then . . . burning flesh. They complete the tableau I saw in my vision, sans future Atti. As before, they're eating; their party has become a cookout. Only now I see what it is they're eating. I'm too stupefied to shudder.

All is quiet as they munch on their game. While they eat,

they hum. It's not music. They're like cats purring. Sated.

Gradually they start to evaporate back into the atmosphere. I don't know why they're leaving. Perhaps they can't be living things for long. The rainbow takes them away from me, wrapping them up like a present, and then they disappear. I try to stand, and I do it without much of a problem. I'm hurtin' all over, but my energy seems to be restored.

Then I see him. Dimly in the firelight. He's up and he's walkin'. Staggerin', limpin', and bleedin' from everywhere, but he's walkin'! We look at each other, him with the only working eye he has right now, but he sees me. I *know* he sees me. I'm scared to death to draw attention to the fact that Clay's walkin' on his own in case any more white men have been hidin' and are ready to reappear now that the haints are gone. So I start moving toward him slowly. And with my mind's voice I tell him, *I love you.*

And he hears me! He says, *I love you, too.* Now I'm cryin', and I have to run to him to nurse him back to health. To do whatever I can—

Thunder. Bouncing off the trees. Hanging in the air. I hear it before I see.

Clay falls to his knees, then slumps over. No movement. No breath. Still.

I run to him and turn him over. His eye is still open. I imagine I can still see the love in it.

But it's all gone now.

A bullet has pierced his chest right in the middle. His heart. Clay lies dead in my arms.

A keening moan ripples through me and outside me. The haints. They know. They're sorry. They made a mistake. They didn't get the right one.

Virgil Hampton stands off to the side with a hunting rifle in his hand. He looks at the fire and the charred remains of his chums. He shakes his head in disgust.

He dares to open his mouth to me again.

"If you'd been a good girl, none a this woulda happened," he calls. "No. You had to use your niggery devilment, didn't ya? Now see what you did? I hate that word. You've reduced me to a common redneck."

Red orange red orange no more purple no more green no more rainbows.

"Despite your attitude, I woulda given you everything. You really blew it, girl."

When it starts, it sounds like a thousand harmless breezes, but the louder it gets, the clearer the sound. They're chanting now. Chanting in rhythm. The same thing over and over, faster and faster. *Happy-happy happy-happy happy-happy happy-happy . . .*

"You know what's ironic? Your boy *was* late. He ran up to your door all outta breath. Only to find you gone. They woulda got to him eventually. No doubt about it. But who knows what might've happened if you'd just waited a little bit longer? So the way I see it, what became of him? That's on you too."

Red orange red orange redorangeredorangeredorange-redorangered—

Happy-happy happy-happy happy-happy happy-happy happy-happy REDREDREDREDRRRRRRRRRRRRR-
RRRRRRRRR

"*Evalene,*" a haint screeches from somewhere in the clouds. "There is only one way. Jubilation comes from VENGEANCE."

Miss Athena and Miss Indigo watch Evalene. The one white man left shot that poor boy like a lame horse.

It's my fault, says Miss Indigo.

It's HIS fault, says Miss Athena.

The man's speaking to Evalene, and she turns her head and, at last, sees her mother and grandmother on the other side of the pond in the dark. Her eyes go flat, and she won't communicate with them. Miss Athena and Miss Indigo summon what strength they have left and send it to Virgil. Miss Athena intends to stop him; Miss Indigo intends to rip him apart. Neither happens. It doesn't work. Miss Indigo peers at her mother in fear.

Is it me? Cuz I haven't used it in so long?

Miss Athena shakes her head. "It's Evvie. She's put up a wall to keep us out."

Miss Athena tries to call on the haints again, but they can't return. She tries to call Evvie once more. Evvie looks across the pond and shoots her response to Grammie Atti like a dagger.

Stop.

"We can't help her anymore. Neither can you. The rest she must do alone," an unseen haint explains. They're invisible, but they're still present, even if they can no longer intervene.

They all watch Evalene. Miss Indigo keeps jubin' to no avail until she falls to the ground in exhaustion. Miss Athena wishes she didn't have to see this next part. For her grand-daughter's sake. But she can't abandon her now.

Gentle. I am gentle. I kiss Clay's lips like so many times before. I lay him down on the ground. So softly. I stand.

"You're lucky I can't quite bring myself to do you in," Virgil says. "You're also lucky cuz I happen to know a law-yer or two. A few senators. If you learn to behave yourself, they might see to it that you don't fry for what you've done to my friends."

I walk. There is no reason to run now.

"Hey! Don't you try anything else! I said I don't wanna kill you, but I will if I have to," he threatens as I get closer.

I stop about two feet in front of him. He's not positioned where I need him, so I throw him to the proper spot.

"Goddamnit, girl!" He stumbles after a rough landing and readjusts the rifle, preppin' to shoot me. I knock him down, belly up, on the bank, hold him down with my own natural weight, wrap my hands around his neck, and squeeze.

He struggles. He tries to talk, but fails. He tries to grab at my face, and he scratches me a few times, but I don't stop. I squeeze tighter. He pulls on the buckskin of my necklace, but I don't care. I squeeze tighter and tighter. And when he starts to turn blue, I loosen my grip. Just enough. This will not be fast.

He chokes and writhes on the ground. He tries to force my fingers from his neck, but I tighten my grip again, and when the blue tint creeps into his skin, I ease up again. He chokes and still tries to talk. This time, because he's perfectly positioned where I need him, I dunk his head in Bottomless Pit and hold it.

Hold it.

Hold it.

Hold it.

Hey, Evvie girl.

Then I release it and he flails like a fish and I shove his head down again and hold it there.

You're like nobody else.

I lift his head, and he's not fighting anymore. *You weak sonuvabitch. Breathe!*

"Breathe, goddamn you!" I shriek.

He chokes up water and takes another breath. He opens those ocean-blue eyes, and they almost look human in their sad resignation.

He looks at me. I let him speak. "We did have fun. You and me once." He hacks the words up with more water and some blood. "I know I made you smile."

I wouldn't survive up there without you.

"Evvie!" Grammie Atti calls out desperately from the other side.

I sniff. I blink. I breathe.

I dunk his head once more. I cry out like the wounded animal that I am, and the sound I make goes on and on until there's nothing left. He's stopped moving.

My hands let go and I sit. I sniff again. Look around.

This is how I've killed Virgil Hampton. Without any magic.

Grammie Atti still stares at me, not makin' a sound. And Mama's there too.

Go home, Grammie Atti. Go home, Mama, I tell them.

You gonna need help with this, Grammie Atti says.

No. Go home.

Grammie Atti leaves.

"I'm sorry, Evvie," Mama calls out.

I stare at her and say nothing. She doesn't move.

Go away.

She sniffles like she's been cryin' a lot, and she slowly fades into the trees. Can't tell if she's really gone or hidin'. Don't matter.

I have no practical tools. So I make do. I spend time collecting rocks. I place them in Virgil's pockets and inside his clothes, and I push him off the bank into Bottomless Pit. Probably I coulda used the jube to float him over to the fire and cook him like the rest. But I didn't. Maybe I hope his corpse is discovered one day, bloated, rotting, repulsive. Maybe I don't give a shit.

At the fire, I kick a few remaining body parts the haints left behind into the hot center, and the flames crackle.

If I'd just waited for him a little longer.

A little longer.

Clayton Alexander Jr.

There ain't much out here but weeds. Still, I find a few wildflowers, and I bring them to Clay. I delicately place them in his hands and wrap the fingers that ain't been crushed around them. I cry without makin' any noise. I find a stick, and I write in the dirt *Evvie loves Clay*.

I lie down next to him and keep cryin'. I wrap my arms around him. We hold each other for a long time. As long as we can.

28

Life

"THINK I FOUND SOMETHIN' THAT'LL fit you," Mama says.

She takes the nightgown off, lifting my arms for me. She secures me into a brassiere and then slides the black dress over my head. She looks me over. Then she sits behind me on the bed and combs my hair. She says things to me. I don't know what. I can't listen anymore.

"You gotta stand up now," she tells me, and I do.

Next thing I know we're in the church for the funeral. I stare down at the hymnals and fans on the back of the pew ahead of us. Occasionally Mama dabs her eyes and mine. I don't hear what the preacher's sayin'. Don't matter. I don't hear all the *amens* and *give us strength, Lords*. They don't matter either.

I do hear Mr. and Mrs. Alexander. They sob. Clay's daddy, like a lost little boy. Clay's mama, like a mad woman. Their cries matter.

The casket is closed. A bouquet of lilacs and carnations lies on top of it. Sittin' just to the side of the flowers is his trumpet. It's to be buried with him.

When we get back home, I crawl into bed and stay there. The twins come in and say things, but mostly they try not to bother me. Sleep is better. Sleepin', I dream about him, and he's still here and he's makin' me laugh and makin' me melt, and I'm real good at wakin' myself up before it all goes wrong. Sleepin', I can't think about everything that's been taken. All the memories we'll never have. All the music he'll never make.

They're tryin'. Tryna break through. Mama first. Mama's been knockin' at the door in my head since I got home that Sunday morning. They say they had to rip him outta my arms, and I screamed and fought. I don't remember. She's tryna read me and get me to talk to her with my mind's voice. But I can't. Grammie Atti's started doin' it too. Even future Atti has tried to check up on me, bless her heart. I just can't. They need to let me be.

The door opens. My back's to it, but I blink my eyes open. The sun seems high in the sky. Probably about noon. Don't matter.

"Baby?" It's Mama.

"I know you hurtin' right now. I know it must feel like you ain't never gonna feel happy again." She pauses for a second.

She might be givin' me space in case I wanna talk. No need.

"You might not wanna hear this, but God's here for you. He's here for all of us. I know he doesn't always answer our prayers the way we want him to. But he will take care of you, and you will have good days again. I promise," she says, and I can hear that she's clearly tryin' not to cry.

"Evvie? It's been four days. You gotta get outta that bed. You gotta take a bath. And I'm probably gonna have to burn that dress." She actually tried to joke at the end of that, which makes everything she just said even sadder.

I do the best I can. I get up and it hurts, and she walks me into the bathroom. I can do it, though. I run my bathwater, and I sit in the tub. When she grabs a washcloth and starts to bathe me, I take it from her. I can do it myself, even though it's hard and it takes me a long time.

"Don't you feel a little better now?" she asks once I'm out of the tub and wearing clean clothes. I make some kinda gesture with my head to acknowledge that I heard her.

"Now you need some food. I made shrimp and grits and biscuits," she says, coaxin' me to the kitchen. Coralene and Doralene appear from behind her, clinging to her hips for comfort as they look up at me, confused and scared. I shake my head.

"Okay. Well. I could make some soup? Or chicken broth?"

The world is moving past me, and before I give any thought as to why, I'm back in bed. Mama starts to cry, and then so do the twins.

"Baby, you gotta try!"

I'm sorry they're all crying. I'm sorry I can't help them. I'm sorry I can't try. My eyes drift closed again, and already it's better.

September. That means school. I can't do the first day, which turns into the first week. The following Monday, Mama and a few of her church lady friends force me out of the bed and take me to a doctor. I don't speak to him, either. He asks me how much weight I've lost in the last few weeks. I say nothing. Mama tells him at least ten pounds, and then he puts me on the scale and she gasps. Twenty. He says if I don't eat, I'll die. I don't need a doctor to tell me this. He says Mama should force-feed me if she has to. He also asks her if she's heard of St. John's Wort.

"Evvie Evvie Evvie. Everybody misses you. A lot." Anne Marie sits beside me on my bed. Today I'm sitting up. Today I'll try to stay sitting up.

She's brought books and papers and explains each to me.

"These are all the assignments you've missed from biology, trig, and history. I've put bookmarks in your textbooks, so you know which units we've done so far," she says. "I'm sorry. Since these are the only classes we got together, these were the only teachers that would let me bring your work home." She looks up at me apologetically.

I glance at the stack. Pages and pages of words that don't mean anything to me.

"I could help you. If you want. So you don't fall behind," she offers. That's sweet. I'm already way behind with no hope of catching up.

"Up to you," she adds. She coughs nervously, and I feel bad that she's here and seeing me like this.

"Please don't give up, Evvie. We need you," she says softly.

I lean back against the wall and stare out the window. Dreamin' of escape.

"Uncle Roland's gone. I was scared and I didn't want to tell my parents about the black eye, but I did. And would you believe he admitted it? Daddy was furious, but felt bad kickin' him out with nowhere to go. He gave him a month to find a place and told me I wasn't to be alone with him again. As if I'd wanna be! Then Mama was makin' plans for our Labor Day picnic. This was before . . ." She trails off. She means before Clay died. They decided not to have the picnic this year.

"Anyways, Mama mentioned havin' you, your mother, and sisters over, and he started stammerin' and sayin' stuff that made no sense, and for some mysterious reason, he didn't want you to come over. Mama told him plain: Evvie's like family and it ain't his house. Next morning, he was gone. Ain't that somethin'? I mean, ain't that weird?"

I try to give her a touch of a smile. I lost track of her situation, and I hate that I did. I'm proud she stood up for herself, though. I'm glad the specter of me unnerved her uncle enough to send him runnin' for the hills. I do care, and I want her to know. I'm tryin'. I hope she knows I'm tryin'.

I can feel her eyes on me. Mine are glued to the parched grass out the window. Not for any reason. Just because they landed there, and I don't have the energy to move them.

"I—uh—I had a soda the other day with this new girl. Pearl. She's from Florida. I'd been wantin' to tell you about her, but . . . Anyway, we had a soda and we talked. She's real nice and funny and smart. She reminds me of you." Anne clears her throat before continuing. "And we walked home and it was dark and . . ." Anne Marie stops to look up at me to see if I'm listenin' to her. I am. I may not look like it, but I am.

"If I tell you, will you promise not to tell anyone else?

I nod.

She moves closer to me and whispers, "She kissed me. On the lips." Then she cowers a little, like she's afraid of what I might say.

I turn my head and look directly at Anne Marie for the first time since she's come into my room.

"What?"

"Thank you, Jesus!" she exclaims, and hugs me. "I got you speakin' again!"

"Yeah, yeah, go back," I say. "You and this girl . . . kissed? Like—*kiss* kissed?"

"I think so. Yeah. Yeah we did. Please don't tell anyone."

"I won't."

"I'm still scared of hell, but I like her. I *really* like her. I don't know what to do."

I feel a lump in my throat. She's needed me, and I haven't been available.

"If there's a hell, you'll never see it," I tell her. "I don't care what anybody says. If nobody's gettin' hurt, and somebody's gettin' happy, you ain't doin' nothin' wrong."

She smiles at me with tears in her eyes.

"I love you, Evvie."

"Oh." I try to chuckle a little. I didn't expect this conversation to get so emotional. "I love you, too," I say.

She tells me all about this Pearl, who is apparently dreamy. For a hot second, I wonder if Anne Marie's ever thought about me in this way, and I feel a li'l funny about it, but I let the thought pass. She's my best friend, and she's happy. It's nice to see someone happy. The good kinda happy that doesn't hurt a soul. And this is the most I've been able to talk in over a month, and I love her for givin' me that.

He's against the back seat, and I'm in front of him, his arm draped over me. It's cramped, but we don't mind.

"Tell me somethin' good," he says.

"Like what?"

"Like somethin' good that I don't know about."

I scratch an itch on my cheek with his stubble.

"Hmm. D'ya know what comets are made of?"

"I do not."

"Ice, gas, and dust," I inform him.

"Wow."

"Does that count as somethin' good?"

I look up at him. He gets a sad, faraway look in his eyes. "I wish we'd talked more about that kinda stuff," he says.

"I didn't wanna bore you," I reply.

"You never bored me."

"I also thought we had more time."

He kisses my forehead. I squeeze his arms around me tighter.

"Wanna see a movie later?" he says.

"Okay. What movie?"

He snickers in a devilish way. "How about *Lolita*?"

"Sure."

He tries to smile as he says, "Wait for me this time."

I open my eyes and stare at the ceiling. I breathe deep. I turn over on my other side to go back to sleep, and tears dampen my pillowcase. The dreams hurt when I'm awake.

Mama's makin' me go to school. I don't know how I'll last. Every day is long and joyless. Anne Marie comes over now a few times a week, and that ain't so bad. I'm learning that life is a thing to get through.

I'm out on my bike. Nowhere to go. Just ridin'. I don't know why I put myself on display, cuz folks keep wavin' and callin' my name, and I ain't talkin' to nobody.

I find myself headin' to the outskirts of town and up that steep hill. To the lookout. I arrive at the top, and I'm winded. The sun's still out, so the lookout seems pretty ordinary compared to how it is at night. I sit in the dirt and gaze out over my town.

Right now? At this second, I'm thinking about death and responsibility. I am responsible for Virgil's death. Virgil is responsible for Clay's. I should've waited for him that night. I don't know if I could've saved him, but I should've waited. I have to live with that. I wouldn't say my mistake makes me responsible exactly. It does, however, make me accountable. Who's responsible for the others? Can haints be held responsible? I don't think so. I think Virgil and I are both responsible for the others. And it don't even matter how awful those men were. I'm still half-responsible. Their suffering can't bring Clay back to me. None of it is a comfort. Virgil's pale, dying face in my memory is not a comfort.

There was a story in the paper. Mama tried to hide it from me, but I saw it. Took up a lotta space. All about the disappearance of Virgil Hampton, a descendant of the Wade Hamptons (the First, the Second, and the Third). The article talked about his accomplishments—two years at Cornell before dropping out (the article said he "took a leave of absence")—and his promising future. As far as I know, none of the others made it into the paper. Clay certainly didn't.

I think I understand what they meant, the haints. In the moment of exacting my revenge, I got a rush, a high, but it was short-lived and it wasn't joy. I may be a disappointment to my ancestors. But I found no jubilation in vengeance.

I hear footsteps near me. I hope they'll just pass me by.

"Evvie?" someone calls.

I turn my head to see R. J. Funny. I must've seen him at school by now, but I can't remember. Feels like I haven't seen him in years.

"Mind if I join you?" he asks. I watch him for a moment and then face forward. After a moment, he sits on the ground beside me. For a long time, neither of us says anything. He's the one that breaks the silence.

"It ain't fair. What you been goin' through. It ain't fair at all."

You don't know what I'm goin' through, R. J.

He doesn't say anything for a bit. I'm grateful that he doesn't need to talk and doesn't try to force me to talk.

"I've lived here my whole goddamn life, and I ain't welcome here. Neither was Clay." He says that last part softly. "How can someplace be your home if you can't be safe there? Why do we put up with it? Just cuz it's where we're born? That ain't a good enough reason. Not for what they do to us."

I keep staring straight ahead, but I am listening to him. He's right.

We sit a while longer. I wonder how long we'll sit here, who will leave first, and if I'll care. A cool breeze blows, and I momentarily think about makin' it snow again. It's a fleeting thought. I don't do that shit anymore. I think back to what Miss Corinthia said. Would she be disappointed in me? Probably not, given the circumstances. But I'm disappointed. I wanted to save lives. Not end them.

I failed.

"I don't have any answers, honestly. I don't know what's right," he finally says, "but if you need somebody to be your punchin' bag for a while? I'd happily accept the job."

I turn and look him right in the eye.

"Or not. I'd just be willing to do whatever it takes to bring you back to yourself again," he says.

I want to say something to him, thank him maybe. But I can't. I don't know why. Instead, a dam breaks inside, and I weep. I throw my arms around him, and he hugs me back.

"It's okay. You cry," he says. "Go on and cry."

I cry oceans, drenching his nice school shirt. When I can't cry anymore, he brings me home. Mama made chicken and dumplin's and offers some to R. J., who accepts. And believe it or not, I'm actually kinda hungry.

29

Gifts

I GO EARLY. FIGURE THAT'S THE BEST TIME to catch her before she gets too busy. When I get there, I hear voices inside, so I just sit and wait.

Them chickens. Always makin' noise. Always lookin' at me when I'm here. They have to know more than they let on. They see everything. I don't envy them.

I can smell some kinda burnin' herb and wonder if they're just gettin' started or finishin' up. I'm sittin' on the bottom wooden step, close to the ground. From under the steps, a little furry thing wriggles out and nudges my foot. A rabbit. She looks exactly like the rabbit that crawled on me the early morning of the meteor showers. It can't be the same one. That would be absurd, wouldn't it? At the same time, I know this one is a girl too, and her size and markings are identical.

The li'l thing hops up to the step so she's beside me. She crawls into my lap and starts tappin' on my abdomen just like before.

"That is such an odd thing to do," I tell her. And she does it again. I can't help but giggle. She's so cute and it tickles. How can this not be the same rabbit? How many of 'em tap-dance on people? Are they a special breed? Never heard of it in my life.

The screen door opens, and the rabbit vanishes back under the steps. A woman in her thirties or forties comes out. She's surprised to see me sittin' there, but then she nods a hello, and I nod back and she goes on her way. I do our old special knock: three times, pause, two times, and without waiting, I enter.

She's not in the kitchen, which is unusual, but I can smell her pipe smoke, so she ain't far.

"Come in here," she calls from the sittin' room. I go through her beaded curtain into the dark room that is nicer than the kitchen, but colder. Energy-wise, not temperature-wise.

"Hey," I say.

She nods and welcomes me to sit on the wicker sofa with the comfy cushions.

"Didn't expect to see you here again," Grammie Atti says.

"Is it all right that I'm here?"

"You can come here anytime you want," she scoffs. "I

mean, I didn't imagine you needed me much anymore. I been tryna call you, ya know?"

"I know."

"Why you ain't answer me?"

"I don't know. Couldn't talk to nobody. Don't wanna use magic."

She doesn't nod or anything, but I can see her thinkin' about how to respond. She slides a dish with cinnamon candies toward me. I take one.

"I actually do need your help with somethin', Grammie Atti," I say, slightly ashamed.

"Ah. Here it comes. What?"

From my bag, I pull out the music box with the colored ballerina. The beautiful box I love so dearly.

"I need this destroyed," I tell her. "I can't have it near me, and I don't know how to do it."

She picks it up and inspects it. She opens the lid, and she's also in awe. It is really a stunning piece of craftsmanship. So unique and detailed. I'll probably never see anything like it again in my life. But I can't keep it. Every time I look at it, I feel like I'm dying, and I don't want anything that's had Virgil's hands all over it anywhere in my life.

"It's a gift from that white man, yeah?" she asks.

I nod.

"You could keep it. If you wanted to. We could put an enchantin' spell on it to cleanse it of his evil."

I shake my head. "No. I can't have it around me."

"All right."

I suck on the spicy candy; she puffs on her pipe.

"What are you gonna do with it?" I ask.

"What does it matter?"

"Just curious."

She takes another inhale.

"Ain't decided yet," she begins. "Usually I put a bindin' spell on an evil object, and then I burn it." She exhales. "Thing is, this ain't an evil object. It passed through the hands of an evil person. There's a difference. Outta context, the object itself has absolutely no power. It's just a pretty jewelry box. Its power lies in the memories you associate with it. And I can't burn your memories," she says. Her voice softens. "Don't worry. If you never want to see it again, you shall never see it again," she promises.

"Thank you," I say. "Thank you for—for all the help you've given me."

She waves my words away. "What'd I tell ya about gettin' all sentimental? My part was easy. You had to do the hard work, and you did. All there is to it."

"Uh . . ." I have more than one reason for being here. This next one is family-related, so who knows how she's gonna react? "I don't know if you remember or not, but Thursday's my birthday. Mama and I are makin' dinner and havin' a couple friends over. You could come if you want to," I offer. I'd like her to come, but I don't want her to feel pressure.

Her eyes widen. I think she's surprised to be invited. But then she just gives me a smile that seems half-wry, half-wistful. "That's kind, but I'm not a birthday party person.

If you're glad to be alive, celebratin' it only once a year just seems stupid. Come over Friday. I'll give ya a special reading. You can find out what your next loop around the sun has in store for ya," she says.

"Okay."

"What else is on your mind?" she asks me.

"You mean you don't know already?"

She chuckles to herself. "Believe it or not, I don't know everything."

Maybe she don't know everything, but she's not wrong. There's more I need to know. I guess there always will be.

"What's the point of Jubilation?"

"The point?"

"Why do we have these abilities? What are they *for*?"

"Survival. You know that as well as I do."

I feel my jaw clenching in anger, and I give myself a moment to get calm. I don't know exactly how to put into words what I'm feeling, and it's fucking frustrating.

"Survival," I begin. "Specifically, the survival of a handful of select colored women, right? This is something we've had since slave days, right?"

"Before."

"Uh-huh. To fend off predators. Usually white ones. Am I getting this all right?"

"Yes, Evalene."

"I used everything I had. You used everything you had. Mama stepped up with everything *she* had. You brought spirits back from the dead, and we STILL couldn't save Clay," I cry. "What. Is. The. POINT?"

She presses her hands together in her lap and gazes out the window.

"I don't know," she says quietly. "And I didn't bring 'em back alone. You had a hand in that too."

I wipe the tears away from my cheeks. I'm tired a cryin', but seems like cryin' ain't tired a me.

"We're human, granddaughter. There's only so much we can do."

Again, I think of my human flaws. If only I'd waited for Clay that night . . .

"He'd still be here if I hadn't messed up in the first place!"

"You didn't put a gun in that demon's hands," she says sharply.

"There's no joy in it, Grammie Atti," I tell her. "It only brings pain."

"Not true, but you hurtin', so it feels true." She stands up and walks through the beaded curtains into the kitchen. I hear her moving things around in there.

She reappears with her arms full of junk, which she drops on the coffee table. She separates out about a dozen tiny poppets all wearing some shade of purple, like the haints. Despite their grotesque faces with sewn-on lips and Xs for eyes, there's something almost sweet about them. She arranges 'em in a group on the table.

"Imagine that these ladies are all of us. Don't ask me how many of us there are, cuz I couldn't tell ya, but there are a lot of us."

Then she takes a handful a bleached chicken bones and makes a triangle around the poppets.

"Now. Here are some threats from the white world. They come in numerous forms, but these represent direct danger."

She stares hard at the ladies on the table until they all stand up and attack the bones, tearing at them, crushing them, sending them flying in every direction. My mouth could probably catch flies, cuz I know it's just hangin' open in awe. Whatever she's doin' here is clearly advanced.

"They did well, didn't they? Predators didn't have a chance. But what about now?" She picks up a canister and pours a thick circle of sugar around the dolls. At once they all collapse, lifeless again.

"They're small, but imagine each grain a sugar is anyone who wants to keep whites at the top and us at the bottom. This can be the grand wizard a the KKK, a sweet white lady who won't let you use her toilet, the white person who claims to be your friend but looks the other way when you're in trouble or somebody tells a nigger joke, or—and this is the saddest of all—a colored person who hates her skin so much, she'd betray you or me for the approval of anybody white. We are surrounded by multitudes that want to keep things the way they are. We can't overpower the whole world," she explains.

I stare at the mess of sugar on her table. The poppets look like defeated corpses.

"So. Our magic will never be enough. They'll always win," I say.

"You think Virgil Hampton considered himself a winner?" she snaps. I look up at her. She's remindin' me that I'm a murderer, and I don't need remindin'. I feel bad and ashamed, because I feel no remorse for taking his life.

I shake my head.

"What I'm saying is we have the power to save lives and we do, but there are no guarantees. Sometimes it ain't gonna work out the way we want it to."

"Mama said somethin' like that about God."

Grammie Atti sighs, with a slight roll of her eyes. "Yeah, well a broken clock is right twice a day."

"Are we broken?"

"No magic is perfection, Evvie. It's just another part a life. You will not win every battle. Any victory is a gift to be cherished."

I knew she wouldn't have a definitive answer. How could she? I can't explain it, but I feel better talkin' it over with her anyway.

"And think about it. If we could make every blessed thing happen exactly the way we want it to, wouldn't we be runnin' the goddamn planet?"

"Yeah. I guess so," I admit.

"Don't try to shut it outta your life like your mother. Goin' that route'll make you unhappy and keep you that way. Find a way to live with it," she says.

I nod and stand. Feels like it's time I should go, but the shit on the table irritates me.

"Grammie, where do you keep your washcloths?"

"Oh please, you ain't a maid," she says. I bend over anyhow to pick up the poppets, but she grabs my hand.

"Sorry. I won't touch 'em," I say.

Grammie Atti looks at me in a funny way, like she's just noticin' somethin'.

"You had a rabbit tappin' on you?"

"*Yes!* It happened right outside today, and it happened like two months ago too! What does that mean?"

She stares at me for a minute, but doesn't say anything.

"Please don't tell me it's bad luck. I can't handle any more," I tell her.

"Ain't said it was bad. Can mean different things. Be prepared for abundance," she says.

"I'd rather have less than more of anything these days."

"Well. We'll see."

I don't know why, but I have an urge to give her a hug or somethin' before I go, but that's not her style. Plus, it would make it seem like I'm never comin' back, and I will be back. I plan to be a regular at Grammie Atti's until she gets sick a me.

When I get to the back door, I ask her one last question.

"Will '63 be a better year than '62?"

"You tell me," she teases.

I step out onto the back porch and go down the steps to the front walk.

"Evalene?"

I jump. I didn't know she was still behind me.

"Yes?"

"Don't ignore me next time I call you," she says sternly, but I can see a faint smile at the corners of her mouth.

"I won't."

"Evvie, I have a secret for you," Coralene whispers.

"Okay. What is it?"

"I have to tell you later, cuz everybody will hear me." Nobody's paying any attention to her. Doralene is showing R. J. and Anne Marie the tooth that fell out of her head earlier, and Mama's tellin' her to get that nasty thing away from the table.

"You can whisper it. They won't hear," I tell her.

She's skeptical but decides to give it a try. "You're my favorite person," she whisper-spits into my ear. Then she kisses my cheek and runs back to the other side of the table before I can say anything. I smile at her and blow her a silly kiss. She beams. It's rare, but every now and then, the twins are kinda angelic.

Since it looks like everyone's done, I start to clear the table.

"No! Let me do it! You're the birthday girl," Anne Marie protests.

"I do it all the time."

"That's my point," she says, takin' plates from my hands. I still help. Gets it done faster. Eventually, it's just me and Anne Marie doin' it. R. J.—bless his heart—is a li'l clumsy in the kitchen and broke a glass. He was immediately excused from duty. And Mama said she had to go "see about somethin'." That's cute. Like I don't know what she has planned.

"Seventeen now. Does it feel good?" Anne Marie asks.

The idea of anything feeling "good" since losing Clay confounds me. So I'm pretty shocked when I find myself answering in the affirmative.

"It does. It's a different feeling," I reply.

Anne Marie studies me as she wipes some crumbs from the table.

"Can you describe it? What you feel?"

"Not in a way that makes any sense," I tell her.

"Tell me in a way that don't make sense then."

I grin at her. "I feel larger. Not heavier or like I've grown physically—"

"Definitely not heavier, you skinny thing. We gotta fatten you up!"

"I just feel like there's more to me than there used to be. That's all."

Anne Marie stops what she's doing and regards me.

"See? Toldja it wouldn't make any sense."

"No, I think I understand," she says, though I can see her tryna puzzle out exactly what I mean.

It's better to expand than to shrink, ain't it?

I glance at her, and she's rinsing her hands in the sink. I don't know why I tried to speak to her with my mind's voice just then. I guess it's possible that I might miss jubin'. Possible. Regardless, it's all right that she can't hear me. Lately I've been usin' my regular voice just fine.

"Here. Have a seat," Anne instructs, pulling out a chair.

"Why?"

"For heaven's sake, Evvie! Just do it," she teases.

I sit down and pretend I don't know what's about to happen.

Mama, the twins, and R. J. enter from the living room singing "Happy Birthday to You." R. J.'s creepin' along all slow cuz he's afraid he'll drop the cake. At last they set it down in front a me, just as they finish singing. I close my eyes.

Tell me about your thing, Evvie.

My what?

You know! Your thing. The thing that gets you excited. The thing that can take the blues away. Stars and such, right?

I open them again, and I blow out all seventeen candles at once. Everyone claps, and the smoke cloud dissipates. I can't believe my mother went through the trouble of lighting seventeen candles. That's what love looks like.

I cut the first piece, and they won't let me cut any more so I just take it. She did a lovely job. It's a ginger ale cake with pistachio frosting. I don't know how she made this without me seeing or where she hid it, but I'm touched. She must've really wanted this birthday to be a nice one.

"Evvie, what did you wish for?" the twins ask me in unison.

"She can't tell you," Mama says. "Then it won't come true."

I take a bite of the delicious fizzy cake.

"No, I can tell you. I ain't superstitious. This is really good, by the way."

"Thank you, baby," Mama says proudly.

"No matter what pain may come to the people in this

room, I wished for you all to find your thing. The thing that gets you excited when nothin' else does. The thing that can take your blues away. That was my wish," I say. They all get quiet, and Mama's eyes get real glassy.

"All right. Birthday rule: there's to be no cryin' while it's still my birthday. Everybody got that?" I say.

"Hmm. Bossy. Sounds like the old Evvie's comin' back," R. J. says with a wink.

"I ain't cryin'," Mama argues. "But that was a beautiful wish." She sniffles a little. "Too bad it won't come true, cuz you said it out loud!"

We laugh and start jabberin' all at once. Mostly about the cake, which is the best thing I've tasted in ages. I'm keepin' my eye on folks goin' for seconds to make sure I have some leftovers for tomorrow. Then I notice Anne Marie and R. J. exchange glances. They are not subtle at all.

R. J. brings in a box from the living room. It's not that big, but I can't imagine how I would've missed seeing it. It's wrapped in beautiful shimmery purple-and-silver paper. Purple-silver. Huh.

I open it carefully, cuz the wrap is so pretty. I expect them to rush me, but nobody does. I remove the last of the paper and look at the box. And for a second, I ask myself am I havin' a dream-vision again?

"Do you like it?" Anne Marie asks cautiously.

This ain't a dream. This is real. I'm holding my very own Tasco-brand telescope in my hands. Something I never thought I'd do.

"When—? How did you—?" I can't make sentences.

"We went in on it together," R. J. explains.

"But I never told you— How did you even know?"

Anne Marie presses her lips together for a second. "Well, you're the only person I've ever met who can identify the Seven Sisters in the sky like it's the moon or somethin'. And—well—somebody else mighta asked me a while back if I'd like to chip in," she finishes.

Clay. He was thinkin' about my birthday long before I was.

"I hope we got a good one," R. J. says.

I hug both of them.

"Thank you," I say through tears, wonderin' if I deserve to be loved this much.

"Evvie, no! You said no cryin' at your birfday," Doralene reminds me.

I release my friends and wipe my eyes. "You're right. No cryin', dammit!" I laugh. They laugh too, and Mama puts her arm around me.

"Is Evvie allowed to cuss now?" Coralene asks.

We try to get back to normal. While the others chat, I read every word on the box before opening it.

"Mama?"

"What?"

"*Is* Evvie allowed to cuss now?"

"Only on her birthday."

* * *

It's late. I'm in the backyard on a blanket, usin' my new telescope. It's amazing how much more I can see with it. On a clearer night, I might be able to discover somethin'. I heard that sometimes amateur astronomers have discovered comets. Just lookin' around up there. I doubt I will, but you never know.

Seein' so much more detail, I know I need some new books on astronomy to put this treasure to good use. Think I'm gonna ask Mrs. Woodley if she could order some new astronomy books for the library. Worst she can say is no.

I set it down to give my arms a rest. I was too eager to get it outside, so I haven't figured out how to set up its stand yet. I close my eyes and enjoy the night breeze.

Thank you for my birthday gift, I say. I open my eyes. It's the first time that I've allowed myself to speak to Clay. It was too painful before. But tonight it feels okay.

I miss you so much.

When I see you in dreams, it's like you're still here, but we both know you're gone.

What's real weird is that lately I feel like you're even more present. Like you're lyin' beside me right now even though I know you're not. And the weirdest part is, it don't make me feel sad. That's strange, ain't it?

The breeze blows a little harder. The kitchen light is out. Mama must've gone to bed.

Anyway. I'm startin' to feel less alone now.

I didn't leave you alone.

I distinctly heard that voice. I know I did.

". . . Clay?"

Clay? Is it you?

Hey, Evvie girl. I didn't leave you alone.

I squeeze the telescope to my heart. I hear him, and he hears me. I'm wide awake. I'm not dreamin'. This ain't a vision. Miracles can happen.

I know that now. I have a lotta people who love me. I'm lucky.

You have more than you realize, m'lady.

I giggle. Afraid to break the connection in case I never get it back again.

And then, I'll be damned if that rabbit ain't back! She crawls right up on me like it's our old routine now and just starts tappin' away at me.

I wish you could see this.

What is it? A rabbit?

I sit straight up, and my eyes damn near bulge outta my head. The rabbit hops offa me but don't run away.

Clay. Can you see me?

No.

Then how did you know it was a rabbit?

Rabbits are signs of abundance. And fertility.

Oh.

Shit.

That's all he has to say. It's why I been feelin' that there's more to me than there used to be: there *is*.

I'll never leave you alone, Evvie.

I lie back down on the blanket and rub my abdomen, curious and scared about what's inside. Dear god, Mama's gonna have a coronary. First she'll wanna beat the livin' hell outta me; then she'll have a coronary. Christ Jesus.

What am I gonna do?

You'll have faith. You'll love each other. You'll believe you can make it work. Because you will.

We go on like that for a while. He makes me laugh a little and melt a little. I end up fallin' asleep outside and wakin' up just before dawn. Just as the sun is risin'. I watch all the colors appear and fade before settling on the gold of the morning. It's a new day. With new obstacles to be sure. But I'll have faith, I'll love, and I'll believe I can make it work.

Because I will.

ACKNOWLEDGMENTS

I'm as grateful as ever to all the fantastic, intelligent, and generous people in my life. Without them, this book would not exist.

This book went through many drafts, including a huge rewrite that briefly made me wonder if I should just quit and cut my losses. I'm glad I didn't. Thank you, thank you, *thank you* to my first-round readers! Danica Novgorodoff, Cori Thomas, and Chris Van Strander—your thoughts were invaluable. Then there was a second version of the book that was VERY different from the first. Thank you, Jackie Kelly for being the fresh pair of eyes on this one and a giant thank you goes to Kia Corthron (my sister and fellow scribe), Tom Matthew Wolfe, and Tasha Gordon-Solmon for reading and giving me in-depth feedback on *BOTH* versions of the book! I appreciate you all infinitely.

I have to thank my peerless agent, the incomparable Laurie Liss, for always having my back and supporting me since the day we met. To Simon & Schuster/Simon Pulse: thank you for taking a big risk on an unknown author by giving me a two-book deal: that kind of encouragement is life changing. A few different editors contributed their time and wisdom to birthing this book. Fiona Simpson, who gave me the tough and correct advice when she suggested I start over; Tricia Lin and Jennifer Ung, who stepped in late in the game to help me reach the finish line: you are fierce women! Thank you, Tiara Iandiorio, for the gorgeous, dreamy cover. Sometimes it takes a coven to make a book real and I couldn't be more pleased with the result.

Thank you to the wondrous staff at the MacDowell Colony for all the little miracles you provide for us artists, like delicious meals. I began the skeletal draft of this book there four years ago in the dead of winter in Garland Studio, which was haunted and also the studio of choice for James Baldwin on more than one occasion decades before. I didn't appreciate the ghost, but the beauty, inspiration, and that electric legacy will stay with me always.

All my readers: without you, all this effort would be for nothing. You have my undying gratitude.

I mentioned Tom Matthew Wolfe above, but I have to thank him again. Our lives have gone though a lot of changes in the last few years and he's remained the kind-hearted, hilarious, and loving guy I married through all of it. Thanks for being my partner in crime.